Summer Dreams at Villa Limoncello

Summer Dreams at Villa Limoncello

DAISY JAMES

CANELO

First published in the United Kingdom in 2019 by Canelo

This edition published in the United Kingdom in 2020 by

Canelo Digital Publishing Limited
Third Floor, 20 Mortimer Street
London W1T 3JW
United Kingdom

A CIP catalogue record for this book is available from the British Library.

Print ISBN 978 1 78863 792 3
Ebook ISBN 978 1 78863 344 4

Look for more great books at www.canelo.co

Printed and bound in Great Britain by Clays Ltd, Elcograf S.p.A.

To my wonderful family and friends

To all those who are pursuing a dream

Chapter One

Villa Limoncello, San Vivaldo
Colour: Sunshine yellow

'Remind me again whose idea it was to organise a Painting & Pasta course at Villa Limoncello?' asked Izzie, anxiety tickling at her stomach as she ran her eyes down her numerous checklists before adjusting the easels in the gazebo for the fifth time in as many minutes. 'What if something goes wrong? What if the guests don't want to learn about watercolour techniques, or how to create mouth-watering Italian patisserie or Tuscan twists on pasta sauces?'

'Relax, nothing's going to go wrong.' Meghan smiled, rolling her eyes at her best friend's familiar refrain from beneath her pink-tipped fringe. 'Carmen and her friends wouldn't have booked if they weren't enthusiasts in both of those things! And there's no one more prepared to deliver a painting course in the whole of Tuscany than you are. God, Izzie, you've even laminated the recipe cards and printed off photographs of the foodie sightseeing tours you've got organised, not to mention prepared all those personalised folders… complete with a picture of each guest on the front just in case they forget what they look like!'

Yet, despite the lists, schedules and colour-coded itineraries Izzie had gathered in her trusty folder, she still couldn't shift that nugget of nervousness lodged somewhere between her stomach and her ribcage.

'Meghan, you know how much is riding on this course being a success. If we can't make the villa pay for itself, Luca will have no choice but to sell it, and after all the renovations and redecorating we've done over the last six weeks, and the extra cash Luca's invested, that would be devastating.'

'It would, I agree – and the villa looks amazing, Izzie. There's no doubt your creativity sprites have returned with aplomb. I absolutely adore what you've done with the bedrooms – just the right amount of Tuscan charm without completely obliterating the floral fiasco the previous owner had going on. God, when I stayed here last time, I thought I'd tumbled down a rabbit hole into a psychedelic dream!'

Izzie giggled. 'I know, who decorates the walls *and* the ceiling *and* the door panels with the same patterned wallpaper? Every time I went into that room, I swear I could almost smell the roses!'

Bringing Villa Limoncello up to the standard demanded by paying guests had been Izzie's dream project. She loved everything about the place; its terracotta roof tiles, the smooth honey-coloured façade, the green paint-blistered shutters, and the brigade of cypress trees marching in tandem down the driveway. She loved the freshly painted walls of the bedrooms, the marble floor tiles that had taken them a whole week to return to their former glory, and the quirky brass light fittings she and Luca had unearthed on a visit to Siena.

However, her favourite part of the property had to be the *limonaia* – the old glasshouse attached to the south-facing gable which housed the plants that gave the villa its name. It was true; after two long years of banishment, her creativity sprites were *definitely* dancing again, and everything she had learned from running her interior design studio had come scorching back. She just hoped that their first five guests agreed, especially as one of them was none other than the award-winning fashion designer Carmen Campbell.

'I'm so pleased you decided to take the leap from Duchess of Dullness to Contessa of Colour and Creativity, as Jonti would say,' continued Meghan, her eyes softening as she reached out to rest her hand on Izzie's forearm to prevent her from rearranging the brushes again. 'Taking some time out in this little corner of paradise was the best decision you could have made after what happened with Anna, and, as your best friend, I can honestly say that Tuscany agrees with you – your eyes are shining, those copper curls of yours are less bird's nest, more Sunday best, and that smattering of freckles across your nose is so cute. However, I suspect the smile on your lips has nothing to do with your daily dose of Italian sunshine, or a reconnection with your passion for interior design, or even the proximity of all the amazing renaissance artists, has it?'

'Meghan…' began Izzie, her cheeks flushing with heat.

'So how are things going with Luca? Gianni tells me that our favourite Italian chef has been at the villa every day for the last six weeks, even coming over before he puts in a shift at Antonio's. Don't tell me you spent all that time discussing new lines in curtain fabric and poring over paint samples?'

'Not all the time, no. There was the new furniture to assemble for the guest bedrooms, the en-suite bathrooms to sort out, the bed linen to wash and iron, the toiletries to source. Then there was the kitchen to refresh, the new oven to install...'

'Izzie, darling, I'm talking about romance here! If I were standing in those sparkly blue sandals of yours, I wouldn't be able to resist a bit of smooching underneath that pergola over there, or a moonlight meander through the vines, or a lunchtime linger over by the wishing well. And don't get me started with what you could do in the *limonaia* – the most romantic place of all. Ahh, if Luca was—'

'If Luca was what?' enquired the man himself, appearing on the steps of the whitewashed gazebo, his dark eyes framed with lashes the colour of liquorice, crinkling at the corners. A whiff of his favourite lemony cologne invaded Izzie's nostrils and she needed every ounce of her willpower to ignore the ripples of attraction cascading through her veins and focus on the task ahead.

'Meghan was just saying how fabulous everything looks for the first painting tutorial, weren't you?'

'Yes, yes, I was.'

Meghan was right, though. There was a connection between her and Luca. Being with him had helped her to greet every day she spent under the Tuscan sun with a smile on her face and a song in her heart after spending two miserable years submerged beneath the mantle of grief, when demons of the past had stalked her every move, her business had collapsed and she'd

4

been forced to take a job as a house-stager at Hambleton Homes, working for a man who was a walking corporate cliché. However, no one had been more surprised than she had when she found herself turning down Darren Hambleton's offer of a pay rise and agreeing to stay on in San Vivaldo to spruce up the villa so Luca could offer upmarket breaks to the discerning traveller – not to mention agreeing to deliver one of the courses!

'Okay, I know there's a lot riding on this first course at *Villa dei Limoni* being a success, but the most important thing is for everyone to have fun – and that includes you, Isabella!'

Izzie adored the sensual cadence of Luca's Italian accent, especially when he twisted his tongue around her name, not to mention the cute dimples that bracketed his lips whenever he smiled, which was often. She also loved how he, and everyone else who lived in San Vivaldo, referred to the villa by its original name, the one it had boasted for over two hundred years until it was inherited by an American relative of the Rosetti family who thought the name-change would speed up its sale.

'So, Carlotta has finished sorting out the bedrooms – apart from Carmen's because there's still a "do not disturb" sign hanging on the door – and she's rushed off to meet Vincenzo for their weekly trip to Firenze. I think they're having coffee with his granddaughter and few of her university friends at Mercato Centrale.'

'Better tell them to watch out if any of them are single!' Meghan smirked. 'Carlotta's matchmaking skills are legendary – they could be engaged by teatime! Look what happened to me and I was only here for three days!

In fact, perhaps I should warn our guests, too? Carlotta did serve them breakfast!'

'I'm sure they'll be fine,' laughed Izzie, feeling some of her anxiety melt away. 'Anyway, there's four women and only one guy – not sure even Carlotta can work with those odds.'

'Maybe she could—'

'Okay, okay, some of us have a restaurant to run!' interrupted Luca, rolling his eyes at Meghan, who had become Carlotta's biggest fan after meeting her dream guy within minutes of chatting to the village's unofficial matchmaker. 'So, Izzie, I've prepared lunch for everyone and left it in the fridge. Please reassure Carmen that I've taken into account the list of food sensitivities her PA emailed through before they arrived, and then all you have to do is take off the covers and serve.'

Meghan giggled.

'What?'

'Well, it's just as well Izzie is only responsible for the painting tutorials this week. I don't think our group of cultivated travellers would be very impressed if they were served with a few rounds of buttered toast and a cup of black coffee instead of the gourmet food they've been promised on the website.'

'Hey – that's not fair!' spluttered Izzie. 'Okay, so I might never be a candidate for a Michelin star, but I'll have you know that I can now whip up a delicious cheese omelette and even, if I'm forced, turn my hand to producing a decent *torte della Nonna*. How can I help it if my culinary expertise lies in the arena of limoncello-based cocktails which, I can assure you, went down very well with every single one of our esteemed guests at last night's welcome reception, *especially* Carmen, who, as a fashion designer extraordinaire, is known for her exquisite taste!'

'Touché!' Luca grinned, before his eyes fell on the pile of folders spread on the glass table in the centre of the gazebo, along with a huge purple arch-lever file. 'Is this the itinerary, by any chance? It's over four inches thick! What have you got in here? We have five guests staying for five nights, Izzie! God, is there anything you haven't got covered?'

Luca flicked through the pages in the master file. Every day of the course had been separated by a colour-coded divider and contained an itemised breakdown of their agenda: details of the techniques they would be covering in each of the daily painting tutorials, the recipes Luca would be demonstrating every evening that would form the *primo piatto* of their meal along with a selection of local wines, as well as information on the museums and art galleries the group would be visiting during the week.

'I hope you're not expecting me to follow these recipes to the letter – that isn't how Italian chefs like to work! We cannot allow our culinary inspiration to be bound by rigid rules and instructions. We need to be free to explore our creativity using the freshest ingredients of the day!'

'Sorry, Luca, I just don't want there to be any hiccups, that's all. Good reviews are so important and if we can build up a reputation for excellence, our guests will spread the word and our bookings will increase.'

'Yes,' agreed Meghan, tossing her long blonde hair over her shoulder and resetting her over-sized sunglasses on the bridge of her nose. 'Then you'll be able to tell Riccardo Clarke, and all the other potential buyers out there who want to turn Villa Limoncello into some kind of Disney-esque version of a Tuscan farmhouse, that it's definitely not for sale.'

Meghan's voice had edged up an octave with indignation, but that's what happened when she spoke about Riccardo, the grumpy owner of the over-renovated B&B next door. He had his eye on acquiring Villa Limoncello's vineyard and olive grove because, whilst his property was well-proportioned and boasted a fabulous swimming pool, it had very little land. In fact, his desire to own the villa had been so great that he'd resorted to underhand methods to persuade the owner to sell. When Gianni Lombardo – the object of Meghan's affections and the estate's talented viticulturist with a fabulous line in operatic arias – discovered the real cause of the leaf blight that had plagued his beloved vines, the air had crackled with an explosion of Italian expletives and Riccardo was now his sworn enemy!

'Okay, let's leave Riccardo out of this, shall we?' sighed Luca, clearly not wanting to be drawn into another of Meghan's lengthy character assassinations of their neighbour. 'Look, I'm already running late, so I'll leave you both to it. Good luck! And Izzie, I know you'll be an amazing art tutor – all you have to do is channel your inner Banksy and you'll be fine. I'll be back at five to start the preparations for tonight's pasta-making tutorial – *spaghetti sugo finto. Ciao!*'

'*Ciao!*'

Izzie tried not to stare as Luca jogged towards the driveway where he'd left his scarlet Alfa Romeo Spider parked under the shade of a sprawling magnolia tree. But how could she not enjoy the way his pale pink shirt clung to his muscular torso or how his espresso-coloured hair sprang up in tufts at the back of his collar, not to mention the snug fit of his black jeans.

'Mmm, gorgeous!' muttered Meghan, her eyes sparkling with mischief as she faked a swoon before clapping her hands in excitement. 'Okay, Izzie, it's action stations! Here come our guests!'

Izzie inhaled a deep breath, relishing the floral tang of the honeysuckle that grew in abundance around the pillars of the gazebo as she ran through the colours she planned to focus on that morning for her tutorial on watercolours – cerulean blue for the endless sky, forest green for the vines that snaked up the hillside, burnt terracotta for the higgledy-piggledy roofs of San Vivaldo, sunflower yellow for the fields of flowers that dotted the panorama.

Tuscany was a truly magical place to hold a painting course, and if she could just corral the battalion of butterflies playing tag in her stomach, she knew her training would kick in and she would enjoy every minute of what lay ahead. She smiled, sending a missive of gratitude to her director of fate for orchestrating her arrival at Villa Limoncello.

Chapter Two

The gazebo, Villa Limoncello
Colour: Translucent aquamarine

'Does anyone know where Carmen is?' asked Izzie as she stood in the middle of the gazebo, keen to get started but reluctant to do so in the absence of the person who had generously booked and paid for the holiday for everyone.

'Carmen's always late for everything!' complained Beth, blowing her long, dark fringe from her eyes and shaking her head in irritation as she shoved her chair backwards. 'We've been friends for over fifteen years and I don't think she's ever been on time for anything! How she manages to run a business is beyond me, let alone win awards! I'll go and find her. Some of us are really looking forward to this morning's painting demonstration.'

'No, it's okay, Beth. I'll go,' called Hannah, already halfway down the whitewashed steps in search of her boss, her ponytail swaying like a tawny pendulum. 'She told me she wanted a lie-in this morning, so she was going to skip breakfast and have one of her super-shakes instead.'

'That girl needs to calm down or she'll spontaneously combust,' muttered Zara, rolling her eyes in annoyance whilst toying with one of the paintbrushes on the easel in front of her. 'She's always running around after Carmen.

I wouldn't be surprised if she's got Hannah doing her laundry whilst we're here, as well as organising her diary and supervising her daily vitamin intake. I thought we were supposed to be here to relax, as a treat for all our hard work. It's hardly a treat if your trusty PA has to be on duty twenty-four seven, is it?'

Zara shook her head in disgust. She collected her long caramel locks in her hands and secured them in a topknot with one of Izzie's paintbrushes to emphasise the elegant sweep of her neck and her tanned shoulders. From her straight-back deportment, there was no mistaking the fact that Zara Connelly worked in the modelling industry; not only was she over six foot tall, but only a professional model could carry off the flimsy tangerine jumpsuit that had probably cost more that Izzie earned in a month.

'Well, Carmen *is* paying for everything,' interjected Tom, raising the vintage Pentax he wore slung around his neck on a leather strap to take yet another photograph of the view. With red hair and freckles, Izzie had some sympathy for the way he constantly dabbed at his forehead with a serviette he must have retained from breakfast. She too had been blessed with pale skin and Titian locks, and just a few minutes in the sun caused her face to resemble a tomato if she wasn't careful – although she drew the line at sporting slashes of green-hued sun cream across her cheeks à la Adam Ant.

'Yes, Tom, we know she is, and it's very generous of her, but that doesn't mean we have to fall over ourselves with avid appreciation, does it?' snapped Beth, flicking the sides of her severe ebony bob behind her ears. As the only one not involved in the fashion business, she had made no concession in her attire for spending the morning in the sun-filled garden of a Tuscan villa, sporting black skinny jeans, a long-sleeved T-shirt, also black, and a pair of black Doc Martens. 'Anyway, correct me if I'm wrong, Mister Accountant, but isn't it all tax deductible?'

'Probably,' muttered Tom, smoothing his sweaty palms over his wildly floral shorts.

'Where are they? I knew I should have gone to look for her, not Hannah!' continued Beth, craning her neck towards the terrace of the villa. 'I wish they'd hurry up; the sooner we get started, the sooner we can make a start on that amazing lunch I saw when I poked my head around the kitchen door earlier.'

'But you've just finished breakfast!' exclaimed Zara, sending Beth a look of such abject horror that Izzie had to clench her fists to stop herself from giggling.

'So what? If that's going to be the standard of the food this week, I just know we're going to have fabulous time! I can't wait to learn how to make fresh pasta, too! And all the home-made Italian sauces – rich carbonara, spicy arrabbiata, creamy alfredo, tasty marinara.'

'Ergh, you can have my share, Beth. I intend to stick to the salads. Carbs are the enemy of the weight-conscious,' declared Zara, patting her non-existent stomach and glancing at Beth's ample proportions from beneath her long, mascaraed lashes, her upper lip curling slightly.

'Well, I'm with Beth. I plan on trying everything that's on offer,' declared Tom, picking up one of the empty paint palettes and attempting to twirl it around his index figure until it flew into the air and clattered to the floor at Izzie's feet. 'Oops, sorry, Izzie.'

Beth and Zara rolled their eyes in unison and then giggled as he leaned forward to retrieve it, getting his camera strap entangled with his chair leg in the process and almost garrotting himself.

'Oh, at last! Here she comes, Her Majesty, the Queen of Sheba!' muttered Beth under her breath before raising her sing-song Welsh voice. 'Come on, Carmen, we should have started twenty minutes ago!'

'Morning all, it's great to see you all raring to go!' Carmen smiled, gliding elegantly into her allocated seat and demurely crossing her ankles before smoothing down the fabric of her floor-length coral-coloured sundress, one of the statement pieces from her current Spring/Summer collection. She slotted her designer sunglasses onto the top of her head and peered round at the gathering with a critical fashion-designer eye. 'Oh my God, Beth, darling, why does it always have to be black with you? It might have escaped your notice, but we're in Italy, it's July and the sun is shining; what's wrong with the cream silk kaftan I bought you in Duty Free?'

Without waiting for an answer, Carmen switched her attention to the laminated programme of events Izzie had propped up on each of the easels.

'Oh, I absolutely love how organised you are, Izzie. Everything itemised, everything colour-coded. Watch and learn, Hannah, watch and learn. You might pick up a few tips for when we get back to the office.'

Carmen turned her back on her PA in time to miss the flush that seeped from Hannah's cheeks down to her chest. Flustered, Hannah plonked herself down on her own chair and began scrabbling around in her over-sized hessian beach bag for her sunglasses to cover her mortification, then looked up expectantly at Izzie.

Izzie glanced at Carmen's assembled entourage and wondered whether any of them actually *wanted* to learn how to produce a watercolour of the Tuscan countryside or whether they would have been happier pursuing a course in amateur dramatics. From what she had seen so far, the dynamics and suppressed tensions between the group members would be enough to stage a two-hour play.

'Okay, so welcome, everyone, to the first painting course to be held here at Villa Limoncello. I hope that by the end of this week you'll be able to take away some new skills as well as a few paintings to display on your walls back home, but, more importantly, that you'll have had lots of fun. On the easel in front of you is a copy of today's itinerary, from which you'll see that this morning we'll be starting with a tutorial in watercolour techniques before moving on to try them out yourselves. After that, we'll adjourn for a typically Italian lunch which has been prepared for us by Luca Castelotti from Antonio's Trattoria over in San Vivaldo, who'll be back later on today to show us how to make home-made pasta, which we'll eat together under the pergola on the terrace.'

Izzie paused, grateful for the encouraging nod of approval from Meghan as she slipped away to spend a few delicious hours with Gianni before she was needed to help serve lunch. Carmen, too, had a wide smile on her face, clearly enthusiastic to make a start on the course she had booked as a thank you and team-building exercise for her staff after being bestowed with an industry award.

'So, without further ado, let's get started. I've prepared a wooden box of must-have artist's tools for each of you to use for the duration of the course and you can take them away with you at the end so that, if you want to, you can continue to paint at home. There's an artist's palette, a set of brushes, two water containers, a sponge to moisten the paper or create texture, a pencil for preliminary sketching, a couple of palette knives, a roll of masking tape, a spray bottle and a packet of tissues.'

'Are you expecting tears?' laughed Zara, rummaging through her painting goodies.

'I hope not! No, they're to dry your brushes and to blot away any excess water from your canvases. Okay, so we'll take this step-by-step and please feel free to ask questions as we go along.'

Nerves gnawed at Izzie's stomach, her throat was dry and her voice a little croaky. Even though she had a degree in fine art from the Royal College of Art, as well as presentation skills from running her own interior design studio, she had no experience of leading tutorials and regaining her self-confidence was still a work-in-progress. After all, until recently, she had lived a life of rigid routine – getting up at the same time, dressing in the same hoodie-and-jeans combo, grabbing a skinny latte from the same café – fearful that any deviation would cause her grip on sanity to falter.

Yet she had made huge strides since arriving in Tuscany six weeks ago. Not only had she successfully orchestrated a celebrity wedding, rejuvenated a crumbling villa and improved her culinary repertoire, these painting courses were proof that, with the support of her new Italian friends – Luca, Carlotta, Gianni, Oriana, who ran the local *pasticceria*, and Francesca, who owned the florist's, amongst others – life could be transformed from raincloud grey to sunshine yellow again. She inhaled a strengthening breath and focused on the blank sheet of paper in front of her.

'So, we start by lightly sketching the image we intend to paint in pencil, like this.'

With a slight tremble in her hand she drew two simple horizontal lines that would become a depiction of the Tuscan panorama spread out in front of them; fields of bobbing sunflowers, clusters of silver-green olive trees, distant villages with honeyed façades and terracotta roofs, all topped by a sky of translucent aquamarine. The view was perfect for a beginner's painting tutorial and Izzie's faith in her artistic abilities jumped up a notch.

How could anyone *not* be inspired by such bucolic magnificence?

Izzie loaded her brush with water and, using broad, light strokes, dampened the paper. Then she dipped her brush into the ultramarine and demonstrated how to create the sky before moving on to paint the hillside in the distance, crowned by the village of San Vivaldo, and finally the frilly emerald leaves of Gianni's beloved vineyard in the foreground. Standing back, she was pleased with what she had produced in just under twenty minutes.

A flutter of optimism percolated in her chest. Maybe she *could* do this!

Chapter Three

'Right, now it's over to you. Watercolour is one of the most versatile mediums to work with, so you can be as detailed and controlled, or as loose and impressionistic as you like.'

Over the next hour, silence descended over the white-washed gazebo, interrupted only by the occasional buzz of a lone Vespa straining to climb the incline towards the village or the soft symphony of the cicadas gearing up for their midday performance, as every one of the guests concentrated on creating their very first masterpiece. As expected, Carmen proved to be the most proficient of the group, with a sharp eye for detail and perspective. Tom was the least accomplished and Izzie spent most of her time urging him to just relax and enjoy the experience instead of focusing on what the final product would look like.

'Oh my God, Hannah. Is that the best you can do?' laughed Carmen, abandoning her own painting – an accurate reflection of the view framed by a ruffle of pale pink honeysuckle – to critique her fellow artists' canvases. 'You have the whole of Villa Limoncello's feast of floral delight, with a backdrop of rolling emerald hills, sunflower-filled fields and clear blue sky, and yet you choose to focus on a broken ceramic pot? It's pretty, don't get me wrong, but it's not really challenging yourself, is it?'

'Actually, Carmen, I'm not—'

'When I booked this course, I wanted us all to step out of our comfort zone, to challenge ourselves and push the boundaries of our creativity. That's the only way to improve, by constantly striving to accomplish new skills, to unleash new ideas and concepts. I think this is a C for effort. What do you think, Izzie?'

Izzie stared at Carmen for a beat. Having googled the fashion designer before she arrived as part of her habitual obsession with detail and overzealous organisation, she had suspected that Carmen Campbell would be a larger-than-life personality, with her signature long blonde hair that rippled in the breeze like a field of ripening corn. Like Zara, she was tall and willowy, but exuded a vibrant energy you could almost touch. However, she was clearly more than just a clothes horse, having had the fore-sight to establish her eponymous fashion house before her modelling career came to an end, and through sheer grit and determination – and not a little talent – she had obviously succeeded in a very competitive industry.

Nevertheless, the way she had spoken to her PA made Izzie uncomfortable, and whilst she had no wish to upset her celebrity guest, she also wanted everyone staying at the villa to feel valued and happy.

'Actually, I think it's a promising piece of work. I like the shades of light and dark in the background and the flowers have a touch of Charlotte Halliday about them. Can I just say that, as with all areas of creativity, whether it's painting, sculpture, music, writing or interior design, the results are subjective. This is not a competition and I would discourage comparisons or grades. We all see things differently; different textures, different colours, different shapes, and we enjoy working in different mediums, too. Some people will find they prefer to work with water-colours or pastels, whilst others might excel in pencil drawing or acrylics.'

'Yes, I'm looking forward to that tutorial the most,' said Tom, squinting at his rather insipid watercolour as if it were a Rembrandt.

'Some artists love creating landscapes, and, as you can see, there's an abundance of inspiration here at Villa Limoncello, but others might choose to make a study of the architectural detail found in the streets and alleyways of Siena, which you'll see from our itinerary is a place we'll be visiting on Thursday.'

'Oh, I'm *so* excited about our trip to Siena,' declared Hannah, her blue eyes widening, any lingering discomfort at her boss's belittling of her work washed away on a wave of excitement. 'I especially want to see the Piazza del Campo – it's supposed to be the largest medieval square in the world. And I want to learn more about the Palio horse race too, and climb the Torre del Mangia, and visit the—'

'Tourist haunts,' muttered Carmen, lining up her brush with the horizon, her silver charm bracelet clanging around her wrist. A waft of heavy oriental perfume floated in the air, which, coupled with the heady aroma of the honeysuckle climbing around the columns of the gazebo, caused Izzie to feel a little light-headed. 'What about you,

Zara? What are you looking forward to the most? One thing I do know, it won't be the variety of pizzas on offer!'

Zara held Carmen's eyes for a moment, and Izzie had the strangest feeling that, instead of irritation at the offhand comment, a splash of fear stalked through her gaze. However, when she glanced back towards Carmen, she saw she was smiling sweetly at the friend with whom she had spent ten long years on the catwalk.

'What I'm looking forward to most,' replied Zara, pulling the paintbrush from her hair and allowing it to tumble down to her shoulders, 'is taking a trip to Florence to feast my eyes on Michelangelo's *David* in all his muscular, marbled glory. I hope the Accademia is on the agenda, Izzie.'

'Don't worry, there's plenty of free time for your own sightseeing trips,' confirmed Izzie, tapping her finger on her bulging purple file. 'All the details are in the packs I gave you when you checked in yesterday.'

'Well, a statue of a five-metre-tall naked guy is not at the top of my list of must-sees,' piped up Tom, adding another splodge of grey paint to his depiction of the villa's newly painted fountain. 'If you want my opinion—'

'Actually, we'd rather not. It's art, darling! We'll all go. Anyway, I told you, no one is diverting from the itinerary. We're here to celebrate the award, yes, but I also want us to use this opportunity as a team-building exercise, to gather experiences and make shared memories that we can gossip about when we get back home.'

'Tell me again why Dalton couldn't come, Carr?' interjected Beth, concealing the switch to a more personal topic with a broad smile. 'I haven't seen him for ages, and he's never around when I come over to your flat – does he even still live there?'

'Oh, Dalton was devastated he couldn't come to Tuscany, but being such an accomplished photographer means he's always in demand somewhere or another,' said Carmen airily, flicking her wrist in dismissal of Beth's enquiry.

However, Izzie couldn't fail to notice the look of annoyance on Carmen's expertly made-up face. Clearly there was something amiss over Dalton's absence that only Beth knew about and Carmen wanted to keep from the others. Gosh, this whole course-running business was turning out to be a minefield! Despite having just met the group, she didn't have to be a contestant on *Mastermind* to know who was in charge. Okay, so Carmen had paid for the trip and that was very generous of her, but that shouldn't give her carte blanche to call out Beth's choice of attire, criticise Hannah's painting abilities or belittle Tom's taste in sculpture. And she definitely hadn't imagined the look in Zara's eyes when she'd mentioned her dislike of pizzas.

What was going on?

'Okay, I think it's time for lunch.' Izzie smiled, anxious to avoid any further deterioration in the atmosphere. 'If you'll follow me, I'll show you to the table in the court-yard, and Meghan and I will bring the food outside.'

'Yum!' declared Hannah, hooking the handles of her beach bag over her shoulder, then linking her arm through Tom's as they all made their way to the shady area at the rear of the villa, where Carlotta had laid a long trestle table with white crockery, sparkling glasses and vases filled with sprigs of fragrant lavender before cycling off for her rendezvous with Vincenzo. 'There's nothing like a morning of artistic endeavour to make the tummy rumble! I'm starving!'

'Me too,' agreed Beth, rushing ahead so she could grab the carved throne-like chair at the head of the table.

'Hey, I think I should sit there, don't you?' Carmen smiled, placing her hands on her hips, her expression making it clear that Beth should move.

'Oops, sorry, Carmen. Didn't see the Queen Bee name card!'

When Beth and Zara had settled into chairs on one side of the table, with Hannah and Tom opposite them and Carmen presiding, Izzie rushed off to the kitchen, praying Meghan had managed to tear herself away from her sojourn in the vineyard and had made a start on preparing the cold drinks. She needn't have worried and she flashed a smile of gratitude at her friend who had used a few days of her precious holiday allowance to fly over to Tuscany to support her in her new venture.

'Hi, Izzie, how was your first tutorial?'

'Interesting would be an understatement!'

'Interesting good, or interesting bad?'

'Let's serve lunch first or I think we might have a mutiny on our hands.'

She saw Meghan wrinkle her nose in confusion, but she picked up a basket heaped with freshly baked focaccia, grabbed a couple of bottles of Chianti and made her way back to the courtyard, the aroma of the warm bread causing exclamations of happiness all round.

'I absolutely adore that smell!' declared Beth, closing her eyes to savour the fragrance.

'Me too,' agreed Hannah, helping herself to a chunk of the rosemary-topped focaccia and bringing it to her nose. 'Mmm…'

'And here's your lunch! Enjoy!'

With a flourish worthy of a Michelin-starred chef, Meghan set a long wooden board crammed with Luca's sumptuous antipasti in the middle of the table. The platter showcased a cornucopia of colours, from the pink of the Parma ham and salami to the creamy white of the *stracchino* and mozzarella, from the rich red of the tomatoes and tiny marinated peppers to the vibrant green of the asparagus spears and the lettuce leaves. A generous helping of olives, both black and green, added further interest, along with radishes, artichokes and chickpeas.

'Wow!' cried Hannah and Beth in unison. Even Tom considered the spread worthy of the removal of his beloved camera for the first time that day, placing it with reverence on one of the vacant seats.

'Before we dive in, I think we should have a toast!' declared Carmen, flicking back her long hair and raising her glass of Chianti in the air. 'To our adventures under the Tuscan sun – both creative and foodie. May we produce canvases worthy of Titian, Raphael and Botticelli!'

'*Salute!*' the group chorused, then fell on the food as if they hadn't eaten for days.

Chapter Four

Izzie followed Meghan back to the kitchen where she fixed herself a double espresso, then sank into a seat at the scrubbed pine table, heaving a sigh of relief that she could at last rest her aching feet. She'd been on the go since five thirty that morning, and without an injection of caffeine her energy levels had taken a nosedive.

'So? Spill the gossip, Iz!' said Meghan, sliding into the chair next to her and meeting her gaze. 'I have to admit you looked exhausted. Tough morning?'

'Not the tutorial part, I loved that, but Carmen wanted to turn it into a competition. I know she has a reputation for being a hard taskmaster but seeing it in practice is a little unsettling. I'm going to have my work cut out keeping everyone's spirits up, and I'll definitely need to replenish my compliments drawer to make up for the constant low-level denigration from the boss.'

'It's a shame Jonti couldn't be here – he'd have whipped Carmen into shape in no time!' giggled Meghan. 'I don't think I've ever seen him so upset after his supervisor refused to authorise his request for a few days off. I thought he was going to have a meltdown, but in true

27

Jonti Montgomery style, he's cooked up something much more subtle for Dastardly Darius that involves access to his Mini and a packet of smoked kippers. He sent his love, though, and made me promise to post lots of photographs on Instagram.'

Izzie smiled, and for some unfathomable reason, tears prickled at her eyes. She adored Jonti – he was more than a fellow purveyor of all things fabric-and sequin-related. With his quirky sense of fashion, from the orange winkle-pickers to the rainbow-framed glasses that enhanced his bright blue eyes and his signature bleached blonde quiff, he exuded a sense of style she'd previously discarded to the realms of a former life. She would have loved him to see the progress she'd made after a few short weeks in Tuscany, ditching her drab khaki sweaters and 'dishcloth-grey' leggings for strappy tops in saffron and raspberry with matching capri pants.

'Well, if things go well this week, there'll be lots more opportunities for Jonti to come over for a visit. If they don't, well, I'll be seeing him back in Clapham by the end of the month.'

'So you're planning to stay in London instead of going home to Cornwall, then?'

Izzie opened her mouth to respond, but found the words were trapped by a sudden sweep of emotion. She might have made progress in the sartorial arena, but when it came to more painful matters, like taking a trip back to St Ives, where every corner held a memory of her twin sister, she had some way to go.

'Sorry, Izzie, I didn't mean to…'

'No, it's fine, really. You're right, I do need to face up to those demons, and I am working on it. In fact, being here at Villa Limoncello, enjoying the sunshine and the food and the…'

'The gorgeous men?'

'Yes, meeting Luca has definitely helped,' she laughed, tossing back the final dribble of coffee. 'How are things going with Gianni? I have to admit, I've never seen him so happy – not only does he practise his operatic talents on the vines, but he's started to sing to the olive trees, too! And for a woman whose relationships usually last no more than four dates, things must be getting serious. This is the third time you've been back to Tuscany in six weeks!'

'Gianni is different from the other guys I've dated. It's like he's a "real" person, not trying to be something he's not, and he's not afraid to talk about, or show, how he feels. He loves everything with a passion; his family, his friends, his vineyard and the fabulous wine he intends to create, his dreams for his musical career, even the local football team, and being with him makes me feel so alive!'

'Have you told your family about him?'

Izzie saw the familiar cloud that floated across Meghan's face whenever her parents were mentioned and instantly regretted her question. She knew exactly how Meghan was feeling because, like her, she too avoided going home to North Yorkshire, but for entirely different reasons.

'No, but I've organised a spa break for me and Mum at the end of July. It'll be easier to talk to her when she's on her own, away from the stables, away from Dad. I'm going to tell her the truth. You're right, Izzie, perhaps there's something in the air here that introduces a new perspective on things back home? When I'm strolling through the vines, or lingering in the *limonaia*, I know exactly what I want my future to look like and it's not breeding racehorses or being a window dresser at Harrods, it's designing and staging catwalk shows!'

'Oh, Meghan, I'm so happy to hear you say that!'

With tears threatening, Izzie leaned forward and wrapped her arms around her best friend, the friend who had walked by her side through the good times and the bad times; when she'd celebrated graduating the RCA with first-class honours, when she'd won an award for her interior design business, when she'd announced her engagement to her ex-fiancé, Alex, and when she'd thought she couldn't make it through another day without Anna in her life. Amongst the many things she had learned over the last two years, one of the most important lessons was how important it was to talk to those people who loved or cared about you the most.

'Okay, I think we should serve dessert, don't you?'

Meghan leapt from her seat and grabbed the wooden tray loaded with two huge cafetières and a silver plate piled high with a selection of Luca's home-made desserts – *sfogliatelle*, lemon *crostata*, almond *cantuccini* and a pyramid of freshly baked cannoli filled with cream and sprinkled with crushed pistachios.

'I'll get the fruit salad.' Izzie smiled, opening the fridge door and relishing the blast of ice-cold air on her cheeks.

She removed a hand-painted ceramic bowl filled to the brim with a rainbow of chopped fruit that Carlotta had prepared that morning, and a jug of fresh cream, then followed Meghan outside to the courtyard where Luca's antipasti had been devoured, along with every last drop of the Chianti.

'I hope you're all enjoying your lunch?'

The group nodded in agreement and there were exclamations of delight when Meghan placed the tray of Italian patisserie on the table.

'Everything you've eaten is organic and locally sourced. If you have time, you might like to take a trip over to the local village, San Vivaldo, where you'll find Antonio's Trattoria where Luca is head chef, and Oriana's *pasticceria*, which is truly a cathedral of sugary magnificence.'

'Sounds like my idea of heaven,' enthused Beth, determinedly ignoring Zara's crunched-up nose and raised upper lip. 'What do you say, Han? Fancy a visit this afternoon?'

'Just try and stop me! Want to join us, Tom?'

'No thanks. I'm stuffed after that lunch – thanks, Izzie, Meghan, everything was absolutely delicious. If it's okay with you, I think I'll take a few more photographs and then shelter from the sun for a while, perhaps make a start on the detective novel I bought at the airport. It's the next instalment of this—'

'And I think I'll stay here at the villa, too, soak up the rays,' interrupted Carmen, tossing back a last mouthful of the fragrant Jamaican coffee Izzie had ground that morning. 'I've got my eyes on a great spot over by that cute little wishing well. Zara, fancy joining me?'

'Maybe, but I think I might take a stroll around the grounds first. Was that a tennis court I saw earlier, Izzie?'

'Yes, it was, although I'm afraid it's not in use at the moment. It's the next item on our renovation schedule, though.'

'Okay, then scoot, everyone,' ordered Carmen, pushing back her chair and making it clear they were dismissed. 'I really need a bit of alone time to align my chakras. I've seen enough of you all for the time being.'

As everyone made their way from the courtyard like a gaggle of geese following their leader, Izzie heaved a sigh of relief and mentally ticked off 'Lunch – Monday' from her checklist.

'Okay, so I think our first meal was a definite hit. Let's hope this evening's pasta-making tutorial goes just as well.'

'As long as you stay out of the kitchen, we should be fine!' giggled Meghan, ducking out of the way as Izzie went to flick her with the tea towel. 'So, now that we've finished up here, I think I might borrow a leaf out of Zara's book and take stroll down to the olive grove.'

Meghan grinned as she slotted a bottle of Chianti and two glasses into a picnic basket that she had crammed with the same foodie treats from lunch and a fresh loaf of ciabatta.

'Having an al fresco picnic?'

'Well, *you* might call it that, but I'd call it indulging in a little bit of afternoon delight!'

Izzie laughed, her spirits soaring at the happiness radiating from her friend. She adored Meghan, and she hoped her dreams to become a creator of catwalks came true. She suspected Meghan had hoped to glean a bit of inside information on potential openings from Carmen, and hadn't failed to see her disappointment when it had turned out the fashion designer would be less than receptive to such an approach.

'Say hi to Gianni for me!'

She waved her friend off, then lingered on the terrace for a few moments to drink in the view, savouring the feel of the sun's warmth on her face and the tranquillity that wrapped its tendrils around her body in a comforting hug. There was something so calming about the shimmering golden light, the fragrance-filled breeze, the delicious food made with the freshest of ingredients, that had ignited the creativity genes that had lain dormant since she'd lost Anna to a brain aneurism.

Her heart still ached over her sister's untimely loss, but she was now at least able to rejoice in the good fortune of having shared her life for the twenty-seven years they'd been together – and the person she had to thank for that progress was Luca Castelotti. Spending an afternoon with him in Florence, a place she had dreaded visiting because it was where Anna had planned to have her hen weekend, had helped enormously. Now, instead of wallowing in her grief, she found herself glancing up at the sky, picking out the prettiest cloud, and imagining her sister floating in its soft midst, watching over her, cheering her on.

She meandered down to the garden, along the gravel pathway bordered by lavender and rosemary plants, and towards the dilapidated tennis court whose net sagged like a widow's stockings, her thoughts flicking down the list of what needed to be done to bring it up to scratch, when she stumbled upon Carmen stretched out on her sun lounger next to the wishing well.

'Oh, sorry, Carmen, I didn't mean to disturb… Carmen? Carmen! Oh my God! Are you okay?'

As Izzie rushed to her side, Carmen crunched forward, groaning in agony, clutching at her stomach, perspiration bubbling at her temples. Izzie reached for her hand, shocked to find it was cold and clammy to the touch.

'It's just a bit of stomach cramp. I'll be okay in a minute…'

'Carmen…'

'Izzie, what's going on? Oh my God, what's wrong with Carmen?'

Izzie had never been so pleased to see Meghan in her life, followed by the reassuring presence of Gianni, who immediately moved forward to support Carmen as she leaned back onto her sun lounger, her face drained of all colour as she continued to press her forearms into her abdomen.

'I'll fetch some water!' said Meghan, and dashed off towards the kitchen, passing Hannah on the way, gesticulating wildly in the direction of the wishing well before disappearing into the villa's kitchen.

'Carmen, what's wrong? What's the matter?'

Carmen attempted a weak smile for her PA, but it was more of a grimace.

'I'm fine, really, I think I might have eaten something I shouldn't have. I don't feel… Oh my God, I need the bathroom. Excuse me!'

Carmen jettisoned from the sun lounger like Usain Bolt out of the starting blocks and sprinted towards the villa with her hand over her mouth, shoving a confused Tom out of her way in her desperation to make it to the downstairs cloakroom in time.

'What's going on with Carmen?' he asked, fingering his camera lens nervously.

Hannah fixed a surprisingly steely gaze on Izzie.

'It's obvious, isn't it? Food poisoning – from lunch!'

34

Chapter Five

Izzie stared at Hannah, her jaw loose, the shock ricocheting through her veins preventing her from responding
to the accusation Hannah had tossed into the air like a
verbal grenade. Her heart hammered out a concerto of
alarm and it was a few seconds before her brain recon-
nected to its modem.

'I'll just go and see if Carmen needs anything...'

'No you won't – I will!' Hannah bristled, her face
almost as pale as Carmen's had been. 'Don't you think you
should be contacting the chef who prepared our lunch to
inform him that his substandard food has made one of us
ill and to warn him that the food inspectors will be paying
him a visit?'

And with that she spun on her heels and flounced off
towards the villa, only to bump into Carmen being fussed
over by Zara, and Meghan and Beth, who were carrying
pitchers of iced water, lemonade and a tray of glasses,
setting everything down on the table under the shade of
the pergola.

'Carmen! Oh my God, you look awful! How are you
feeling?' cried Hannah, rushing to her side and taking

Carmen's other arm to help Zara guide her into one of the sun-bleached director's chairs.

'Well, I'd feel better if everyone stopped gawping at me like a bunch of gobsmacked goldfish. I just need a few minutes to... Oh no, hang on...'

Carmen leapt from her seat again and shot with lightning speed back into the villa.

'I hope you're happy!' cried Hannah, flashing her eyes at Izzie and Meghan before dashing off in Carmen's wake so she could loiter outside the bathroom door like an over-zealous Rottweiler protecting her owner from any more undeserved strikes.

'I'd better call Luca,' muttered Gianni, the lines on his forehead deepening with concern as he extracted his phone from the pocket of his scruffy denim shorts and walked towards the *limonaia* so he could make the call in private.

Izzie glanced at Meghan, panic swirling through her chest, her throat dry and constricted. Food poisoning? How could that be possible? She and Carlotta had invested hours in a marathon of extreme cleaning the previous day; not one microbe of bacteria would dare to rear its ugly head, and she knew Luca had been meticulous in his preparation of lunch. However, she was also aware that mistakes could happen.

'Does everyone else feel okay?' she asked, looking around at Zara, Beth and Tom.

'I'm fine,' said Beth, patting her stomach beneath her black T-shirt that announced a recent Black Sabbath tour. 'But then I've got the constitution of an ox! Don't worry, it's typical of Hannah to jump to the worst conclusion before thinking things through.'

'What about you, Tom?'

'Oh, I'm the same as Beth. I'll eat anything and everything that's put in front of me – the more exotic the better. Lunch was delicious, and I particularly liked the pickled artichoke. And I can't wait to start the pasta-making course. Oh no… you don't think it'll be cancelled, do you?'

'Well, if Carmen doesn't insist on it, then Hannah probably will,' grumbled Beth, crossing her arms over her chest and sticking out her bottom lip like a petulant toddler. If Izzie hadn't been so upset about the current developments, she would have laughed.

'Anyone else want a glass of this delicious-looking lemonade?' asked Tom, holding the pitcher aloft, his bushy ginger eyebrows raised in question, completely at ease with continuing to partake in Villa Limoncello's home-made beverages despite Carmen's sudden indisposition.

In fact, everyone accepted a drink, but Izzie noticed Zara eyeing the contents of her glass suspiciously, her fingers trembling slightly on the rim.

'Are you feeling nauseous, too?'

'How can *she* have an upset stomach?' snapped Beth, rolling her eyes in Zara's direction. 'She only ate a couple of tomatoes and a few sprigs of grilled asparagus at lunch, and, as far as I know, you can't get food poisoning from that!'

'So you *do* think it's food poisoning, then?' said Zara, rubbing her non-existent stomach as though anticipating an explosion at any minute.

'Well, what else can it be?' demanded Hannah as she re-joined them on the terrace, pouring herself a glass of lemonade which she downed in one.

'Although you don't think it was caused by the lemonade?' Beth smirked, the only one seemingly unmoved by her friend's dietary distress. 'I see you've decided to leave your guard post?'

'How can you be so flippant, Beth. You know Carmen has sensitivities to certain foods! What if she's having an allergic reaction to one of the ingredients?'

'Then she'll use her EpiPen. Look, Hannah, Carmen's a grown woman who has managed to get to thirty-five without falling into a sinkhole or coming out in hives because she's sniffed a packet of peanuts! It's a stomach upset, get over it!'

'Excuse me!'

Zara shoved back her chair and rushed into the villa, leaving a trail of sweet jasmine perfume behind her.

'Oh no, another one bites the dust.' Beth grinned, taking a leisurely sip of her lemonade. 'I think you might be waving goodbye to your culinary fantasy tonight, Tom.'

'Well, if we all have food poisoning, none of us will want to do a cooking course, will we?' snapped Hannah, looking at Beth as though she had just suggested they take a trip to the moon. 'That would be ridiculous! Who wants to learn how to make pasta from a chef who's just poisoned us all with contaminated food?'

Izzie gulped down her anxiety as her desire to introduce a modicum of common sense to the unfolding drama prevailed.

'I think it's a little premature to be jumping to conclusions about what might have caused Carmen's illness. It could be a bug she picked up from the plane, or she could have eaten something she brought with her, like those energy drinks she has at breakfast. We don't know yet.'

'I agree with Izzie,' said Tom, hope scrawled across his face as he twisted the strap of his camera around his index finger.

'Well, how does that account for Zara?'

'Oh, well, yes, I suppose…'

Heat flooded Izzie's face as she considered their options and realised that the only sensible thing to do was to cancel that evening's pasta-making tutorial and see how Carmen and Zara were later in the evening.

'So, Luca's on his way over,' said Gianni, taking a seat at the table and combing his fingers through his messy mop of dark curls before helping himself to a glass of lemonade, running his tongue along his lower lip to collect a trail of sugar granules.

'Good,' said Hannah, her cheeks recovering some of their colour, which only served to enhance the dark shadows of exhaustion beneath her eyes.

'I think we need to keep an open mind until he's had the opportunity to check everything out. He's confident that it's unlikely to be anything you ate at lunch – everything was freshly prepared this morning, taking into account everyone's dietary preferences and, to be honest, it's much too quick to be food poisoning.'

'Thanks, Gianni,' said Izzie, the heavy block of concrete that had taken up residence in her chest easing slightly.

'And both Gianni and I ate everything on the lunch menu and we're fine,' added Meghan, sending Gianni a wide smile that caused Izzie's stomach to flutter.

'Hey, Zara? Are you okay now?'

Izzie watched Zara glide across the terrace towards them, her chin raised, her head steady, placing each foot precisely in front of the other, hips swaying elegantly as though she was still modelling the latest summer fashions on a runway.

'I'm fine. Nothing to worry about. I haven't been sick or anything – just felt a little faint, that's all. I think it's a mixture of the shock and the sun. I don't have food poisoning.'

'Okay, so does that mean you're feeling up to a trip to San Vivaldo, then?' asked Beth, tossing the sides of her bob behind her ears in a familiar gesture. 'I really think we should make the most of our time here. Want to tag along, Han? I don't think Carmen will be surfacing for a while.'

Hannah glanced from Beth to Zara, indecision flickering across her face.

'No, no, I think I should stay here. Carmen's asked me to look into the process of reporting a food-poisoning incident to the authorities. I really don't think any of us should leave until we—'

'Look, Hannah, Izzie and Meghan will be here if she needs anything and you'll be at the end of a phone. Come on. This is supposed to be a holiday not a work trip! Carmen shouldn't be expecting you to be at her beck and call! All you've done since we arrived here is run after her; unpacking her clothes, lending her your hairdryer because she's not capable of remembering her own, making up her vitamin drink! Take some time off from all the worrying – it'll do you the world of good. It's just a stomach bug. She'll be fine.'

Hannah glanced at Izzie and Meghan, weighed up Beth's arguments and whether she could trust the fate of her boss to the people Carmen held accountable for her indisposition in the first place.

'I... no, sorry I can't. I need to stay here in case she needs me.'

Without further ado, Hannah stalked back into the villa to maintain her vigil at Carmen's bedroom door whilst making enquiries into the whereabouts of the local Health & Safety offices. Beth shook her head and heaved a sigh of defeat.

'What about you, Tom? Want to join us?'

'Absolutely! You're right, Beth, we need to make the most of being here. It's been ages since I had a holiday, and heaven knows when I'll get another chance to have a break from work.'

Izzie saw a flash of sympathy scorch across Beth's and then Zara's expressions and she found herself wondering about Tom's background. All she knew was that he was Carmen's accountant and business manager with an obsession for taking snapshots of anything that moved.

'Come on then, race you to the car!'

Izzie watched them go, the cause of Carmen's sudden illness already relegated to inconsequential as they chattered animatedly about their trip to the local village. When the hire car disappeared through the wrought-iron gates, she couldn't hold onto her emotions any longer and tears collected along her lower lashes.

'Oh my God, two days in and we've already managed to poison one of our guests, and not just *any* guest, either. It has to be Carmen Campbell, the award-winning, internationally acclaimed fashion designer! Once the news leaks out, we can wave goodbye to organising any more courses at Villa Limoncello.'

'Izzie, it's not—'

'Which means that Luca will be forced to sell the villa—'

'Izzie, I think we should—'

'And we'll have to go back to London.'

'Izzie…'

'And what about Antonio's? If this does turn out to be food poisoning, it's bound to have ramifications for the restaurant. What if that's closed down, too? Oh my God! It's all a complete disaster!'

'Izzie, I'm sure that's not going to happen,' soothed Meghan, passing her a paper napkin to dry her eyes. 'We need to talk to Luca, then we should have a serious chat with Carmen. All we know at the moment is that she's got a stomach upset – nothing more. What did she eat on the plane? Did anyone else have the same, did they stop on their way over here, did she bring anything with her, what was in the vitamin drink she had for breakfast? My money is on that – it looked like swamp water.'

Izzie's sensible side knew that Meghan's questions were reasonable, but that didn't calm her anxiety monsters, who'd managed to break free of their straitjackets and launch into a feeding frenzy. Was this her fault? If it *was* lunch, all she and Meghan had done was remove the covers and serve. Or was she blowing everything out of proportion? She forced herself to relax, to corral her worries and shove them back into their box until they knew more.

The crunch of tyres on the gravel brought a surge of relief. She squinted into the sun and watched Luca's scarlet

42

Spider make its way to the front steps of the villa, scattering a confetti of pebbles into the air as the tyres came to an abrupt stop. Within moments, Luca had leapt from the driver's seat, his handsome face wreathed in concern. Despite the gravity of the situation, Izzie experienced a sharp fizz of attraction deep in her soul when he deposited the customary kisses on her cheeks.

'So, tell me exactly what happened.'

Luca sank into a chair next to Gianni, crossing his ankle over his thigh and giving the impression that all was well with the world, yet his dark mahogany eyes were filled with unease. He hadn't had time to change out of his chef's whites and to Izzie he looked even more attractive than he did in his jeans and T-shirt.

'Izzie found Carmen over by the wishing well complaining of violent stomach cramps before she dashed off to the bathroom. She's recovering in her room, watched over by Hannah, her PA, who is adamant that it's food poisoning from something they ate at lunch, and she's threatening to call in the authorities, so we'll probably have to cancel this evening's pasta-making tutorial, and perhaps the whole course as well.'

'And what does Carmen want to do?'

'We haven't spoken to her yet,' said Izzie, twisting the napkin between her fingers.

'Well, I think that's the first thing we need to do when she's feeling up to it.'

Silence meandered through the air as each of them contemplated the repercussions of what had happened. Izzie watched Luca rub his palm across his stubbly jawline, his brow knitted with anxiety, and she experienced an almost overwhelming urge to rush up to Carmen's room

43

to interrogate her on the precise details of her diet over the last twenty-four hours.

'So, Gianni, want to help me make a start on sterilising the kitchen for the second time in two days?' asked Meghan, indicating Luca's bowed head with her eyes and giving Gianni a nod filled with meaning.

'Oh, right, yes, good idea.'

Izzie waited until they were out of earshot then turned towards Luca. 'What are you thinking about?'

'It's strange, don't you think?'

'What do you mean?'

'Well, if it *is* food poisoning – how come everyone else is fine? I assume everyone ate lunch, not just Carmen?'

'Yes, in fact Beth, Hannah and Tom hoovered up every last morsel. Zara didn't eat much, but I don't think that's unusual, and Meghan took a picnic to share with Gianni and they're both fine. Do you think Carmen's reaction could have something to do with her food intolerances?'

'Well, first of all, what I said earlier was true. I'm fully conversant with every food allergy, intolerance and sensitivity, and you know how meticulous we were in sourcing and preparing the ingredients. Carlotta has been catering villas for decades and there's no one more fastidious when it comes to hygiene practices. There is no way anything we served at lunch could have been contaminated with any kind of nut or nut derivative.'

'So what do you think happened?'

Luca met her eyes, causing her stomach to perform an instantaneous flip-flop as he hesitated over formulating his next sentence.

'Luca?'

Then it dawned on Izzie, and the bottom of her stomach dropped like a penny down a well. 'Are you suggesting... Are you saying that you think someone... someone might have put something in the food?'

Luca didn't reply straight away, just fixed his gaze on the distant horizon where the rolling emerald hills met the azure of the sky, his jaw clenched, his head shaking slightly.

'I'm just thinking of alternate scenarios, that's all. It's a possibility, but not the food in general, otherwise, as you said, everyone would have been affected.'

'You think someone *wanted* to make Carmen ill? But why would they do that?'

'I have no idea, but if that's true then whoever it was is going to have me to answer to. If it's meant to be some kind of practical joke to send the cat away so the mice can have a good time without her, then I'm... I'm... God, Izzie, I could lose everything if even the slightest rumour of this spread.'

Izzie thought her brain was about to explode as she tried to assimilate everything that had happened and what Luca seemed to be suggesting. So much for organising a relaxing course in the Tuscan countryside, spending the mornings in creative contemplation, the afternoons snoozing and gossiping in the sun with her best friend, and the evenings learning how to make home-made pasta from someone as talented, and handsome, as Luca. Now it looked like her time would be taken up with worrying about whether someone was intent on sabotaging the course and why they would do such a thing.

'What do you think we should do?'

'I'm not sure.'

'Well, maybe we should start by asking a few questions…'

'Exactly what I was thinking, but we should do it surreptitiously. Without Gianni and Meghan knowing either. If someone did introduce something into Carmen's food or drink, then this is a serious matter. And it could only be one of the other guests, don't you think?'

Izzie stared at Luca, understanding for the first time the severity of the situation, especially bearing in mind Carmen's sensitivities to certain foods. Things could have been a lot worse than a stomach upset! Anxiety began to coil around her veins, tightening the guy ropes around her lungs until she forced herself to focus on their options, otherwise she would be looking her sanity in the rear-view mirror.

'So what you're saying is that we should don our metaphorical deerstalkers?'

'Our what?'

'Become amateur sleuths.'

'Something like that,' said Luca, a distant flicker of amusement entering his eyes for the first time since he'd arrived at Villa Limoncello.

'So, who's your money on? Tom? Beth? Zara? Surely not Hannah?'

'Well, you know more about the guests than I do. You spent all morning in their company, immortalising this stunning panorama in paint. What do you think?'

'Oh, God! If you're asking me who I think is the most likely person to want Carmen confined to her room, based on this morning's session in the gazebo I would have to tell you – it's all of them!'

46

Chapter Six

The kitchen, Villa Limoncello
Colour: Delicious ruby red

'All of them, are you serious?'

'Yes, and I'm sure Meghan will agree with me, too. In fact, if Carmen spoke to me the way she speaks to Hannah and Tom, then I might have contemplated doing the same thing!' Izzie gasped, slapping her hand over her mouth and meeting Luca's eyes. 'Sorry, I didn't mean that. I just...'

'Don't worry, I think I can strike you from the list of suspects – for the time being.' Luca smirked, his eyes softening.

'Lists! Yes, that's it. Hang on!'

'Izzie...'

But it was too late. Izzie was already jogging into the villa to collect her trusty arch-lever file crammed to bursting with every stationery-lover's dream – everything she needed for a successful painting /cookery course in the Tuscan countryside down to the last detail.

Except it hadn't worked out that way, had it?

She paused on the doorstep, her eyes once again drawn to the view; the terracotta gables of San Vivaldo nestled on the crown of the hill, the parallel tramlines of the vines snaking across the fields, the clock-tower punctuating the sky in the distance. It was late afternoon, yet the day's heat still lingered in the air and the cicadas pressed on with their relentless sonata regardless of the traumatic happenings in their midst.

Who would have thought something like this could happen in such idyllic surroundings?

She recognised the nugget of dread nestling in the pit of her stomach. It was the same feeling she had carried with her for two long years when, no matter what she did, whether it was an enjoyable experience or not, lurking on the periphery of her consciousness was the unassailable knowledge that everything she accomplished would be tinged with sadness. The only way she had been able to cope with the struggle to bedtime was by adhering to her fixed routine, allowing no margin for random surprises or else she would collapse in a heap on the floor.

Only by breaking that cycle and coming to Italy had she been able to move forward; small steps, granted, but meaningful ones. Her last-minute dash to help Meghan's brother Brad Knowles stage a wedding at the villa had proved to be the catalyst to moving forward – never forgetting what had happened, she couldn't do that, but learning how to stitch her grief into the tapestry of her life in order to create a new picture that could, at some point in the future, include happiness.

After the success of the wedding, she'd been delighted when Luca had asked if he could engage her services to help him update the villa, and then host the first Painting & Pasta course. She had leapt at the chance to spend more time with him and to continue with her sunshine therapy. Villa Limoncello had worked its magic and reignited her love for interior design, the profession she had trained for and was passionate about. She adored fabric, soft furnishings, paint effects, stencilling, glass-painting and anything that involved the use of her glue gun – all things that she and Luca had discussed and created together to get the villa ready for paying guests.

She had briefly floated the idea that the villa should simply host the courses, and their students could make arrangements to stay elsewhere, such as the upmarket B&B next door, but Gianni had been horrified at the mere suggestion – and, of course, she didn't blame him after what had happened.

So it looked like if she wanted to stay on in Tuscany to oversee the autumn and Christmas courses they had planned, then she had to help Luca uncover the truth. They didn't have a lot of time to get to the bottom of what had happened because if allegations of food poisoning were to be splashed over Tripadvisor, then they would struggle to attract new bookings and if it couldn't generate an income, the villa would have to be sold. But it was worse than that – if the villa was sold, that would include the vineyard and the olive grove which meant Gianni would lose his job. She couldn't bear that – Gianni treated his vines like his babies! And, whilst her own feelings had to come at the bottom of the list, she definitely did not want to return to her former, colourless life in London that Meghan and Jonti had labelled 'snoring boring'.

'Okay, let's make a start on a list. Agreed?' said Izzie, her spirits edging up a notch at the thought of doing something positive. She opened her file and removed a fresh piece of paper and a pencil.

'Very professional, Signorina Poirot!'

Luca smiled, pulling his chair closer to Izzie, so close that she could smell the delicious lemony cologne that would always remind her of her sojourn in the Italian countryside and the man sitting next to her that had made it so special. She inhaled a slow breath, lowering her eyelids slightly to savour the fragrance before pulling herself together. If she wanted to save Villa Limoncello, then she had a job to do!

'Okay, so there are four potential culprits – Zara, Beth, Hannah and Tom.'

Izzie wrote their names across the top of the page, then paused, levelled her eyes at Luca, and burst out laughing.

'I have no idea what to do next!'

'What's the matter? Did you miss the most recent episode of *Midsomer Murders*?' asked Luca, his tone light, but Izzie knew he was worried.

'What do you think we should do?'

'I think we should carry on with the planned itinerary until we can speak to Carmen. After all, everyone will go along with what she wants, especially as she's the one who organised the whole thing. We'll continue with the pasta tutorial, keep our ears open to the general banter, and maybe we'll learn something.'

'Sounds like a plan. Let's go and see how Meghan and Gianni are getting on with the cleaning.'

Izzie gathered up her paperwork, slotted it back into her file and hugged it to her chest as they made her way across the terrace towards the kitchen. On the threshold, she stopped abruptly, causing Luca to bump into her and sending her stumbling into the room.

'Oops,' giggled Meghan, pulling out of a passionate embrace, her eyes sparkling, broad grins stretching both hers and Gianni's lips. 'Just celebrating the end of our impromptu cleaning marathon! No germ would be stupid enough to even take a short break in here, never mind a holiday! You could make the pasta on that floor!'

'Thanks, guys.' Izzie smiled.

'Okay,' announced Gianni, striding purposely to the door and leaving a trail of footprints in his wake. 'Better get back to the day job. *Ciao!*'

'*Ciao,*' chorused Izzie and Meghan, watching from the doorstep as he fired up his rust-blistered quad bike and trundled through the garden towards his beloved vineyard, a blast of Italian opera rippling through the air.

'Ahh,' sighed Meghan, performing a pirouette of satisfaction. 'I'm so relieved that we're back on track – it would have been such a shame to cancel everything. I'm *so* looking forward to learning how to make fresh pasta!'

'You're right, Meg. It's going to be lots of fun.'

'Makes a change from your staple diet of buttered toast, eh?' teased Meghan, slipping her arm around Izzie's waist as they returned to the kitchen, where Luca had already laid out seven separate sets of ingredients on the scrubbed pine table.

'Hey, everyone! We're back!' announced Zara, bursting into the kitchen, her hair mussed up around her face, her cheeks sporting splashes of red.

'San Vivaldo is amazing!' giggled Beth, dropping her handbag onto one of the counters, her eyes a little unfocused.

'Don't mind them,' said Tom, rolling his eyes at the two women as he brought up the rear, weighed down with several shopping bags from Bianca's, the local lingerie shop, his ever-present camera bouncing at his chest. 'They've discovered the local delicacy.'

'Which one?' asked Izzie, raising her eyebrows.

'Limoncello!' declared Zara, gathering her long caramel hair in her hands and tossing it over her shoulder. 'Well, how could we not sample the very thing this villa is named after – that would be sacrilege! And it's absolutely delicious and I intend to take several bottles back home with me.'

'Actually, the previous owner used to make her own limoncello here using the lemons from the *limonaia*.'

'What's the *limonaia*?' asked Beth, slumping down onto one of the kitchen chairs and tipping her head backwards so her hair fell away from her face to reveal flushed cheeks.

'It's the huge glass conservatory on the south gable of the villa where Maria Rosetti spent decades cultivating her lemons. You're welcome to take a look, but please don't pick the fruit – it's easy to damage the plants and some of them are over two hundred years old. However, you might be interested to know that I've made a few bottles of limoncello from Maria's original recipe which is just about ready for drinking.'

'Well, that's the best news I've heard all day!' giggled Beth.

'So, the pasta tutorial is still going ahead, then?' asked Tom, his gaze taking in the ingredients on the table. 'Does that mean Hannah has seen sense and is not going to call in the food police?'

'Not yet!' said a voice from the door. 'I'm waiting to see what Carmen wants to do and she's still asleep, but I really don't think it's a good idea to hold the pasta-making lesson until we can be absolutely sure that—'

'Now that everyone is here, can I ask if anyone else has experienced similar symptoms to Carmen whilst you were in San Vivaldo this afternoon?' interrupted Meghan, her eyes seeking each one of their guests separately. 'No?' When everyone had shaken their heads – including Hannah, albeit reluctantly – she continued, 'Then I don't think there's any reason why we shouldn't just carry on with the itinerary, is there?'

'I agree,' said Beth, eyeing the ingredients in front of her and rolling up her sleeves. 'Anyway, I'm starving!'

'Me, too,' confirmed Tom, before casting a glance across to where Zara seemed to be swaying a little, clearly still experiencing the after-effects of her foray into limoncello-tasting. 'Izzie, is there any chance of some strong, black coffee?'

'Sure, coming right up.'

Izzie got busy with the coffee machine, sending the scent of aromatic ground coffee beans into the kitchen, and when everyone had a cup of the thick dark elixir in front of them, Luca cleared his throat to get their attention.

'Okay, if everyone's ready…'

'What about you, Hannah? Are you staying or are you going to sit in your room all night staring at the walls?' asked Beth, tossing back her tiny cup of espresso in one gulp, before helping herself to another one.

'I think I'll stay. At least that way I'll know what's going into my dinner!'

Beth rolled her eyes but remained silent, and everyone else decided to ignore her.

'Okay, so welcome, everyone, to *Villa dei Limoni*'s inaugural pasta-making tutorial. Let me first of all assure you that all the ingredients we will be using this evening are of the highest possible quality and have been sourced from reputable suppliers within a two-mile radius of where you are standing; the vegetables are fresh, the semolina is organic and the eggs are free-range. Also, for everyone's peace of mind, the kitchen has been sterilised once again. So, before we start, I want you all to wash your hands and put on your aprons.'

There was a scramble for the kitchen sink, and then *oohs* and *aahs* as the students pulled on their aprons – each one embroidered with the words *Villa Limoncello*, a motif of a lemon and personalised with their names. Izzie was relieved to see that the espresso had done its job of calming everyone's nerves, and she smiled with pleasure when they took their places at the table, Tom apologising profusely when he accidentally nudged one of the eggs onto the floor.

'Sorry, I'll just…'

'No!' snapped Meghan, clearly not wanting to allow Tom access to the cleaning materials. 'Leave it, I'll do it!' She swiftly cleared the area, resprayed the tiles with anti-bacterial spray and returned to her allocated place between Izzie and Zara, whose eyes were now completely focused on the task.

'Okay, this evening we will start with one of the simplest of pastas – spaghetti – with a *sugo finto* sauce, which translated means "fake meat" and is a rich tomato sauce made from the freshest vegetables, or what we call *soffritto*, sautéed in red wine. In the past, meat was a luxury and only eaten rarely, which means we have many recipes suitable for vegetarians. So, we'll start with the pasta. I'll demonstrate the technique and then assist you whilst you prepare your own, then we'll move on to the sauce. As this is the first evening, I've already made dessert – *schiacciata alla Fiorentina* – from a recipe handed down from my great-grandmother, which I hope you'll enjoy. All the recipes I'll be showcasing this week are in your individual folders, all courtesy of Izzie, who I think you'll agree has done a fabulous job.'

Izzie felt a blush creep into her cheeks, followed by a soupçon of pride, which forced the afternoon's traumas into the crevices of her mind. As she followed Luca's simple instructions, she began to enjoy the process of incorporating the egg into the flour with a fork, smiling as the mixture came together into a dough.

'I have to admit, Luca, whilst I love pasta, and the sauce sounds delicious, dessert will always be my favourite part of any meal – and that cake over there looks scrumptious!' said Beth, eyeing the pale yellow sponge cake that had been sprinkled with icing sugar and decorated with Florence's emblem, the lily.

'The digestif is my favourite part!' declared Zara, pushing up the fluted sleeves of her aquamarine blouse. Worn with a pair of flared white linen trousers, she looked as though she'd just stepped from her yacht in Portofino for a film premiere, not standing in the slightly careworn kitchen of a Tuscan farmhouse elbow-deep in flour. Yet, despite her declared aversion to all things gluten-filled, it was evident she was having fun.

After demonstrating the kneading method, Luca prowled around the ancient table, making suggestions, guiding palms, correcting technique. 'Right, we'll leave the dough to rest and get on with the sauce. Italians are very particular about which sauce we have with which pasta. For instance, we would never pair a meaty sauce like Bolognese with spaghetti. So, for the *sugo finto* we will peel the vegetables, then gently sauté them in a little olive oil before adding the red wine and tomatoes.'

When there were seven separate sauces, in varying degrees of accomplishment, the group got busy with rolling out the pasta dough and feeding it through their pasta machines, which made for some hilarious results.

'Oh my God, Tom, that looks like something my little brother would make with his playdough set!' laughed Hannah, her intention to scrutinise every ingredient for lurking bacteria forgotten as culinary creativity took over. 'Although I have to admit, your sauce is definitely better than mine!'

'I'm sure it'll taste fabulous, though,' interjected Izzie, keen to avoid the carousel of criticism that had marred that morning's watercolour session and maintain the jovial atmosphere currently swirling around the kitchen.

'How long do we cook the pasta for?' asked Beth, perspiration bubbling at her temples as she leaned over a pan of boiling water, her home-made spaghetti held aloft.

'That's where fresh pasta differs from the dried variety you buy in the shops. It'll only take a couple of minutes. So, is everyone ready?'

'Yes,' the students chorused.

In no time at all, they were sitting around the table sampling their first authentic Tuscan meal made from scratch by their own fair hands. Izzie beamed around at the group, the earlier drama a distant memory as she handed round the still-warm *pane Toscano* and filled everyone's glasses with a locally produced Chianti Gianni had recommended.

'I hope you like the wine. It's from a winery in the next valley, but Gianni is hoping that next year our guests will be drinking wine made from the grapes from the Rosetti vineyard here at Villa Limoncello.'

'It's wonderful,' said Zara, reaching out to refill her already empty glass.

'And this is the best pasta I've ever tasted,' declared Tom, his face wreathed in surprise. 'Even though I do say so myself! How's yours, Han?'

'It's…' Hannah paused and shot a quick glance in Luca's direction. 'It's delicious.'

'So, not sub-standard?' asked Beth, a glint of mischief dancing in her dark brown eyes.

Hannah bristled as she twirled her spaghetti around her fork, gifting Tom with a smile of gratitude when he came to her rescue by diverting the conversation to another topic.

'So, Luca, what's on the foodie agenda for the rest of the week?'

'Well, tomorrow morning we'll take an excursion to the street market in San Vivaldo where we can taste-test the best cheeses Tuscany has to offer, some fabulous sliced meats such as *finnochiona*, which is local salami flavoured with fennel, and a delicious extra virgin olive oil that is pressed within metres of the town. We can also try out a few of the local wines if you like; Chianti, Brunello, Morellino di Scansano and Montepulciano, and there'll be a selection of dessert wines too.'

'Will there be ice cream?' asked Beth, earning herself an eye-roll from Zara, who Izzie noticed had probably produced the most accomplished dish out of all of them, apart from Luca, but hadn't even tasted a mouthful, preferring to stick to the watercress and rocket salad that Meghan had prepared with a sprinkle of pine nuts and a lemon juice-based dressing.

'Of course there'll be gelato,' laughed Luca, his eyes crinkling attractively at the corners. 'Tuscany has the best gelato in the whole of Italy! And there'll be plenty of time for you to explore on your own before we come back to the villa for lunch and your second painting tutorial in the afternoon.'

'What are we learning about tomorrow, Izzie?' asked Tom, who had turned out to be Izzie's most enthusiastic student, if not the most talented.

'Pastels.'

'Great!' he said, leaning back in his chair and rubbing his stomach in satisfaction after eating an enormous slice of Luca's grandmother's *schiacciata alla Fiorentina*, before checking himself. 'Oh, would you like some help with the washing up?'

'No, thanks, Tom. Luca and I will handle that. Why don't you take your coffee out to the terrace?'

Izzie smiled, her heart softening at Tom's thoughtfulness – he had obviously been well-trained at home and she wondered where that was, whether it was with a partner or his family, and why this was his first trip abroad for such a long while when he clearly had a well-paid job. She hoped that everyone would get as much out of their experience at Villa Limoncello as possible, but even more so in the case of Tom. Her mind wandered to the list she had started earlier and whether she could strike off Tom's name – he really didn't seem to have it in him to slip something in his boss's food so food they could enjoy a Carmen-free beak. In fact, from what she had seen of his relationship with Carmen so far, she would say that, if anything, he was terrified of her.

Then she realised that if she discounted Tom, there was no reason why she shouldn't discount the others, too. Zara and Beth had been friends with Carmen for years, and Hannah seemed to have a touch of the mother hen about her, despite the evidence of exhaustion being on constant call was causing her.

Perhaps this was all just an unfortunate accident and she and Luca had jumped to conclusions.

Chapter Seven

The pergola, Villa Limoncello
Colour: Honeysuckle white

By the time Izzie had hung up her tea towel and declared the kitchen squeaky clean again, darkness had crept over the horizon and the cicadas were well into their evening finale. Outside, fairy lights twinkled amongst the tendrils of honeysuckle climbing the pergola, and a myriad of amber flames flickered in the storm lanterns she'd borrowed from Francesca, San Vivaldo's floral genius. The whole terrace resembled a magical grotto, a place where serenity reigned and romance could blossom, just not between the current contingent of guests who were busy finishing the promised bottle of home-made limoncello.

'Right, I'd better make tracks,' said Luca, whipping off his apron and folding it carefully. 'I've left Carlos in charge of the restaurant tonight and I want to make sure everything is in order before we close for the night. Are you sure you'll be okay?'

'Sure, I have Meghan, don't I?'

Then an unsettling thought popped in her brain like an exploding kernel of corn and a shiver of alarm shot down her spine causing goose bumps to ripple along her forearms.

'What?'

'Oh, it's nothing.'

She plastered a bright smile on her lips and set the kettle to boil in case anyone wanted another coffee before retiring to bed. She had no intention of sharing with Luca her fear that if someone really had targeted Carmen that morning, then maybe they would try again that night?

'Okay, see you tomorrow then. I'll meet you under the clock tower in the piazza at eight.'

'No problem, and I'm sorry about… well, today's turn of events.'

'Stop apologising, Isabella. Whatever's happened here is definitely not your fault.'

Luca held Izzie's gaze, then took a step forward, his mouth inches from her, his proximity sending spasms of desire through her body. He really was the most attractive man she'd had the pleasure of meeting since arriving in Tuscany, with his sexy come-to-bed eyes, skin the colour of liquid caramel, and the way his hair curled into tufts at the collar of his chef's jacket. Oh, and the way her name – *Izz-a-bel-la* – rolled from his tongue could definitely cause an ice maiden to swoon!

However, the kitchen of Villa Limoncello, with four guests chatting over a nightcap on the terrace, was not the ideal place to indulge in a passionate embrace so she took a step back, hoping her rueful look left Luca in no doubt that she would have liked nothing better than to melt into his arms and stay there until the morning.

'See you tomorrow then. *Ciao!*'

She followed him to where he'd left his Spider, then lingered on the front steps, watching the vehicle's red tail lights disappear from view, straining her ears until the roar of its powerful engine faded into the night air. Luca's presence at the villa filled every corner with cheerfulness and energy and his absence had left a discernible void, and Izzie realised with a start that her feelings for him had moved beyond the spark of physical attraction.

She thought back to the wedding that had taken place in the gazebo, to the kiss they had shared next to the wishing well, and she relished the fizzle of desire that shot out to her extremities whenever she lingered on that memory – something she had done regularly over the last six weeks.

But, while her future at Villa Limoncello remained uncertain, was it a good idea to cross the boundary from friendship into romance? And as they had both suffered a great deal of hurt in their personal lives, was she really ready to launch into a new relationship that would inevitably have to end when she went back to London?

However, her circling doubts didn't stop her from dreaming about the way his muscular contours moulded perfectly to hers when they had kissed, or how his dark brown eyes seemed to scorch deep into her soul whenever their gaze met, or how his lemony aftershave made her senses zing, or how her lips tingled when he whispered something to her that he didn't want others to hear. She had a great deal to thank Luca for and she resolved to do everything she could to protect his reputation, as well as that of Villa Limoncello as a fantastic venue to hold an intimate wedding, or join a painting or pasta-making class, or to take part in a yoga retreat, a creative writing course or a wine-tasting session.

As she made her way back to the kitchen, she stooped down to retrieve a single blossom of honeysuckle that had fallen from the frilly canopy that crowned the pergola. She raised it to her nose, closed her eyes and inhaled the intense floral scent before tucking it into her curls so she could enjoy its perfume a little longer. She heaved a sigh, reaching up to massage her temples to try to alleviate the tension that had been building over the day. Her feet and shoulders ached, but her discomfort vanished when she arrived at the kitchen and saw Meghan trying the shove a plastic bowl into the washing machine.

'Meghan, darling, you must be exhausted. Why don't you go over to Gianni's for a nightcap? I'll watch over the guests. Don't be too late, though; it's an early start in the morning if we want to make it to the market in San Vivaldo on time.'

'Thanks, Izzie, but I think I'll just grab a brandy and go up to my room. My eyelids feel like they're weighed down by concrete. Are you sure you'll be okay?'

'Of course. Shoo! I'll give you a knock at six thirty.'

'Ergh, that's almost inhumane! Actually, if it's okay with you, I think I'll give it a miss – I really want to spend as much time as I can with Gianni, and he told me he'd show me how to drive the tractor tomorrow. How do you think the pasta–making tutorial went?'

'Well, at least no one is complaining about being poisoned, so that's a good sign. And Hannah seems to have relaxed and entered into the spirit of things – and I did notice that she finished every mouthful of her pasta and her share of that wonderful salad you made!'

'Do you think she'll follow through with her threat to call in the health and safety guys?'

'I think it'll depend on what Carmen wants to do, so we'll just have to wait and see what happens in the morning. Where is Hannah, by the way? She wasn't sitting with the others on the terrace.'

'Gone to check up on Carmen with a cup of her favourite chamomile tea. I think she was planning on going straight to bed afterwards. It's been a very long day and everyone is exhausted. Night, darling, love you.'

Meghan leaned forward to brush a dusting of flour from Izzie's copper curls, deposited a kiss on her cheek and trotted towards the staircase.

'*Buona notte! Sogni d'oro!*' called Izzie before sauntering back out to the terrace, wishing she could have followed in her friend's wake, but as the host she was determined not to retire to her sunflower-bedecked bedroom until every guest was safely tucked up in bed.

Two down, three to go!

'Okay, that's me done for the night!' said Tom, appearing from the direction of the pergola as though he'd read Izzie's mind. Despite the lateness of the hour, and the lack of natural light, he still carried his camera round his neck like a particularly chunky medallion. 'Thanks for an amazing day, Izzie. I've learned so much and eaten like a king. I can't wait to see what you've got in store for us tomorrow.'

Tom hesitated for a moment before looking back over his shoulder to where Beth and Zara looked as if they were settled in for the night in the company of a bottle of grappa.

'Hey, Beth, Zara? Don't forget we've got an early start tomorrow!'

To Izzie's surprise the two women shoved back their chairs and trotted towards her and Tom, both a little unsteady on their feet.

'*Buona notte!*' declared Zara, bending forward to deposit air kisses on both Izzie's and Tom's cheeks. Beth rolled her eyes, but linked Zara's arm so she could guide her towards the villa without tripping over her heels.

'Don't forget. Seven thirty on the front steps.'

'Wouldn't miss it!' enthused Tom, ushering Beth and Zara through the door and up the stairs.

Izzie remained on the terrace, allowing the silence to envelop her as she extinguished the candles in the storm lanterns and performed her final check of the grounds before she could retire to her own bed. She paused next to the fountain that had been hewn from a huge chunk of pale pink marble and depicted a particularly chubby cherub holding what looked like a bunch of grapes. Her feet cried out their objection to the stresses and strains of the day – which certainly hadn't panned out as she'd hoped.

But then life never did – she knew that more than anyone.

Chapter Eight

The garden, Villa Limoncello
Colour: Peacock green

Market day dawned with clear aquamarine skies and the
promise of another sunshine-filled day. Izzie jumped from
her bed with a spring in her step and a song in her heart
– until memories of the previous day's trauma raised their
noses above the parapet and dampened her spirits.

Since arriving in Tuscany, she had made a pact with
herself to squeeze every moment of happiness out of every
new experience instead of dragging her sorrows in her
wake. Her surprise trip to Florence had helped her to take
the first step on the road towards accepting that her sadness
was normal; in fact, it was an essential part of the grieving
process. She had learned that she had to embrace the fact
that even though Anna was no longer with her, she was
still an important part of her life, her guardian angel; and
that it was her responsibility to relish every moment – and
that was exactly what she was doing.

She knew how fortunate she was; Tuscany was not only
a beautiful part of the world with enough art and culture
to fill every spare minute of every day, but she had met
so many amazing people who had taken her into their
hearts and ushered her along the path towards healing

her heart. She had made other changes, too. Instead of existing on a diet of coffee and buttered toast she had expanded her culinary repertoire into herby omelettes, delicious focaccia, and had now added home-made pasta to the lengthening list.

She flung open the shutters, welcoming in the fragrant morning air, enjoying the faint top note of crushed lavender whilst the birds launched into their first chorus of the day – thankfully minus the backing track of jackhammers and chainsaws now that Riccardo had completed the renovations on the B&B next door and it was finally open for business. She crunched up her nose in sympathy for his future guests – that was unless they were *actively* seeking an alternative holiday experience with a Basil Fawlty-esque character as their host.

Izzie stepped into the shower, enjoying the sensation of the water pummelling her neck and shoulders as she tried to wash away the tension of the last twenty-four hours. She dressed quickly in a pair of white capri trousers and ballet flats – the cobbles in San Vivaldo's piazza did not go well with heels – and skipped down the stairs to the kitchen to enjoy a solitary breakfast before her guests descended.

She prepared a cup of espresso that was strong enough to revive the dead, checked her watch and calculated that there was just enough time to take a stroll around the garden to savour the ambient tranquillity of the villa – something she had got into the habit of doing since she had waved goodbye to the wedding entourage last month.

Six thirty – it really was the best time of the day. It gave her the opportunity to ponder the important things in life, to count her blessings, as well as chat to her sister without anyone thinking that she had lost her grip on reality.

She sauntered out to the terrace, smiling at the veil of mist still lingering in the avenues between the vines. Glancing to her right, her eyes caught on the tennis court, still dilapidated, its net sagging like Nora Batty's stockings, and she decided to take a peek so she could start a list of what needed to be done to bring it up to scratch for future guests to use.

Maybe they could offer a tennis retreat for beginners?

She had taken only two steps onto the cracked court, where an abundance of weeds grew through the gaps like a giant's nasal hair, when a rustle in the leaves caused her to pause, her senses on high alert, her heart hammering out a concerto of alarm.

'Hello?'

'Oh, Izzie, sorry, I didn't mean to disturb you.'

'Ah, Carmen, no, it's okay, I just wasn't expecting anyone to be up and about this early in the morning.'

'I've always been an early riser – it's when I come up with my best designs! And I *have* spent a lot of time stuck in my room sleeping!'

Izzie smiled at the former supermodel, dressed in a flowing silk kimono in a vibrant peacock green, her golden hair piled on the top of her head in an elegant up-do. She looked every inch the queen of fashion – apart from a slight peakiness around her pale blue eyes. Like Zara, she possessed an easy grace; every movement seemed to flow smoothly into the next and Izzie felt like a gangly puppet clipped of its strings standing next to her. It was obvious why she had been such a success on the catwalk.

'Are you feeling better?' Izzie asked, leading Carmen towards the patio outside the *limonaia*, where she indicated a pair of rattan chairs that might have seen better days but blended perfectly with the rustic charm of the villa, especially after she'd upholstered them with an offcut of lemon-bedecked fabric she'd found at the market.

'Well, without going into detail, I don't think there's anything left to come out.'

Izzie grimaced and to her surprise Carmen laughed. 'Sorry, too graphic?'

'A little. What do you think caused it? Do you think it was food poisoning?'

'What else could it be? All I had for breakfast was one of my vitamin shakes, which haven't caused me any problems before, and then whatever I ate at lunch. I assume you got Hannah's emails about my sensitivity to nuts?'

'Yes, and I can assure you that Luca has been scrupulous in his preparation of every recipe, as well as the preparation for the pasta-making tutorials and the desserts. And Carlotta and I scrubbed and sanitised every surface, every cupboard, every implement, every pot and pan in the kitchen before you arrived. It's so clean in there you could perform open heart surgery.'

'Well, that's great to hear.' Carmen smiled as she settled into her chair, her kimono parting to reveal a long expanse of tanned thigh. 'It's more of a sensitivity than a full-blown allergy, but still, I have to be careful. To be honest, though, the symptoms I experienced yesterday were nothing like the reaction I have when I accidentally consume something containing nuts, so if Luca was as meticulous as you say he was in that regard, then it must have been food poisoning.'

'It's just that, as far as I know, no one else has been ill and everyone ate the same at lunch.'

'Yes, that's what Hannah said when I spoke to her about reporting the incident to the food and hygiene authorities last night, but I told her that it was up to me to decide what to do, not her, or anyone else for that matter.'

'Yes, of course it is.'

Izzie could feel the muscles in her stomach tighten and her breath quicken as waited for the axe to fall. Was Carmen about to insist on cancelling the course whilst they waited for the food inspectors to arrive?

'You know, I've been looking forward to this trip for weeks, especially the painting tutorials. I was hoping that my inspiration for next year's Spring/Summer collection would be fired by the vibrant colours of the Tuscan countryside, the olive groves, the vineyards, the tiny terracotta villages dotted around the hills, not to mention all the amazing architecture, the marble statutes and all the wonderful Italian artists there are to appreciate.'

Izzie waited for Carmen to continue, but the only sound to pierce the tranquillity of the early morning was that of a lone bumblebee collecting that day's quota of sweet nectar. It was no good; the suspense over what Carmen planned to do was making her feel lightheaded and, even if it was going to be bad news, she wanted to know.

'I'm really sorry this has happened, Carmen. Do you want… do you want to cancel the rest of the course?'

'I don't think that would make me very popular with the others, do you? No, I think we should stick to the itinerary and make the most out of the time we have left here. I'll let you know when I've reached a decision about reporting the food poisoning.'

Carmen pushed herself out of her chair, straightened her shoulders and glanced down at the slender gold watch on her wrist.

'Right, it's seven o'clock, just enough time for a quick shower and I'll be on the front steps at seven thirty as planned, raring to go. I'm actually really looking forward to visiting the market in San Vivaldo – it'll be a good opportunity to fill the coffers of creativity! *Ciao!*'

'*Ciao*,' muttered Izzie, anxiety nibbling at her stomach as she noted that her celebrity guest had neatly avoided confirming one way or another whether she intended to involve the food hygiene authorities.

Izzie leaned back in her chair, sipping her coffee and listening to the creatures who called the garden at Villa Limoncello their home welcome a new day as she watched Carmen float towards the house, the sleeves of her kimono flapping in her wake like a pair of exotic fairy wings. A surge of relief rolled over her and she sent up a missive of gratitude to the director of fate that Carmen had not suffered any lasting effects from her flirtation with the food demons – if indeed that was what had happened – and that the Painting & Pasta course was going ahead as planned.

However, whilst she would have loved to move on from all the drama, she couldn't forget that if Luca's suspicions were right, one of their guests had put his future livelihood at the restaurant and the prospect of running more courses at Villa Limoncello in jeopardy. She resolved to continue her covert investigation into what had happened, just in case Carmen did decide to call in the inspectors.

The bells on the clock tower in San Vivaldo echoed across the valley, telling the residents that it was seven thirty – time for their trip to the market. Izzie had just pushed herself up from her seat to say a quick hello to Carlotta, whom she had just seen arrive on her bicycle with her little dog Pipo in the front basket, when another, more ominous thought occurred to her.

If someone had really wanted Carmen to miss out on all the fun and it hadn't worked the first time – would they try again?

Chapter Nine

The piazza, San Vivaldo
Colour: Creamy ricotta

'Okay, thanks for being on time, everyone. I know it's early, but it really is the best time of the day to experience all the fabulous produce that's on offer at the market,' said Luca, looking altogether too good-looking for eight o'clock in the morning as they gathered on the veranda of Antonio's Trattoria. If he was surprised that Carmen, and indeed Hannah, had joined them for the foodie tour, then it didn't show, and he continued with his prepared introduction as if no one had accused him of poisoning one of their contingent the previous day. 'So, this evening we'll be making *tortelli*, which is a type of filled pasta similar to *ravioli*, so I want us to mould our culinary expedition around the ingredients we'll need to make two vegetarian versions.'

'And what about dessert?' asked Beth, the only one of the group not to have made a concession to the rising summer temperatures, choosing to stick resolutely to her faithful black jeans-and-boots combination.

'Oh God, is that all you think about?' tutted Zara, who that morning was modelling a lemon chiffon maxi-dress with a ruffled neck and hemline. Standing next to petite

Beth, she looked like Big Bird's more weight-conscious sister.

'You'll be pleased to know that I have something special planned for dessert tonight.' Luca smiled, earning himself a cheer from Beth and Tom whilst Zara simply rolled her eyes and Hannah just looked suspicious.

'Okay, so if you'd like to follow me, we'll start the tour.'

Izzie had been to San Vivaldo's market several times, yet she never grew tired of exploring the stalls that were manned by the local artisans themselves offering a vast array of produce as diverse as hand-tooled leather goods, thick bolts of upholstery fabric in the colours of the Italian flag, freshly picked bunches of fragrant basil leaves and huge flagons of extra virgin olive oil pressed from the olives grown in the region; a veritable feast for the eyes as well as the taste buds.

Their first stop was at a stall selling every kind of fruit, vegetable and salad item Izzie could think of, and a few more besides. To her right were potatoes, carrots, green beans, artichokes, huge bulbs of fennel and courgettes complete with their saffron-coloured flowers. To her left were pyramids of apples, oranges, lemons, mangoes and melons, interspersed with grapes, bananas, fresh figs, plums, apricots, peaches and strings of garlic. Luca greeted the stallholder and rattled off a brief conversation in high-speed Italian before turning back to the group.

'Okay, so things are a little different in Italian food markets. We don't handle the produce, we don't sniff it or squeeze it or even select our own like you do in the UK. We tell the *fruttivendola* what we need for that evening's meal and she will select the ingredients for us. In the case of fruit, we indicate when we intend to eat it and the

76

stallholder will choose the perfect stage of ripeness for us which in our case it is *da mangiare oggi, per favore*.'

Luca grabbed the brown paper carrier bags filled with what he needed for that evening's pasta and they continued on to the next stall showcasing a vast array of local cheeses – *pecorino* studded with walnuts and black truffles, *caprino* made from goat's milk and rolled in herbs or ground pepper, and Izzie's favourite, soft, creamy ricotta. The sharp, slightly acidic aroma caused Zara and Carmen to crinkle their noses in unison, then giggle.

'I love cheese!' declared Tom, raising his ever-present Pentax to snap a few shots until he caught the stallholder's look of disapproval. 'Sorry, sorry. What's Italian for sorry?'

'*Scusi tanto*.'

'*Scusi tanto*,' repeated Tom, in a broad Lancashire accent, his cheeks burning.

'Hey, look at this stall,' called Hannah, who had broken away from the group to browse one of the stalls selling hand-painted ceramics. 'Isn't this gorgeous!' She held up a small bowl decorated with a kaleidoscope of colours, but predominantly yellow. 'Oh, and I know my gran would love this!' This time she held aloft a large ceramic spoon covered in tiny painted lemons.

'You have a good eye, Hannah,' said Luca, smiling at the young Italian teenager who was staring at Zara as if there was royalty amongst them. 'Stefano's father is a very talented artist and every item is hand-made as well as hand-painted.'

Hannah beamed with delight at Luca's compliment as she reached into her huge bag to retrieve her purse and make her purchase. Stefano took his time wrapping the wide-brimmed dish and the ceramic spoon in paper printed with drawings of the Tuscan countryside, sneaking glances from beneath his lashes as Carmen and Zara perused his merchandise before moving on to the handbag stall, both much happier now they'd left the food stalls behind.

'Okay, that's everything I need for tonight's pasta demonstration, so if you'd like to explore on your own for a while we'll meet over there, outside *Pasticceria da Oriana*, where we'll each select a delicious treat for this evening's dessert.'

'I saw Oriana's when we were here yesterday – how can we be expected to choose just one treat?' declared Beth, running the tip of her tongue along her lower lip as she stared at the window of the Italian confectioner's shop that looked more like an artist's masterpiece than a bakery with its neat rows of cannoli, mixed fruit tarts and myriad flavours of Italian biscotti.

Izzie grinned. 'You can choose as many as you like, Beth.'

'Oh my God! Really? Come on, Han – let's start shopping! I'll show you where I got *the* best saffron-flavoured ice cream you've ever tasted, and have you ever tried a Campari spritzer?'

Before Hannah could refuse, Beth had grabbed her hand and made a beeline for the gelateria.

'I think I'll take a look at the florist's shop over there,' said Carmen, pointing to Francesca's, where the window was festooned with a garland of colourful bunting and displayed a unique selection of blooms that you wouldn't find on any London high street. 'Want to tag along, Zara? I'd really appreciate your advice on the colour palette I'm planning for next summer.'

'Sure,' said Zara, although Izzie noticed a certain reticence in her manner as she followed in Carmen's wake. Strange, she thought; for two woman who had been colleagues and then friends for as long as they had, and who were on holiday together in a gorgeous Tuscan farmhouse, their relationship was surprisingly lukewarm.

'Tom? Do you want to...'

'No! Oh, sorry, I mean, I've got a couple of phone calls I need to make, so I'll catch you later,' muttered Tom, flicking his eyes from the gelateria to the florist's shop, unable to meet Izzie's gaze as he fingered his mobile phone before making a purposeful decision to head in the opposite direction, towards the medieval church on the corner.

Izzie watch him retreat, his head bent, his shoulders hunched as though he carried the woes of the world on his shoulders. She wondered what had caused his hangdog demeanour, but then she chastised herself. She had no room to talk, having only just emerged from her own personal mist of melancholy. She hoped that Tom's sojourn in the sun would do the same for his outlook on life and all its challenges as it had for her own.

'Fancy a coffee?' asked Luca, his eyebrows raised in question.

'Yes, please.'

They made their way back to the trattoria that Luca had purchased after his brief entanglement with the banking industry, a profession that had made his parents proud but him miserable. Despite the long hours he spent in the kitchen, he had never been happier, and it had been a timely lesson to Izzie that she should always follow her dreams, not those expected of her by others.

'*Due caffè, Carlos, per favore.*'

Luca guided Izzie to the far corner of the wooden veranda and as soon she was settled in one of the padded chairs, he checked that they couldn't be overheard, and met her eyes.

'I see Carmen has joined us for the tour this morning. Have you had chance to talk to her about what happened yesterday?'

The hope in Luca's eyes caused Izzie's stomach to perform a somersault of sympathy. She could only guess at the turmoil he'd endured after the events of the previous day. 'Yes, I bumped into her this morning while I was taking a stroll through the garden.'

'And? Does she think it was food poisoning?'

'She's not sure.'

'And what about calling in the authorities?'

'She's still thinking about it. I did point out that as no one else was ill, it was unlikely to be that, and I really hope she's going to give us the benefit of the doubt. However, she was adamant that she doesn't want to cancel the course – that's why we're back on schedule this morning.'

'Did you stress how careful we were about sourcing the ingredients, that we're absolutely certain there's no way any of the food we served could have been contaminated?'

'I did, and I agree with you, but I could hardly tell her that we think one of her friends might have tampered with her food, could I?'

'No, I don't suppose you could.'

A spasm of distress streaked through Izzie's chest. The whole thing was starting to freak her out. When she had agreed to host the Painting & Pasta course at Villa Limoncello, she'd expected to spend the week teaching painting techniques, orchestrating sightseeing trips and indulging in the pasta-making tutorials, with time off in between to gossip with Meghan about her blossoming relationship with Gianni, and listen to more of Carlotta's matchmaking stories. Instead, here she was trying to piece together who amongst their guests might want to spoil Carmen's Tuscan break and why.

'I'm sorry, Luca.'

'It's not your fault!' declared Luca, grasping her hand, the cute dimples that bracketed his lips reappearing on his face as his eyes filled with excitement. 'Actually, I had an ulterior motive for bringing you here this morning. I have a special surprise for you!'

'A surprise? What kind of surprise?'

Luca's smile was infectious and Izzie's spirits edged up a notch as he leapt from his chair and held out his palm for her to take. 'Come!'

'Where are we going?'

'My artist's studio!'

'Your studio?'

'*Sì*, the kitchen of Antonio's trattoria – where culinary masterpieces are created!'

Izzie laughed as she slipped her hand into his, enjoying the sparkle of electricity that shot through her veins when their fingers touched. Whenever she was with Luca, all her problems seemed to melt away on a tide of exhilaration and she was grateful he had taken time out of his very busy schedule to make something to cheer her up. She knew he disapproved of her tendency to skip breakfast, so she suspected it was one of his legendary blueberry and almond cakes that went so well with a rich dark espresso.

'Okay, so before we go in, I want you to close your eyes.'

'Close my eyes?' she giggled.

'For maximum impact!'

Izzie let go of his hand and covered her eyes.

'Ready?'

'Ready.'

Luca pushed open the door into the kitchen, and in an instant a medley of aromas tickled at her nostrils – freshly ground coffee, warm, buttery pastries, maybe a top note of something floral – and her stomach growled in anticipation.

'Can I open my eyes now?'

'Yes!'

At first, all she could see was the stainless-steel surfaces, the pyramids of shiny copper pans and the huge multi-burner hob that dominated the space like a crouching dragon ready to pounce. When her gaze finally fell on what Luca had created, she gasped.

'Luca, it's…'

'It's a triple-layered English rose cake, flavoured with rosewater and sandwiched together with whipped cream and fresh raspberries,' he announced, his chin raised proudly as though describing one of Leonardo da Vinci's famous sculptures. 'Do you like it?'

'I love it!'

She stared at the exhibit of culinary artistry for a moment, taking in the frothy confection drizzled with dark pink icing and topped with… A sudden surge of emotion swept over her and she raised her eyes to meet Luca's, her heart fluttering in her chest, tears prickling at her lashes.

'Are they...'

Luca nodded.

'Oh my God, how did you... where did you...'

But she couldn't continue. She was having difficulty breathing and her throat had tightened around something hard that no amount of swallowing could dislodge. Luca slid his arm around her waist and pulled her close, whispering a stream of melodic Italian into her curls as she brushed away the tears from her cheeks.

'Thank you, Luca,' she whispered, reaching out to touch one of the sugared rose petals scattered on the top of the cake – rose petals in a rich orange-red colour from a particularly special flower that had been bestowed with the same name as her beloved sister – Annabel. Luca had presented her with more than just a cake, something sweet to make her smile as they shared a coffee together on the veranda outside; he'd created a homage to Anna in the best way he knew how, filled with kindness, compassion and love.

'I had a little help from Francesca.'

Izzie nodded, her thoughts scooting to her friend who owned the florist's in San Vivaldo and who had played a huge part in ushering her along the road towards accepting that her grief was normal and that a new future could be created, a future in which she cherished what she'd had with Anna and was not overshadowed by the misery of her absence. And she knew exactly what her sister would say if she was standing there in Luca's pristine kitchen staring at any kind of Italian dessert.

'Let's dig in!'

She smiled at Luca's delighted expression, tinged with a soupçon of relief, and she realised how nervous he had been about presenting his creation to her and what her reaction was going to be. She needed to show him how much she appreciated his thoughtfulness, so before she cut into the cake and made a wish, she stood onto her tiptoes and brushed his lips with hers.

'Luca, I...'

But that was a far as she got because Luca had pulled her into his arms, their bodies so close she could feel the ripple of his stomach muscles through her flimsy cotton T-shirt. She felt his gaze scorch deep into her soul as he lowered his mouth towards hers and kissed her, slowly, carefully at first, and then with a fierce passion that caused her nerve endings to sizzle as joy and desire spread from the top of her curls to the tips of her toes, leaving her breathless and a little disorientated.

Now that was better than any cake-induced sugar rush!

Chapter Ten

Pasticceria da Oriana, San Vivaldo
Colour: Sugar-pink candy

'Oh my God! Look at the time! I think we're going to have to take a rain-check on the coffee and cake or we'll be late for our rendezvous with Carmen and the others!' said Izzie, surprised at how the time had flown since they'd arrived at Antonio's, but could think of no better way of spending their hour 'off-duty'.

'Okay, just give me a couple of minutes to speak to Carlos about today's menu and then we'll make our way over to Oriana's.'

Luca held the kitchen door open for her and she watched him make his way over to the bar, where Carlos was busy at the coffee machine preparing a couple of cappuccinos for the two holidaymakers perched on the stools in front of him, engrossed in their guidebooks. From their sturdy attire they clearly planned on spending the day hiking in the hills rather than wandering around the cathedrals of consumerism in Florence.

She strolled to the edge of the veranda to wait for Luca to return, taking a moment to appreciate the architectural splendour that surrounded the restaurant; a battalion of triple-storeyed buildings with honeyed façades, faded green or brown shutters, and Juliet balconies that cast welcome shade onto the streets below. Terracotta urns congregated on doorsteps, crammed with geraniums in scarlet and salmon pink, and even a collection of brightly coloured sweeping brushes had a touch of modern art about them.

She checked her watch and was about to hurry Luca along when she heard a voice she recognised drifting up from the shady alleyway to the rear of the trattoria. She strained her ears to tune into the conversation just as Luca appeared at her side.

'Carlos says—'

'Shhh!'

Izzie placed her finger on her lips, then indicated downwards to the street below. Luca creased his forehead in confusion.

'What?'

'Shhh, listen…'

'Look, Helen, I'm trying, believe me, but it's not as easy as that.'

Izzie exchanged a glance with Luca, who immediately understood what she'd been getting at, and they both moved nearer to the edge of the veranda, stooping a little so they could hear better.

'Is that Tom?' Luca mouthed.

She nodded, the dulcet twang of his Lancashire accent unmistakeable.

'I know, I know, I did do that, but it hasn't worked. Look, I'll try again tonight.'

There was a pause and Izzie felt her chest tighten. Try what again?

'*Okay, don't worry, I'll call you. Send Mum my love, won't you? Yes, you too. Bye.*'

Izzie hadn't realised she'd been holding her breath throughout the one-sided conversation and she exhaled before meeting Luca's eyes.

'What do you think that was all about?'

Luca shook his head.

'You don't think… when Tom said that he'll try again tonight…'

'I don't know what to think, but if we don't leave now we'll be late.'

'But what if…'

'We'll talk to him, just not now, okay?'

'Okay.'

It was the most natural thing in the world for Izzie to slip her hand into Luca's when he offered her his palm and, with their kiss still fresh in her mind, she relished the tingle that remained on her lips as they headed towards the piazza together. As soon as the group came into view, though, she dropped his hand, not wanting to cause wagging tongues.

'Come on!' cried Beth, almost pogoing on the spot with excitement as soon as she saw them. 'Let's get inside!'

When Luca pushed open the door of the *pasticceria*, Beth, Hannah and even Carmen rushed inside to inspect the merchandise in all its sugary glory. Huge glass display cabinets showcased a medley of confectionary, from *brutti ma buoni* to cannoli filled with sweetened ricotta, from *pizzelle* with hazelnut spread to *ricciarelli* dusted in powdered sugar – each one was an individual miniature work of art that sent the taste buds zinging.

'Wow!' exclaimed Carmen, her eyes wide with delight. 'This place is amazing!'

'I could actually spend the rest of the day here!' said Beth, pushing her nose up against the tallest of the glass cabinets, which contained trays of candy-coated almonds and bonbons in a rainbow of colours.

Unsurprisingly, Zara hung back, loitering on the threshold, her expression filled with distaste at the over-whelming array of sweet treats on show. Clearly, she viewed their scheduled visit to the San Vivaldo bakery as some kind of torture to be endured and Izzie found herself wondering when she had last allowed the evil that was sugar to cross her lips.

'Who needs to visit art galleries and museums when there's such artistic talent on show right here?' continued Beth, clearly already on a sugar-infused high before anything had even passed her lips. 'And best of all, every-thing is edible! Oh, look at those slices of real, home-made tiramisu, and those tiny doughnuts oozing crème pat, and all these different types of cannoli. How am I going to choose which ones to pick? Tom, what do you think?'

'Mmm?'

'Which of these delicious desserts tickles your taste buds?'

Tom stared at Beth for a moment as if she were speaking a foreign language. Izzie knew his thoughts were lingering on the phone call he'd just taken, but he rallied well and went to stand next to Beth to select a dessert.

'Hi, Izzie, how are the painting tutorials going?' whispered Oriana, sidling up to her whilst Luca slipped into his role of tour guide to inform the group of the origins of the ubiquitous cannoli.

'The painting side of things is going great, thanks.'

Izzie glanced at her friend, whose smile was as sweet as her merchandise – what Oriana couldn't do with flour, butter and eggs wasn't worth knowing. However, her talents weren't confined to the baking arena; Oriana was also a yoga instructor and ran her own studio from a room at the back of the shop, and she had the figure to prove it.

'Does that mean you might find some time to come along to one of my yoga sessions? You've been here for six weeks and I still haven't seen you yet.'

Izzie smiled at her friend who combined her passion for physical fitness with a twist of culinary magic. With a figure so svelte she could give Carmen and Zara a run for their money, she sported a pair of navy skinny jeans, a pristine white apron with the shop's logo of a tiny pink angel embroidered on the front and exuded the scent of an English summer garden. Their friendship had been sealed at their very first meeting when Oriana had corrected Izzie's mistaken belief that she was working on a film shoot for Meghan's director brother, when in fact the wedding being held at Villa Limoncello was a real-life celebrity affair!

'Sorry, I've been so busy getting the villa ready for our paying guests.'

'Is Gianni still on the warpath with Riccardo?'

'Yes, he and Luca are treating him like the Big Bad Wolf and to be avoided at all costs. There's no way they would agree to allow anyone taking a course at the villa to stay at the B&B – even if it was the last place on earth,' said Izzie, rolling her eyes.

'Can't blame them, I suppose, although continuing the feud isn't good for the village. Everyone knows what

Riccardo did, and everyone agrees that it was despicable, and of course, we're all aware why he did it, but it does seem a strange thing to do to your neighbour when you've got plenty of money to move elsewhere.'

'I agree with you, Oriana, but I think there might be another reason why he did it.'

'Like what?'

'God, I've got enough to worry about with the villa's guests! Riccardo will have to wait!'

'What do you…?'

'Okay, everyone, have you made your final choices?' asked Luca, as Oriana's assistant handed over a huge confectioner's box to him.

'You didn't tell me Oriana did vegan cakes,' Zara said to Izzie, a wide smile on her face.

'Yes, she even made a seven-tier vegan cake for a local wedding last month.'

'Awesome!'

It was the first time Izzie had seen Zara animated over anything edible and she was happy to see Carmen, Hannah and Beth crowd round her to take a peek at her choice and promise to taste-test it when they got back to the villa.

However, the one person who hadn't joined in the culinary critique was Tom. Clutching his white confectioner's box as though his life depended on it, he stood next to the door, his gaze fixed on an indeterminable point in the distance, his thoughts elsewhere. Clearly, the earlier phone call had affected his mood, but when he caught Izzie's eye, he looked away quickly and pretended to be enamoured by the extensive selection of nougat wrapped in cellophane and ribbon in the shop window.

'Is everything okay, Tom?' asked Izzie, equalling his stride as they made their way back to the hire car, the words *I did do that, but it hasn't worked* echoing through her brain.

'Yes, fine, thanks. The trip to the market was great, and our visit to Oriana's was really instructive. I had no idea that cannoli were symbols of fertility or that they originated in Sicily! I've chosen three different varieties; one filled with mascarpone and the others with ricotta flavoured with rosewater and Marsala wine! I can't wait to try them. I love ricotta!'

Despite Tom's attempt to divert her enquiry and inject some jollity into the conversation, she could tell from the nervous twitch at the side of his mouth, and the way he fidgeted with the strap of his camera, that something was not right.

Could Carmen's illness have had something to do with Tom after all?

Chapter Eleven

The tennis court, Villa Limoncello
Colour: Burnt umber

'So, how was the trip to the market?' asked Meghan, returning to the kitchen with a wooden tray tucked under her arm, having delivered lunch to the guests, who had chosen to eat under the pergola on the terrace as if a change of venue would reduce the risk of a repeat of yesterday's turmoil.

'I think everyone enjoyed it, but the visit to Oriana's was definitely the highlight of the morning.'

Izzie paused, fighting the urge to blurt out everything that had happened in San Vivaldo, desperate to share the heavy burden of anxiety with her best friend. She wanted to recount the telephone conversation they had overheard in detail and hear her thoughts, ask if she thought Izzie was going crazy. But Luca had asked her not to mention their suspicions to Meghan or Gianni, and of course, she understood why. Meghan had many fabulous qualities, but discretion was not one of them.

'Is everything okay?' asked Meghan, peering at Izzie from beneath her raspberry-tipped fringe, her eyes filled with concern, which made Izzie feel even worse.

'Yes, I'm just...'

'There's nothing to worry about, you know. There is no way anyone can get food poisoning from Carlotta's home-made minestrone soup and freshly baked ciabatta. I promise you that I followed her instructions to the letter, and I even washed all the glasses and plates again, just to be sure. And when I took lunch outside, everyone helped themselves to a huge bowl, even Zara.'

'Thanks, Meghan – I'm sure it can't happen two days in a row.'

But it could if someone was intent on targeting Carmen! Tom's words rang in her ears – *I'll try again tonight*. Oh God! Her stomach performed a somersault of trepidation and she knew that the only way to stop herself from having a complete meltdown was to keep busy.

'I think I'll pop over to the gazebo to make sure everything is ready for this afternoon's tutorial.'

'Need any help?'

'No, no, you've done enough today already. Why don't you have lunch with Gianni?'

'Well, if you're sure…'

Izzie saw Meghan glance at her sideways as she hung up her apron, then pause for a moment before shrugging her shoulders and dashing out of the kitchen door. She knew she hadn't fooled her friend into believing that nothing was wrong. Meghan knew her better than anyone, but she just hoped she had put her jitters down to the fact that she was worried about a repeat of the previous day's lunchtime shenanigans.

She gathered up her trusty file containing the afternoon's itinerary and made her way along the winding garden path towards the gazebo, enjoying the sensation of the lavender stalks brushing against her naked shins and sending spurts of delicious woody scent to her nostrils. She climbed the three steps to the raised whitewashed platform and began to check each easel for the implements they would need for that afternoon's session on using soft pastels. When everything was perfect, she slumped down into one of the striped director's chairs and tipped her face towards the sun, waiting for her emotions to slow from raging stampede to a sedate trot.

But it was no good – if she had been worried about the effect a food poisoning incident could have on the future of Villa Limoncello as a place to relax and sample the culinary delights of a Tuscan paradise, then what would happen if word got out that their guests were being targeted by a random poisoner! This latter scenario was much more gossip-worthy and she could imagine the San Vivaldo grapevine buzzing with zeal.

'Hey, Izzie, are you ready for us?'

Izzie hadn't heard the group approaching and Hannah's enquiry made her jump. She quickly dragged her thoughts back to the present, scrambled up from her chair, and forced a welcoming smile onto her lips, determined to remain professional despite the challenges.

'Absolutely!' she replied, aware she sounded a little flustered.

'Okay, everyone, same seats as yesterday, please,' said Carmen, dropping her oversized satchel on the floor next to the easel with the most shade. Izzie noticed she had changed into yet another fabulous outfit – a fitted halter-neck dress in a rich mulberry colour and a pair of bronze gladiator sandals to match her designer handbag.

'Right, if everyone's ready—'

'Actually, if we're going to be here for the next couple of hours, I think I need to reapply my sunscreen,' interrupted Zara, rummaging around in her huge raffia tote for her tube of factor fifty sun block, her quirky earrings-and-necklace combo sending shards of silver light dancing onto the roof of the gazebo. 'Oh, God, I must have left it in my room! Can we just hang on a couple of minutes while I go and fetch it?'

'Zara, we should have started this tutorial twenty minutes ago...' groaned Beth, flicking the sides of her bob behind her ears in the familiar gesture of irritation. 'Why don't you just—'

'It's okay, it's okay, you can borrow mine,' sighed Carmen, putting down the laminated instruction card she'd been using to fan her face and passing her satchel over to Zara. 'Help yourself.'

'Thanks, Carmen.'

Zara spent a few seconds fiddling with the complicated silver clasp, then lifted the flap and peered inside.

'Agggh! Oh my God! Oh my God!'

Zara tossed the satchel to the ground, shot out of her seat, and flung her hands in the air, her face filled with horror and revulsion. A cacophony of confusion erupted as the rest of the group – apart from Carmen – followed suit, knocking over their chairs and backing away from the handbag as if it were about to explode.

'What is it, Zara? What's... what's in the bag?' stammered Izzie, her stomach churning with panic, goose bumps prickling her skin as she ran her palms across her forearms, wondering if she should do something – but she had no idea what.

Fortunately, she was saved from having to attempt a heroic response because, as the group continued to look on, a giant, luminous-green grasshopper jumped out of its shadowy hiding place, paused to see what all the commotion was about, then bounced away to continue its adventure elsewhere.

'You're frightened of a little grasshopper?' laughed Carmen, the only one brave enough to bend down to gather up the spilled cosmetics and hand the tube of sun cream to Zara. 'What did you think it was going to do to you? Wrestle you to the ground and use you as a trampoline?'

'I... no, it was just such a shock, that's all,' muttered Zara, colour flooding her face at her overreaction to the presence of a harmless insect as she resumed her seat in front of her easel. 'Sorry, Izzie, I suppose you see grasshoppers, and all kinds of other creepy crawlies, every day here in Tuscany – we don't get many in Hammersmith.'

'Or Cardiff,' added Beth, sinking down into her chair with a shudder.

'Okay, now that the cabaret is over, do you think we can start the tutorial?' asked Carmen, fastening her satchel, completely unaffected by the presence of a foreign insect amongst her belongings. 'What are we learning about today, Izzie?'

For a moment, Izzie just stared at the group, half-formed questions ricocheting around her brain as she tried to make sense of what had just happened. How on earth had a grasshopper got itself locked in Carmen's handbag? Didn't they usually confine themselves to leaping around the garden in hot pursuit of their next tasty morsel? Why hadn't Carmen noticed it earlier?

Had… had someone put it there?

With everyone waiting expectantly for her to launch into her introduction, she forced herself to focus on the tutorial, but she just couldn't face the thought of staying in the gazebo. So, for the first time in a very long time, she made a snap decision to deviate from her carefully crafted itinerary, and, if she hadn't been so distracted by unfolding events, she would have congratulated herself for having the courage to go 'off piste' – it was progress indeed.

'Yes, okay, so this afternoon's session is all about working with soft pastels, but before we make a start, I think it might be a good idea if we took our easels over to the tennis court where there's a lot more shade and there's the wishing well, the *limonaia* and the marble fountain to use as inspiration for our drawings.'

'Great,' said Tom, the first to jump up and grab his easel, before turning to look over his shoulder at the others. 'Well, what are you waiting for?'

Hannah giggled. 'Okay, Picasso, we're right behind you!'

A crescendo of chatter followed as the group scraped back their chairs, collected their easels and artist's paraphernalia and made their way towards the dilapidated tennis court. Izzie actually liked the rustic shabbiness of the old court; there was something quite romantic about the many matches that must been played there during its long lifetime, and whilst it wouldn't be hosting Wimbledon any time soon, it made a great alternative venue for a painting class. Whilst Beth and Hannah set up their easels next to each other, discussing their dislike of all members of the insect family, Zara doused herself with an extra layer of sun cream and Carmen took her time positioning her easel in the perfect spot, the recent drama completely forgotten.

'Hey, Tom, maybe pastels will be your preferred medium?' Carmen grinned.

'Possibly.'

Tom seemed to be in a world of his own, his pallor even more noticeable than usual which emphasised his freckles and the sunburnt tip of his nose, and despite the photogenic qualities of the tennis court, his camera hung redundant around his neck. Izzie didn't have to be a psychiatrist to work out that something was troubling him, and she wondered why none of the others had noticed.

'Well, I've already chosen what I'm going to immortalise in colour!' exclaimed Hannah, tossing her long ponytail over her shoulder and raising her sunglasses onto the top of her head. 'That wishing well over there is so cute!'

'Maybe you could add a unicorn or two?' suggested Beth, rolling her eyes at Hannah and earning herself a warning glance from Carmen.

'Let's try not to be too judgemental today, shall we?'

Beth spluttered at the hypocrisy of Carmen's statement and opened her mouth to retaliate – which Izzie suspected would include the words 'pot', 'kettle' and 'black' – but Beth thankfully thought better of it.

Izzie managed to disguise a sigh of relief. She had enough on her plate without the session turning into a schoolyard fracas instead of a restorative adult painting class for the discerning traveller. It was time to take control

– something she had achieved a gold medal for in her personal life. Routine, schedules, itineraries, lists, plans, they were all things that enabled her to retain control and live her life without the risk of her demons stalking her path from dawn to dusk. Even though her stay in Tuscany had helped her to loosen her tenacious grip on her obsession with those false crutches, she was grateful she had them to fall back on in times of stress.

'Okay, so using pastels requires a totally different technique than the one we learned about yesterday when we were working in watercolour. You've each been given a box of semi-soft pastels in a variety of colours and you'll also notice that the paper we are using is rougher in texture – that's because pastel doesn't stick well to smooth paper.'

Izzie selected a pastel in rich burnt umber and broke it in half.

'So that you can get a feel of how the pastels work, let's experiment together. First, swipe your pastel across the paper and notice how much of the pigment is transferred depending on the pressure you apply and on whether you use the tip or the side.'

Izzie demonstrated and then watched her students try out the technique for themselves.

'Great. You'll have noticed that, unlike watercolours or oils, pastels are not mixed before putting them onto the paper, so to create the required tonal effects for the landscape here at Villa Limoncello, we can use several different techniques, such as hatching, like this, or blending with a fingertip, or using cotton wool balls – which you'll find in today's artist's packs – or some artists use erasers or tortillons. You might also be interested in other techniques, like scumbling, which is where we lightly drag a layer of pastel over the top of a more vibrant layer, and there's feathering, which looks like this, and dusting, although I wouldn't recommend that technique for easels.'

Izzie paused to check that everyone had grasped the rudimentaries of using soft pastels, pleased to see that their papers were covered in colourful images of various horticultural subject matter.

'Okay, it looks like you've all got the hang of the difference between using pastels and watercolours, so why don't you help yourself to a fresh piece of paper and make a start on your own sketch? You can either stay in the tennis court with me, or take your easels over to the wishing well, or the marble fountain, or you could even have a go at drawing one of the lemon trees in the *limonaia*. Don't forget to start by lightly sketching your picture using an ordinary graphite pencil until you are happy with the composition before adding colour. I'll circulate and answer any questions you might have or make suggestions on improvements.'

'See you later!' Hannah was the first to lift her easel and scuttle off towards the wishing well, purposely not looking in Beth's direction so that she didn't have to see the inevitable eye-roll. Beth headed in the opposite direction towards the terrace, nervously glancing from left to right in case a battalion of grasshoppers were getting ready to launch an attack.

'Well, I'm going to paint in the *limonaia*,' announced Carmen, tucking her easel and paint box under her arm. 'It's such a beautiful place. So inspiring. Want to join me, Tom?'

Izzie saw Tom hesitate, his eyes darting from the tennis court to the wishing well, to the patio outside the *limonaia*, and again she wondered what was going on with him and why he seemed so nervous around Carmen. She thought he was on the verge of agreeing to join her, but instead, with cheeks glowing like hot coals, he shook his head.

'If it's okay with Izzie, I thought I might take advantage of the shade over by the magnolia tree and paint the gazebo. Well, not paint the actual gazebo, but, well, you know what I mean…'

Tom bundled up his equipment and almost ran from the tennis court.

'How about you, Zara?'

'Erm, actually, I thought I'd stay here in the tennis court. I love how those weeds protrude from the cracks in the tarmac and the net sags in the middle like a pair of old socks. It'll make a great picture to hang in my bathroom at home.'

'Okay, no problem.'

As Izzie watched Carmen stroll towards the *limonaia*, her dress floating in her wake like a bridal train, she couldn't shift the feeling that all was not quite right between the two friends. Whilst Zara's tone had been light, she'd detected a weird undercurrent of unease in her body language, and she wondered whether anyone else had noticed it. Hannah and Beth knew them both much better than she did – surely they had seen the fleeting flashes of fear in Zara's eyes whenever Carmen suggested they spend time alone together?

Ergh! So much for a relaxing, carefree week with a group of happy, smiling tourists eager to shake off the stresses and strains of life back home with a few days of creativity and delicious Italian food. It seemed like every one of their guests had some sort of issue they had packed up and brought along with them in their suitcases. Yet wasn't that exactly what *she* had done when she'd left London for Villa Limoncello at the end of May? Her emotional baggage had been so heavy that she had struggled to poke her head above the cheerfulness parapet.

Nevertheless, after the grasshopper fiasco, she was now convinced than there was definitely more to the food-poisoning incident than an inadvertent slip in hygiene practices. Someone was targeting Carmen, and she had no intention of allowing anyone to jeopardise the success of Villa Limoncello, or Gianni's vineyard or Luca's restaurant, not to mention her own future in Tuscany. She was now more determined than ever to uncover the truth.

Chapter Twelve

The kitchen, Villa Limoncello
Colour: Stinging-nettle green

'So, tonight we're making *tortelli*,' announced Luca, drying his hands on a tea towel before slinging it over the shoulder of his white chef's jacket.

'Mmm, sounds delicious!' said Carmen, beaming as she tightened the strings of her apron around her slender waist and went to stand in front of one of the piles of ingredients Luca had set out on the kitchen table for each of the students. 'I can't wait to plunge my hands into a mound of flour!'

'Sorry, Carmen – as we learned how to make pasta last night, I wanted to concentrate on the fillings for the *tortelli* this evening. I made the dough earlier and it's resting to allow the gluten to be released, which makes it easier to roll out.'

'What fillings are we making?' asked Hannah, who had changed into a pretty floral sundress with spaghetti straps and, for the first time since she'd arrived in Tuscany, had left her hair loose, held back from her cosmetics-free face by a flamingo-coloured Alice band.

'We're making two fillings, both vegetarian: *funghi*, which is made with porcini, shitake and chestnut mushrooms, and *ricotta e ortica*.'

'Wow, I'm drooling already!' declared Beth, pushing the sleeves of her black T-shirt up to her elbows before taking her place at the table between Carmen and Hannah.

Izzie switched her attention to Zara, who was wearing a pair of what could only be described as knitted hot-pants – in an eye-watering fuchsia – and was staring at the individual balls of pasta dough lined up on the bench as though they were the enemy. Her upper lip curled slightly, the look in her eyes made it clear to everyone that she'd love to launch into a lecture on the evil that was carbs, but, catching Luca's raised eyebrow, thought better of it.

'It all looks very complicated,' murmured Tom, wrinkling his nose as he tried to study the laminated recipe card Izzie had made for each of them. 'And it seems like an awful lot of trouble to go to just to make dinner. It's much easier to grill a steak and make a few oven chips.'

'But not as delicious!' said Beth, picking up a fork to taste the fresh ricotta cheese they'd bought at the market that morning. 'What are the leaves in this bowl, Luca? They look like nettles!'

'That's because they are,' said Luca, laughing when he saw the look of surprise on Beth's face.

'As in *stinging* nettles?'

'Yes, they'll be mixed with the spinach in this bowl, then blanched and added to the ricotta, along with a couple of eggs, a generous helping of parmesan and a pinch of nutmeg to make the *ricotta e ortica*.'

The next thirty minutes flew by as they concentrated on Luca's step-by-step instructions on preparing the two fillings. When every student had made a bowl of each, Luca handed them a ball of pasta dough and they watched him roll it out before cutting it into two uniform strips eight centimetres wide.

'First, we place several teaspoon-sized portions of the mushroom mixture, or the ricotta mixture, on one of the pasta strips, like this. Then, we cover it with the second strip and press with our fingers to make sure there's no air left in the individual parcels or they will burst open when we cook them. Next, we cut the *tortelli* with a toothed wheel and place them gently a plate dusted with semolina.'

Luca moved around the table, offering suggestions and words of encouragement as everyone had a go at making the two kinds of *tortelli*. The noise level increased from a low murmur when they were concentrating on rolling out their pasta dough, to cacophonous as they giggled at their respective attempts at producing parcels as uniform as Luca's. By the end of the lesson, there was enough pasta to stage a banquet fit for a member of the Medici family.

As Meghan had handled lunch, Izzie had sent her off to have dinner with Gianni, so it fell to her to help Luca tidy up the culinary detritus and set the table for dinner whilst their guests took a stroll in the garden with an Aperol spritz – a bright orange cocktail made with Aperol, prosecco and soda water with a slice of orange and lots and lots of ice. When they took their places in the court-yard and tasted their individual creations, topped with a generous helping of Luca's home-made Tuscan ragu, everyone declared it to be delicious – apart from Zara, who still couldn't bring herself to indulge, preferring to stick to the artichoke and couscous salad with white wine vinegar dressing and a side of watercress.

Eventually, when everyone had eaten their fill, including finishing off the desserts they had selected from

Oriana's, they adjourned to the terrace with their coffees –
or in Carmen and Tom's case, a glass of Vecchia Romagna
– to watch the sun slip behind the hillside over to west
as the cicadas sang a fond farewell to another perfect
summer's day.

'So, where is Dalton at the moment, Carmen?' asked
Beth, biting into one of the hand-made chocolate petit
fours Izzie had picked up in San Vivaldo.

'He's on a perfume shoot in the Grand Canyon, of all
places,' said Carmen, her eyes fixed on the distant horizon
as dusk chased away the golden shards of sunlight. 'I spoke
to him this morning but all he wanted to do was complain
about the heat and the fact that their hotel's air-con was
broken.'

'Did you tell him about your brush with food
poisoning?'

'Yes, but I don't think he was listening.'

'Well, you know what he's like when he's on an assign-
ment, Carr. Absolute focus and commitment. I'm sure if
he'd been here in Tuscany he would have been at your
bedside, wiping your fevered brow.'

'Really? This is Dalton we're talking about.'

Izzie took a seat on the paint-blistered bench next
to the kitchen door and glanced at the two women
over the rim of her coffee cup. Seeing them standing so
close together, their profiles clear against the darkening
sky, she was struck by their stark differences. Not only
was Carmen over a foot taller than Beth, her silhouette was slender, almost muscular, alongside Beth's more
soft, curvaceous figure. But their profiles weren't the only
contrast; Carmen wore her flowing tresses loose, like a
swaying cornfield in the summer sunshine, whilst Beth's

ebony hair had been chopped into a severe, chin-length bob. Then there was their choice of attire; Beth had stuck with her usual 'anything as long as it's black' mantra whilst Carmen sported a wide-legged yellow jumpsuit – like a canary discussing that day's exploits with a blackbird!

'Well, compared to Jacques, Dalton is the perfect boyfriend material,' said Zara, strolling over to join Carmen and Beth in their discussion. 'Since we split in January, I've had four dates and not one of them made my heart flutter. Izzie, do you know if Luca has any single friends that could make my heart sing and senses zing?'

Izzie felt her cheeks redden at Zara's casual assumption that she and Luca were an item, when she thought they had been discreet about their blossoming relationship. After working alongside each other for six weeks, preparing the villa to host its first guests, her attraction to the handsome chef had deepened, and there had been plenty of kisses beneath the pergola, or next to the wishing well, or in the lemon-scented *limonaia*.

'The person you *should* be speaking to is Carlotta!' laughed Izzie.

'Carlotta who helps out with breakfast?'

'Yes, she's the village's unofficial matchmaker.'

This got Zara's, and Beth's, attention.

'If you're not careful, she'll be flicking through her Rolodex of available men within a fifty-kilometre radius of San Vivaldo for a potential introduction! Look what happened to Meghan – she'd only been at the villa for thirty minutes when Carlotta sprinkled her magic dust and ushered her in the direction of Gianni!'

'Oh, that's like Carmen and Dalton!' exclaimed Beth, glancing towards the pergola where Hannah was topping up Tom's coffee from the cafetière. 'You introduced Dalton to Carmen, didn't you, Hannah?'

Izzie wondered if she was the only one who saw the way Hannah's face blanch as she reached out for her wine glass and took a gulp of rich, red Chianti to delay her response and feign an attempt at nonchalance.

'Yes, yes, I did,' she said, forcing a smile onto her lips, yet Izzie could see from the tightened jawline and narrowed eyes that something was amiss.

'Carmen, why don't you tell us again how you met Dalton,' pressed Beth, either oblivious to Hannah's discomfort or enjoying it.

'No, no, I'd rather…'

'Oh, go on, Carr, it was so romantic,' said Zara, pulling out the chair next to Tom and helping herself to a glass of the Italian brandy as she settled in to hear the story that she had no doubt heard many times before.

'Yes, go on, please,' said Izzie, her interest piqued, until she saw Tom roll his eyes and an urge to giggle rippled through her chest.

'Okay, okay, Beth's right, I do have Hannah to thank for guiding Dalton into my life.' Carmen smiled, her eyes glazing over slightly as her thoughts scooted down the memory superhighway to the day she had met her fiancé. 'We met when I was organising a surprise party for Hannah's thirtieth birthday at the Ritz. Dalton was Hannah's next-door neighbour at the time, and I cajoled him into helping me set the whole thing up. You could say we bonded over a session of extreme cake-sampling when we were trying to choose which birthday cake to order.'

'Lovely…' muttered Tom, clearly bored with the turn in the conversation.

'Anyway, the next day we literally bumped into each other at the local deli, Dalton asked if I wanted to have dinner and, as they say, the rest is history.'

'Tell everyone how he proposed!' said Beth, clapping her hands with excitement.

Izzie cast a quick glance at Hannah from beneath her lashes and could have sworn the girl had turned a sickly shade of green, her face frozen into a mask of faked interest. However, as the last breath of sunlight had just faded from the sky, she could have been mistaken.

'Actually, I think it's time we let Izzie and Luca—'

'But Izzie wants to hear this too, don't you, Izzie?' said Beth, nodding her head at Izzie vigorously.

'Absolutely.' Izzie smiled, although having recently experienced a broken engagement she worried her expression might mirror Hannah's – perhaps that was why Hannah was looking like she was about to expire!

'Well, I thought we were on our way to pick out a present for Dalton's mother's birthday – her favourite store is Tiffany's and he had his eye on this cute silver necklace he knew she would love. When we got there, the manager whisked us away to a private room upstairs which had been set up with a huge black-and-white photograph Dalton had taken of me when we were in Paris, with the Eiffel Tower in the background. There was a bottle of Laurent-Perrier in a silver ice bucket, and pink rose petals scattered on every surface. I was speechless at first, but then he produced this amazing solitaire and crouched down onto one knee. I almost fainted from the surprise! I had no idea he was going to propose!'

'And she said yes!' announced Beth, topping up her glass from the carafe on the table. 'Let's raise a toast to Carmen and Dalton!'

'*Salute*,' chorused the gathering.

'To love!' added Zara. 'That elusive emotion we are all hoping to find. I can't wait for Carlotta to come over tomorrow – maybe she can introduce me to one of the hot Italian guys in that Rolodex of hers, or maybe she has a single friend, or nephew, or next-door neighbour! Oh, did I tell you how my father prosed to my mum?'

As the group were engrossed in Zara's story, then in Beth's as she told them about her cousin being whisked off to New York for a proposal in Central Park, it was a while before Izzie realised that Hannah had slipped away from the table.

What was going on there?

Then Izzie recalled that Hannah had worn a similar expression of discomfort the previous day when Izzie had asked Carmen why Dalton hadn't been able to accompany them on their trip to Italy.

Could Hannah be envious of what Carmen had with Dalton, or was it something altogether closer to home?

She wondered how long the two of them had been neighbours before Carmen had glided into his life – the supermodel with great looks, a fabulous figure and her eponymous, award-winning fashion business. There was a chasm of difference between the two women.

Could Hannah have had feelings for Dalton? Was that why she had struggled to remain in the conversation when it had turned to Dalton and Carmen's engagement?

Izzie paused to consider the possibility, until another thought occurred to her. If that was the case, then was it such a leap to add Hannah's name to those suspected of sprinkling something into Carmen's food?

Izzie groaned. Her list was growing. In fact, it now included everyone apart from Beth, and that was only because she hadn't had chance to have a chat with her on her own. Ergh, she really needed to get Luca by himself, not in the hope of a moonlight meander through the vineyard, but to talk to him about what she'd witnessed that afternoon in the gazebo, otherwise her head would explode with all the questions that were circulating in her brain.

Chapter Thirteen

The limonaia, *Villa Limoncello*
Colour: Zingy lemon

It was another hour before the rest of the guests floated off to bed, clutching their chosen nightcaps, to allow Izzie and Luca to finish the washing up and return the kitchen to its pristine glory. Even though the tidiness monsters no longer circled her with the tenacity of the past, Izzie still couldn't retire for the night until everything was in its allocated space ready for the next morning's breakfast.

'Looks like everyone had a great evening,' sighed Luca, picking up a left-over bottle of Chianti and ushering Izzie out of the kitchen and along the terrace to the *limonaia*, where they slumped down into the ancient rattan chairs and exhaled exhausted breaths. 'You have no idea how relieved I am that Carmen decided to join in tonight's pasta-making tutorial with the rest of the group. I hope that means she's decided not to report us to the *aziende sanitarie*.'

However, as much as Izzie wanted to share in Luca's optimism, she knew things had become more serious, not less. She watched as he poured them each a glass of the rich, ruby-red wine the region was famous for, loving the way the collar of his chef's jacket lay open at his neck to reveal a tuft of dark chest hair, and his jawline sported an attractive smattering of stubble. When he met her gaze, his eyes narrowed with concern.

'Izzie? What's the matter?'

'It's just…'

Izzie paused, not wanting to spoil the feeling of serenity she always experienced whenever she spent time amongst the lemon trees in their glasshouse home. Even at midnight, the warmth of the day still lingered amongst the ancient plants, each one adorned with pendulous yellow baubles sending a citrussy tang into the air. She loved it there, it was her favourite place in the whole of Tuscany – just ten minutes in the exotically perfumed *limonaia* and all the problems of the world melted away, only it wasn't working its magic that night.

'Come on. Spit it out. I can see from your face that something is nibbling at you.'

'Oh God, where do I start!'

Her thoughts ricocheted around her brain like a brigade of out-of-control boomerangs. Again, an image of her mother floated across her vison and Izzie was reminded of those words of wisdom she'd always uttered whenever Izzie or Anna had come home from school bursting with stories that needed to be shared. *Start at the beginning!*

'I think we might need another bottle – this is going to take some time!'

'Okay.' Luca's mahogany eyes switched from amusement to seriousness as he leaned forward to place his forearms on his knees and meet her gaze. 'What's going on?'

Izzie recounted in as few words as possible what had happened at that afternoon's tutorial, her suspicions that it wasn't just an unfortunate incident, and that someone was targeting Carmen.

'So I was right! Carmen's sudden illness wasn't caused by food poisoning!'

Izzie saw Luca's lips tighten and she heard the note of anger in his voice. But who could blame him? Whoever was responsible for what was happening clearly had little regard for the effect their actions would have on his livelihood.

'It was probably just a prank, someone wanting to confine Carmen to her room…'

'But it was so reckless! Everyone knows she has food intolerances – what if she'd suffered an adverse reaction to whatever they used to make her ill?'

'I agree…'

'And how did they make sure she was the only one affected?'

'Actually, I've been thinking about that. I reckon it was put into the vitamin shake – everyone knows that Carmen has it instead of breakfast. It looks like swamp water and probably tastes the same, too – she wouldn't have noticed if anything had been added. Carmen wanted a lie-in on Monday morning so Hannah made it for her and left it on the bench in the kitchen – anyone could have tampered with it.'

Luca jumped out of his chair. 'We have to tell Carmen about this immediately, and Hannah, so that they know that it wasn't food poisoning!' He took several strides towards the door where he paused to wait for her. 'Are you coming?'

'Apart from it being after midnight, I think we should think this through first.'

'Why? That's ridiculous! What is there to think about?' Luca stared at Izzie as if she was suggesting they took a flight to the Antarctic.

'Who would do such a thing?'

'I don't know, but when I get my—'

'Like you said before, I think we should keep this to ourselves, just for the time being, that way we'll be able to gather more information about who could be responsible, because at the moment I think it could have been any one of them!'

'What do you mean?'

Izzie sighed and waited for Luca to resume his seat, battling to keep her emotions in check.

'I really wanted this week to be perfect. I wanted everything to go according to my carefully prepared plan so that we'd be able to organise lots more courses and I could stay here at the villa, enjoying the Tuscan sunshine, the art galleries, the museums, the street markets…'

'But we have to say something! What if Carmen *does* decide to call in the authorities? It's not only the *Villa dei Limoni* that's at risk, but the trattoria, too! My reputation would be…'

'There's something else.'

'What?'

'Hannah.'

'You think it was Hannah who spiked her drink?'

'Possibly, it's just a hunch.'

'Another hunch?' Luca rolled his eyes as he laced his fingers through his hair at the back of his head, allowing an elongated sigh to escape from his lips.

'Just listen.'

Izzie recounted what she had observed at the dinner table and her theory as to why Hannah could be involved. She also decided to throw caution to the wind and add her concerns about the icy atmosphere between Zara and Carmen in the tennis court earlier.

'*Dio mio!* It's like something from a murder mystery movie! Are you sure Meghan's brother isn't lurking in the magnolia bushes out there, pointing his camera at the idiots who think this is real life? You know, before you arrived in this little slice of Tuscan paradise the most exciting thing that had ever happened was Gianni falling into the pond... with you rolling around in a field of sunflowers a very close second!'

'That was totally your fault!'

Izzie laughed, relieved to see the smile had returned to Luca's face at the mention of the incident where she'd ended up sprawled in a field under the gaze of a very bemused donkey, after being run off the road by Luca when he'd seen her riding his ex-fiancée's sugar-pink Vespa, which he'd believed to be locked safely in one of the villa's outbuildings. It was a particularly inauspicious first encounter, but her life had improved greatly from that moment onwards.

'Anyway, I think it would be a good idea if we kept quiet for a day or two and see what else we can find out. If we say anything now, we might *never* uncover what's going on. Do you really think who did this is going to confess and beg for forgiveness?'

'So let me get this straight. You think Hannah could have done it because she was in love with Dalton before

Carmen lured him away, Zara's in the frame because her relationship with Carmen is unusually lukewarm, and…'

'Yes, and don't forget Tom.'

'Tom?'

'The phone call we overheard outside Antonio's.'

'Argh, this is turning into an absolute nightmare! What on earth made me think it would be easy to run a few creative courses where guests could learn a new skill whilst they relaxed and recharged their batteries? Give me a busy restaurant any day!'

Izzie pushed herself up from her chair and went to join Luca at the door, sliding her hand into his and giving it a sympathetic squeeze.

'Come on, I'll make us coffee.'

She hadn't realised it had been raining and Luca had taken just one step onto the patio when a gust of wind caught the awning above the *limonaia*'s door and sent a barrage of rainwater over his head, missing her by inches. He gasped, spluttering from the shock of the unexpected dousing.

'Oh… my… God!'

With his arms held out at his sides and his jaw loose with incredulity, he spun round to face Izzie, who couldn't stop the grin from stretching her face.

'Hey, what are you laughing at?'

With his dark eyes filled with mischief, Luca reached out to grab her hand and, to her surprise, instead of racing towards the warm, dry kitchen, he hooked his arm around her shoulders and pulled her towards the footpath that lead to the gazebo.

'Luca!'

Arm in arm, they ran through the raindrops, laughing and giggling, stumbling along the uneven path as thunder tumbled over the hills in the distance. Rain continued to sprinkle down from the inky black sky, but unlike back home in London, it was like taking a stroll in her morning shower. Luca's jacket was now as wet as her T-shirt and clung to his firm torso like a second skin, emphasising his impressive physique. Breathless, she skipped towards the steps of the gazebo, anxious to take cover before she was drenched to her underwear, but to her surprise, Luca stopped short of the shelter and dragged her into his arms.

'Hey, I'm getting soaked!'

'*Balla con me!*'

'Dance with you? But it's raining! We're getting wet!'

Izzie tried to pull away, but Luca held onto her, his eyes scorching into hers, his lips curled into a playful smile, laced with challenge.

'But...'

'*La vita non si tratta di aspettare che la tempesta passi... Si tratta di imparare a ballare sotto la pioggia!*'

It took Izzie a couple of beats to understand what Luca had said but when she did, she moved into his arms, tears sparkling at her lashes, her heart melting with gratitude for this thoughtful, kind, passionate man who had zipped into her life and shown her that dancing in the rain was exactly the way she should honour her sister, not buried beneath the boulder of pain her loss had delivered.

With tears mingling with the raindrops, she moved into his arms, surrendering to his lead as he sent her pirouetting in what was now merely drizzle, laughing with delight as he seized her waist, lifted her feet from the ground and twirled her around and around and around, until she was dizzy from all the emotions cascading through her body. When Luca eventually set her back down to the ground, gasping for breath, he paused to look at her, scouring her eyes for confirmation that his feelings were mutual, then his lips were on hers, hot, urgent, filled with unbridled passion, as though nothing else in the world existed apart from that moment, that connection, that merging of body and mind.

She returned his kiss with a passion she hadn't known she possessed, relishing the somersault of attraction tumbling through her lower abdomen, savouring the thrill of desire that sizzled through every vein in her whole body, tingling out to her fingertips. A whiff of Luca's cologne met her nostrils and she almost swooned with happiness, at being there, in the rain, in the garden at Villa Limoncello, in wonderful, glorious Tuscany, but most of all with someone who made her feel whole again.

She cast a glance up to the clouds in the sky and knew for certain that Anna was there, riding on the fluffiest one of all, smiling down on her, signalling her approval and sending Izzie her love.

Chapter Fourteen

The pool house, Riccardo's B&B
Colour: Shimmering turquoise

The following day, Izzie left Carlotta to sort out breakfast and field questions from Zara about her legendary skills as a matchmaker, whilst she set up the easels in the vineyard. It had taken all her skills of persuasion to get Gianni to agree to allow their guests to use the slopes for their next painting tutorial, as well as her solemn promise that she would make sure that no one touched even a single leaf.

She did have sympathy with him for being so nervous about strangers descending on his precious vines. It was only last month that he had discovered the identity of the person responsible for the sabotage of his beloved plants. Initially, Gianni had thought his vines were the target of a particularly virulent disease that caused the leaves to crinkle and die – until Izzie and Luca had discovered that their neighbour Riccardo had been dousing them with a solution of home-made weed killer.

Gianni had not wanted to let him get away with what he'd done, had insisted they call in the police. But Luca had wavered, taking into account the fact that the man had recently lost his wife. It had been Eloisa's dream to own a farmhouse in Tuscany, but, sadly, she had not survived the vicious scourge of breast cancer long enough to see the B&B renovated and open for business. Riccardo had promised to seek professional counselling as atonement for his sins, having put his slip in integrity down to the cloak of grief that had clung to him with the tenacity of a barnacle. However, while Luca had relented, Gianni still grimaced with dislike whenever Riccardo's name was mentioned in conversation, which Izzie made sure was as infrequent as possible.

'Hey, Gianni, are you happy with the easels being set up like this?'

'Sure,' he said, jumping down from his rust-blistered quad bike and shoving his hands into the pockets of his extremely short shorts. 'Provided you tell every single one of your would-be Canalettos that they are not, under any circumstances, to touch the grapes – not one!'

'It's a painting tutorial, not a grape-picking class!'

'Just saying,' he said gruffly, scratching at his stubbled chin until he met Izzie's gaze, his usually laughter-filled eyes heavy with solemnity. 'Is it true, Izzie? Meghan told me that one of the guests is accusing Luca of poisoning her with his cooking.'

'Yes, it's true, but…'

'Well, as I've just found to my cost, some things are not all they seem, and I've been thinking…' Gianni paused, unable to meet Izzie's eyes as he scuffed the toe of his dirty work boot in the crushed seashells beneath his feet.

'What?'

'Do you think someone could have tampered with her food?'

Izzie let out a gasp of surprise which she managed to turn into a cough. How had Gianni heard about that? Had

Luca said something to him earlier despite asking her to keep it quiet? It had been his idea to keep his suspicions between the two of them, not hers, but then Gianni was his best friend.

'Tampered with her food?'

'Yes, maybe someone wants to sabotage the courses we're running here at *Villa dei Limoni* so that Luca has to sell – and guess who would be waiting in the wings, rubbing his palms with anticipation!'

'Ah,' sighed Izzie, unable to keep the smile from her face.

'It's a possibility…' said Gianni defensively.

Izzie knew where he was going with this and she supposed it *was* a possibility, and whilst Gianni had a different perpetrator in mind, he was spot on with his deductions.

'And you think that might be…'

'Riccardo! If he's done it once, then he can do it again!'

'How do you think he managed that?'

'Well, it's obvious. Carmen was found writhing in agony on a sun lounger over there by the wishing well, which, as you know, is right next to the boundary between the villa and the B&B. Riccardo could have easily leapt over the wall, put something in her drink and all he had to do was to stand back and wait for the explosion – so to speak!'

Gianni threw his hands in the air to illustrate his theory and the image it conjured up in Izzie's mind caused her to splutter in amusement.

'But why would he do that, though? He's never met Carmen – and how could he have known that she would be sunbathing right there, at that precise time, and that she wouldn't hear him when he approached her?'

'Erm, I...'

'I know how upset you are about what Riccardo did to the vineyard, and I am too...'

'And Luca!'

'And Luca, but do you really think he would target one of our guests? It's a huge leap from spraying a few vines with vinegar to poisoning someone's drink. If anyone was going to do that it would be someone who knows her.'

Izzie stopped abruptly, immediately regretting what she had said because she had confirmed that Gianni's hypothesis was right – just not agreed with his choice of culprit.

'So you *do* think someone targeted Carmen?'

'It's an alternate explanation for her stomach upset.'

'And does Luca agree?'

'Yes, but really we don't want to make a big thing—'

'But that's preposterous!' Gianni threw his hands in the air again. 'I'm not going to stand by while someone threatens the future of the villa. I have huge plans for the renaissance of the Rosetti vineyard, to create a wine as fabulous as the original.'

'Please, Gianni, will you talk to Luca before saying anything? Please?'

Gianni's face relaxed as his anger faded. 'Okay, okay. I'll talk to Luca, but when I find out who did this to us, I'll...'

Izzie watched him leap back onto his quad bike, rev the engine and race away down the avenue between the vines like Lewis Hamilton's older brother, taking a corner so sharply that it required all his strength to remain in control of the mechanical beast. She heaved a sigh, performed a final check of the easels and the painting accessories they would need for that day's tutorial, then made her way back to the villa.

When she reached the terrace, she checked her watch and was surprised to see there was still an hour to go until she was expecting the guests to make their way to the vineyard. She glanced over towards the wishing well, and, for a reason she couldn't fathom, her feet led her in that direction.

At the stone wall that separated the villa from the B&B next door, she paused to appreciate the beauty of the property. Through a wide arbour framed with a flurry of yellow roses, the place looked like something from an upmarket travel magazine – with its smooth, honey-coloured façade, its freshly painted shutters and its pots of dancing geraniums – all in complete contrast to its cousin next door, although Izzie knew which property she preferred. Despite its careworn appearance, Villa Limoncello held a certain rustic charm, a magical ambience that no amount of cash could recreate.

Without thinking, she hopped over the wall and sauntered towards the pool house, a miniature version of the B&B, with terracotta roof and shutters painted an identical shade of forest green. However, the highlight of her unauthorised excursion into her neighbour's garden was the fabulous rectangle of turquoise, its surface glittering in the early morning sunlight. She'd swap the B&B's swimming pool for the villa's tennis court any day!

'Assessing the competition?'

Izzie swung round and came face-to-face with Riccardo, his piercing blue eyes holding hers as he waited for an answer. She didn't know what she had expected, but she was shocked at his appearance; his salt-and-pepper hair, usually neatly barbered, was dishevelled, his shoulders drooped, and the smudges of tiredness beneath his eyes were clear evidence that he was having trouble sleeping.

'Of course not.' She smiled, hoping to skip over the fact that she was trespassing because she didn't have the spare capacity in her brain to add a run-in with Riccardo to her worries. She had enough problems with her guests.

'Good.'

To Izzie's surprise, instead of chastising her, or cross-examining her on the reason for her presence, Riccardo turned away to continue his early morning constitutional. However, he'd only taken a few steps when he seemed to change his mind and spun back around to meet her gaze, obviously engaged in an internal struggle over something.

'I wanted to say… I wanted to say I'm sorry. I… I don't know…'

Riccardo ran his roughened fingers through his hair, giving him the appearance of a mad scientist disappointed with the results of his latest experiment. From his uneasy body language, it was clear to Izzie that he wanted nothing more than to escape the awkward conversation, and yet he thrust his hands into the pockets of his tailored shorts and clenched his jaw in determination.

'I'm sorry. What I did was unforgiveable.'

'Then why did you do it?'

Riccardo averted his eyes, but not before Izzie saw the familiar flash of sorrow lurking in their depths. A cauldron of emotions swept through her chest – grief could make people do some strange things and she recognised a fellow sufferer when she saw one. It was the reason she found it difficult to hate Riccardo, like Gianni did, and could find it in her heart to forgive him for what he'd done to the villa's vines.

'I know what I did was wrong, and I know you probably won't believe me when I say that I have no idea what made me do it. It was a complete aberration, like some kind of automaton had taken over control of my actions. Oh, I'm not making excuses, and I don't blame Gianni for hating me – I'd hate me too. However, in my defence, I only wanted to worry the owner of the vineyard. The villa had been empty for two years – left to rot! All my enquiries as to who owned it had fallen on deaf ears so I just took the situation into my own hands – I thought the owner would be happy to get rid of it.'

'It's an extreme way to get someone's attention, killing off their precious vines that have been on the estate for centuries.'

'I didn't kill them.'

'You sprayed them with weed-killer!'

'Not the vines, I sprayed the *leaves*, just the leaves – I had no intention of contaminating the land. The solution I used was my own recipe – a mixture of industrial-strength vinegar and lemon juice, both completely organic. It's what I always use to get rid of the weeds in the B&B's garden. Yes, it dries out the leaves in the sunshine, but it does not affect the actual vine itself.'

'Okay…'

This was news to Izzie. She thought back to the heated altercation that had taken place between Luca, Gianni and Riccardo when they had confronted him with the evidence Izzie had stumbled across that had led them to the truth of what was causing the unidentifiable 'crumbling leaf disease'.

'So, why didn't you tell Luca and Gianni that?'

Riccardo simply shrugged.

No matter how hard she tried she couldn't figure the guy out. From their very first encounter on the day she arrived at the villa when she'd inadvertently blocked his access to the B&B, he'd been grouchy, off-hand and rude, and she had wondered whether his guests would appreciate their sojourn in the Italian countryside with a host who could give the Grinch a run for his money. Yet, when Gianni had severed the villa's electricity cable just hours before the celebrity wedding was due to start, Riccardo had come to their rescue, allowing them to hook up to his own supply. She had asked for his help and he had given it willingly. An idea sprang into her head and she wondered if she dare ask again.

'Do you have any B&B guests staying at the moment?'

'No, I'm about to leave for Rome. Got a meeting with my editor. Why?'

'I was wondering...'

Riccardo followed the direction of her gaze and for the first time during their conversation the corners of his lips twisted into a wry smile.

'Ah, you want to use the swimming pool, eh?'

'Not me, my guests.'

'How can I refuse? It's thanks to your well that it has water in it!'

'You don't mind?'

Riccardo shook his head.

'Thank you. I'll bring you one of Luca's home-made tiramisus!'

'Not necessary,' said Riccardo gruffly, before turning back towards his house, his head bent as though he carried the troubles of the world on his shoulders.

Izzie watched him go, sympathy nipping at her heart. She knew from friends in San Vivaldo that Riccardo, otherwise known as Richard Clarke, the best-selling English crime writer, had been wrestling with the demons of writer's block since his wife's death. Maybe that was why he had an appointment with his editor, and she truly hoped that his trip to the Italian capital would help him to find a route to solace so his creative juices could flow once more.

Having lost someone close herself, she felt a connection with Riccardo, a mutual understanding of the pain that seared through the very fabric of your being when a loved one was snatched from the centre of your life too soon. She knew from personal experience that his grief would never go away, but over time it would get easier to live with; that he could learn to weave his loss into his everyday life so that his wife remained, if not by his side, then certainly in his heart. She was working on achieving that and she hoped Riccardo could too.

As she meandered back to the gap in the boundary wall, she knew that Riccardo's contrition over the vineyard incident was genuine and was absolutely certain that he had nothing to do with Carmen's sudden illness – he hadn't even known that Villa Limoncello was hosting guests that week. She and Luca would have to look elsewhere for the person responsible, and as it was Wednesday that left them only three days short days to unravel the mystery.

Chapter Fifteen

The vineyard, Villa Limoncello
Colour: Olive green

'So, welcome everyone to day three of Villa Limoncello's painting course. This morning we'll be learning how to paint using acrylics, which are great for beginners because they're very forgiving – if you're not happy with what you've done, then you can paint over it almost straight away.'

'That's a bonus!' giggled Zara, tossing a glance in Tom's direction.

'Acrylics are also very versatile; you can use them on a wide range of surfaces, not just on paper but on wood or leather or fabric, and they can be applied using brushes, rollers, palette knives, or even sprayed or splattered onto the canvas.'

'Splattered? Now that sounds like fun!' said Beth, her eyes widening with mischief. 'You mean like a water fight but with paint?'

'Sort of,' laughed Izzie. 'But with the intention that the paint lands on the canvas, not on each other. Another benefit of using acrylic paint is that we can vary the consistency to suit our preference – high viscosity, which is achieved by adding gel or paste, will produce a result

133

similar to oils, or low viscosity, which is achieved by diluting with water, will look like watercolour.'

'I think this is going to be my favourite session,' said Carmen, fingering the tubes of multi-coloured paint with interest. 'I might have a go at painting the hessian I brought back from Bangladesh last month before I make it into bags.'

'Okay, let's get started.'

As they worked in companionable silence amidst the whispering vines, Izzie was struck by how picturesque the location was for a morning of artistic endeavour. The air was warming up, yet there was still a light breeze tickling at the leaves and sending up eddies of dusty soil. All around her the cicadas were busily performing their morning symphony interspersed by the occasional whine of a single Vespa struggling to make it up the hill to San Vivaldo.

It was idyllic, and for a brief moment she felt as if she were playing a role in a film, until reality poked its head above the parapet to remind her that there was more going on here than a simple celebration and a team-building exercise between friends and colleagues. She was indignant that whoever was responsible had chosen their stay at Villa Limoncello to act on their grievances. She also had a great deal of sympathy for Carmen, who had booked and paid for the whole trip only to be struck down within hours of arriving. It really was indefensible, and, leaving aside the effect of those actions on the future of Villa Limoncello, for Carmen's sake she was determined to expose the culprit.

'How are you getting on?' Izzie asked, leaning over Carmen's shoulder for a closer look at her canvas and being gifted with a whiff of rich, oriental perfume.

'Great! I'm loving these acrylics!'

Izzie smiled at Carmen's enthusiasm. She was relieved that she was enjoying the painting tutorials, and that she hadn't mentioned the unfortunate stomach incident since arriving in the vineyard dressed in a rich butterscotch sundress, with a complicated cat's cradle of ribbons the only fabric covering her breasts. She looked so polished that she wouldn't have looked out of place on stage at the Oscars!

'You should definitely try them out in the studio, Carr,' said Zara, adding a dash of burnt sienna to her palette along with a generous dollop of yellow ochre and mixing well.

Like Carmen, Zara was photoshoot-ready, wearing a long, pleated column in dark apricot, complemented by a statement necklace-and-earring combo fashioned from huge copper & silver orbs that glittered under the Tuscan sun like sunbeams from heaven.

'Maybe if you added a bit of shading just there?' suggested Izzie, pointing at Hannah's painting.

'Like this?'

'Yes, see how it brings the building into the fore-ground?'

'Great,' replied Hannah, her voice a little clipped.

Out of all the guests, Hannah was the only one Izzie hadn't clicked with. There was something about her that caused her hackles to prickle; a bubbling, barely contained anger seething inside her just waiting for the perfect moment to explode. Of course, Hannah probably still thought either Luca or Izzie herself was responsible for poisoning her boss and was annoyed that Carmen hadn't yet called in the authorities.

Izzie decided that it probably wasn't the right time to try to talk to her about it, so she moved further down the row of vines and paused at Beth's easel, surprised to see just how accomplished her painting was, certainly on par with Carmen, who was still the most talented artist in the group – except now it looked like she had a challenger for her crown.

'Your composition is perfect, and there's certain Monet-esque quality to those flowers.'

'Thank you, Izzie, that means a lot.' Beth beamed, dabbing her paint brush at the part of her painting that depicted the sunflower-filled field beyond the olive grove to their right.

To Izzie's relief, Beth had chosen that morning to depart from her fixation with all things black by adding a flash of colour in the guise of a gorgeous dark emerald leather satchel that brought out the colour of her eyes. On closer inspection, Izzie saw that the wide straps had been hand-embroidered with turquoise, jade and gold stitching in the shape of peacock feathers. It was understated yet beautiful, the perfect accessory for Beth, and Izzie wondered if it was one of Carmen's designs, although if it was, the handbag was a departure from the bold, brash primary colours she usually favoured.

'Is your bag one of Carmen's creations?'

'No, it's not!' Beth snapped, her paintbrush hanging in the air as she turned to face Izzie, her eyes filled with indignation and annoyance. 'This satchel is *actually* one of my own designs. I went to fashion school too, you know.'

'Oh, I didn't mean, I'm sorry...'

'No, no, I'm sorry. I shouldn't have said that. You just touched a bit of a nerve, that's all.'

'Did I?'

Beth reached down to pick up her bottle of water and took a long draught, wiping her mouth with the back of her hand as she pondered whether to expand on the reasons for her outburst. Izzie remained silent, hoping she might be about to learn something about Beth and Carmen's friendship.

'Carmen isn't the only one with a degree in fashion design, you know. We were at uni together, we just graduated in different years. Carmen shot off into a lucrative career in modelling, whilst I went in a different direction. I could hardly follow her, could I? I'm only five foot three in heels!'

Izzie didn't know what to say. If she were honest, she thought Beth's figure was more appealing than Carmen's, but it was no business of hers – despite the note of resentment in Beth's voice.

'Did you want to join her in that industry?'

'No way!' Beth laughed. 'No, not at all. That life doesn't interest me in the slightest – although the travel would have been amazing and the clothes... well, wow! No, I'm only interested in the design part of the industry.'

'Do you work in the fashion business?'

'No, I work in retail. I design handbags in my spare time.'

'And take it from me, every single one she creates is amazing!' said Carmen, coming to look at Beth's painting. 'Hey, that's really good, Beth. I knew you'd be the most talented artist amongst us!'

'Always the element of surprise,' muttered Beth so that only Izzie could hear.

Suddenly Izzie experienced another spasm of sympathy for Carmen. She was gorgeous, in demand from magazines and photoshoots, wore some fabulous clothes, ran a successful business that challenged her creativity every day, had a wonderful fiancé whom she clearly loved, enough money to splash out on a trip for her friends – and yet all those around her seemed to do was resent her for it. Hannah resented her relationship, Beth resented her business success, maybe Zara did too, and Tom as her accounts manager – perhaps he resented her wealth? It seemed no matter how generous Carmen was, she still couldn't win the approval of her friends and colleagues.

As the sun rose higher in the cerulean sky, Izzie realised her students were beginning to wilt and she knew it was time to wrap up their third painting session. Every single one of them had created a vibrant, individual image of the panoramic scenery and she was proud of what they had achieved as beginners, especially Tom, whose picture of Gianni's abandoned, rust-covered tractor was very proficient for someone who didn't know what acrylics were before the tutorial.

'Okay, I think we should end this session before we expire or burn to a frazzle. You've all worked really hard this morning, produced some fabulous works of art, and I hope you've enjoyed the session.'

'Yes,' came the chorus.

'Thank you. So, as you'll see from the itinerary, this afternoon is free for you to do whatever you want – and as a special treat I've managed to negotiate a complimentary pass to our neighbour's pool on one condition.'

'What's that?' asked Beth, her eyes filled with curiosity.

'No one is to tell Gianni. Riccardo is not his favourite person for reasons we don't need to go into.'

'Yay!' cheered the group, except from Tom, who wrinkled his nose.

'Never been particularly keen on swimming myself.'

'Even under the Tuscan sun?' asked Carmen, already packing away her easel.

'Don't worry, Tom,' said Zara, tucking her paint box under her arm. 'I'll give you a lesson.'

'Me too,' added Hannah, slipping her hand into his in a gesture that surprised Izzie but the others didn't seem to notice.

'As there's no pasta-making tutorial tonight, we've booked an evening out at an organic farm with a spectacular view of San Gimignano – a walled hilltop town famous for its medieval architecture. It's been nicknamed the Manhattan of Tuscany because of the fourteen towers that form its skyline, so don't forget your cameras. If everyone could be on the terrace for pre-dinner drinks at six thirty that would be great.'

'What's on the itinerary for tomorrow, Izzie?' asked Carmen.

'Tomorrow we have our trip to Siena where we'll be learning the techniques of pencil drawing.'

'Oh, I'm really looking forward to that one!' said Zara, smiling with excitement. 'Come on, last one in that pool pays for dinner.'

'I think it's already…'

But Zara was already hot-footing it from the vineyard towards the villa to change into her bikini, and Carmen gave chase like a schoolgirl running after her best friend in a game of tag. Beth stared after them as she finished packing up her satchel and sauntered slowly in their wake, her face clouded with an expression Izzie couldn't decipher.

'Will you be joining us at the pool?' asked Hannah, making it clear to Izzie from the tone of her voice that she would like nothing less than spending any extra time with her.

'No, there are things I need to do here at the villa.'

'Okay, come on, Tom.'

'I really would prefer to spend some time in my room, Han. I think I've caught the sun this morning and I—'

'Then you can sit under an umbrella and watch us!'

'Okay.' Tom blushed, clearly uncomfortable but not willing to continue with his refusal.

'Don't worry, I'm sure we won't be blinded by your milk-bottle legs!' shouted Beth over her shoulder.

Izzie could see the embarrassment scrawled across Tom's features. Being the only man in the group, and one who was not as body-confident as the rest – maybe with the exception of Beth – who could blame him, especially when three of the women got to see the male form in all its muscular glory every day of their working lives. She saw him cast a glance over his shoulder at her as he trotted reluctantly at Hannah's side, looking like a lamb being dragged to the slaughter.

Chapter Sixteen

Izzie heaved a sigh of relief as she watched the group disappear for their afternoon of watery fun. She couldn't wait to spend some time away from the villa. Carlotta had done all the chores, with a little help from Meghan, whilst she'd been presenting the tutorial and as the group was dining out that evening there was no prep to do for that evening's meal, so she too had the rest of the afternoon to her own devices. She had hoped Meghan would join her for a trip to Pisa, but when she saw the sparkle in her eyes in anticipation of spending some quality time with Gianni, she didn't want to intrude.

She smiled, her heart blossoming with affection for her best friend, gratitude flooding her veins for the support and kindness she had shown to her during the time when grief had challenged her sanity. Meghan also had her own monsters to slay and Izzie hoped that spending time here in Villa Limoncello would help to give her the confidence she needed to confront her issues and share them with her parents.

She loved Meghan and it hurt to see her refusal to talk to her parents about why she'd needed to escape from their successful stud farm in North Yorkshire to the bright lights of London. Because Brad had forged a successful career as an award-winning film director, it seemed he'd used that to avoid his familial duty of carrying on the family business, which meant it had fallen to Meghan to face the pressure of expectation alone. However, unbeknown to Mr and Mrs Knowles, there was a fatal flaw in their plan for their daughter to return home to help train the next Grand National winner – she hated everything to do with the equine world. In fact, it was more than that; she was terrified of horses and had not yet found the courage to admit that to anyone except Izzie and their friend Jonti.

Meghan's parents saw her behaviour as a rejection of her heritage and were confused at her persistent desire to continue in her job as a window dresser for Harrods when she could be instrumental in producing the next rosette-winning thoroughbred. And, as was always the case with these things, the longer the situation festered the more they pressed and the harder she dug in her heels. Izzie struggled to understand why Meghan didn't just tell them about her phobia, to explain how she came out in goose bumps whenever she went within two feet of the smelly beasts, but Meghan had told her that, as pragmatic as ever, they would simply arrange a course of therapy to eradicate the problem and Meghan was adamant that her future lay in the realm of design, not racing.

Izzie grabbed her duffel bag, slung it over her shoulder and made her way to the outbuilding where she stowed the sugar-pink Vespa that had become a valued friend. Whilst the vehicle looked more like something Barbie would use to visit her pet unicorn, it held a special place in her heart as it had been the catalyst for meeting Luca

– despite having ended up on her bottom under the doleful gaze of an Italian donkey for her trouble.

She wheeled the scooter along the cypress-lined driveway and, once she was through the wrought-iron gates that protected the villa from unwanted tourist invasion, she slung her leg over the seat and pointed the handlebars in the direction of San Vivaldo, where she hoped to persuade Oriana to share a coffee with her. Maybe she should enquire about her next yoga session too – it was time she started a new fitness regime. After the loss of her sister, every ounce of energy she possessed had been used to simply make it through the day and, come six o'clock, the very last thing she'd wanted to do was labour over an exercise bike or take an aerobics class.

She thought of the many sunshine-filled days she had spent with Anna during the summer holidays when her sister had been released from her duties as the village's beloved primary school teacher; combing the beach for shells, swimming in the sea, surfing the waves that Cornwall was famous for. They had returned home, exhausted from their excursions, yet still keen to indulge in their love of all things Italian, from fashion and food to, latterly, planning their trip to Florence as part of Anna's hen weekend celebrations before her long-awaited wedding to her childhood sweetheart Josh.

Sadly, neither of those celebrations had happened and the whole village had mourned the passing of someone who had been taken far too soon. If it were possible, Izzie had been even more heartbroken to witness the confusion and distress on the faces of the children Anna had taught, whom she had treated with patience and affection, helping not only with their education, but with encouraging them to be considerate members of the community by arranging regular bake sales for the local hospice, organising beach litter picks and coordinating the annual village fayre.

As Izzie navigated the serpentine roads, the breeze whipping her hair across her cheeks, the sun warming her face, the fragrant air tickling at her nostrils, gratitude flooded her heart at being blessed with such a wonderful twin sister for almost twenty-seven years – longer than some people had with their siblings. Despite the ache of her loss, her spirits lifted, and she cast up a missive of thanks to the gods of good fortune, even more determined than ever not to waste a moment of her time pondering sadness. The next thing she knew she was riding into the piazza, removing her helmet and shaking out the tangles from her unruly copper curls.

'*Ciao*, Izzie, how're things going over at Villa Dei Limoni?'

Izzie smiled at Francesca, the owner of San Vivaldo's florist's shop and all-round horticultural maestro, whom she had met when overseeing the celebrity wedding that had brought her to the villa in the first place. The bridal arrangements she had created had been works of art in themselves, especially the spectacular floral chandelier that would not have looked out of place in Versailles.

'They're going okay, thanks. I've got the afternoon off, though, so do you fancy a coffee?'

'Would love one!'

Izzie grinned. She had bonded with Francesca immediately – the village's florist reminded her of Meghan with her raspberry-streaked hair and quirky dress sense, but also her wide smile and innate kindness. She loved the way she was fluent in Italian, complete with the customary gestures to illustrate her emotions, but spoke English with a broad West Country accent – just like Izzie herself did – because her mother was from Devon. She thought of the rose petals Francesca had supplied to Luca for his triple-layered rose cake and her heart gave a jolt of appreciation for her thoughtfulness.

'So, tell me about the classes.'

'Well, the painting side of things is going okay.'

'That makes it sound as though there's something that isn't?'

Izzie hesitated. Could she confide in Francesca? How could she do that when she'd agreed with Luca that she wouldn't talk to Meghan about what was going on? But, on the other hand, if she didn't spill everything that was churning through her mind to *someone*, she might just combust from the pressure. Her temples throbbed, and her throat felt like it had a miniature pineapple lodged in it with the effort of keeping everything to herself. Francesca had been supportive when she'd opened up to her about her sister, as well as discreet over the secrecy surrounding the celebrity wedding Villa Limoncello had recently hosted.

'Izzie? Is something wrong?'

'It's complicated.'

'My favourite thing! Come on through to the back, I'll make us some coffee and you can tell me all about it. I knew there was something going on as soon as I saw you.'

Izzie groaned. She had always worn her troubles on her face. Anna had been the one who had learned how to hide those things – maybe it was a necessary skill that all primary school teachers had to perfect.

'Is it that obvious?'

'Yes, but only because you've been so happy these last few weeks while you've been sorting out the villa with Luca, so the transformation is noticeable. You look like you're carrying the world's woes on your shoulders.'

Izzie smiled at her new friend, loving the sound of her Devonshire twang regardless of the fact that it caused a stab of homesickness. She hadn't made the trip back to St Ives for some time, her fragile emotions making it difficult to witness the intensity of her parents' grief. However, now that she was starting to feel stronger, more positive about her future without Anna by her side, she was beginning to toy with the possibility of either taking a trip to Cornwall when she got back home or inviting her parents over to stay at Villa Limoncello. She knew her mother in particular would love the garden and be blown away by the *limonaia*.

One of the people who had helped her to gain a new perspective on her life was sitting right opposite her at the huge scarred wooden bench where Francesca selected, cut and arranged her flowers with exquisite taste and unparalleled artistry – and her face was filled in concern. Izzie inhaled a breath, savouring the perfume of the Casablanca lilies that sat in a tall glass vase awaiting their fate. The whole room had the appearance of an artist's studio, where the tools of the trade were wire cutters and industrial-sized scissors, with vases instead of water pots, ribbons and bows instead of paints, and cellophane instead of ornate frames.

'*Ecco!* One coffee, the solace of the worried! So, come on, Izzie, the sooner you divulge the details, the better you'll feel!'

Izzie took a sip of her cappuccino, its rich aroma adding another dimension to the cornucopia of scents that floated through the air in Francesca's floral paradise, and suddenly all she wanted to do was divulge the whole saga.

'One of the guests at the villa thinks they got food poisoning from the lunch Luca prepared,' she blurted before going on to explain what had happened, how upset she was and how she feared that it would spell the end of their dreams for Villa Limoncello to become a vibrant part of the community again after years of neglect. 'So, if Carmen does decide to splash the whole thing over the travel review sites and social media when she gets back home, then we can wave goodbye to an avalanche of repeat bookings, but what I'm more worried about is Antonio's Trattoria.'

'I wouldn't worry too much about that, Izzie. Antonio's has been an institution in San Vivaldo for the last sixty years – most customers are locals and they won't be swayed by what a group of visitors have to say about one isolated incident at the villa. Whatever happens it will be forgotten about after a few weeks.' Francesca leaned back in her chair, hugged her coffee cup between her palms and narrowed her eyes. 'Do you have another theory for your guest's stomach upset?'

Astute as always, thought Izzie, but she wasn't ready to float half-formed accusations in public without the evidence to back them up. It wouldn't be right. And maybe she and Luca had got it wrong and there *had* been something wrong with the food. She forced a wide smile on her lips.

'No, no, nothing like that. Thanks for listening, Francesca, I feel loads better.'

'No problem.' Francesca smiled. 'Now, have I told you about Carlotta's most recent success? Who needs Tinder when we have our very own matchmaking maestro living amongst us?'

Izzie spent the next hour giggling with Francesca, exchanging gossip and theories for Carlotta's romance triumphs and who she would bring together next. Eventually, she drained the last mouthful of her coffee, pushed herself up from her tall stool and leaned forward to embrace her friend and deposit the regulation kisses on her cheeks.

'Izzie, you know I'm here anytime if you need to talk.'

Izzie saw Francesca give her a look of such heartfelt compassion that she almost crumbled from an upsurge of emotion. For a moment she couldn't speak, couldn't formulate the right words to thank Francesca enough for her support, her understanding and her friendship.

'Thank you,' she managed to croak before giving her friend another hug and leaving the shop as quickly as manners would permit.

Kindness; who would have thought that it was one of the toughest things to deal with?

Chapter Seventeen

The garden, Villa Limoncello
Colour: Dusky magnolia

Izzie steered the little pink Vespa between the gateposts of Villa Limoncello, the brigade of cypress trees welcoming her like a guard of honour at a wedding. She smiled to herself as an intense feeling of homecoming spun through her body – she had only been at Villa Limoncello a short time but already it felt like she'd been there for years.

With Luca's help, her Italian was improving every day, especially the words for foodie treats like *panzanella*, *torta di ceci* and *castagnaccio*, a chestnut cake unique to the region flavoured with pine nuts and sultanas and sprinkled with olive oil and rosemary – delicious! Her culinary skills, non-existent before she arrived in Italy, were improving too, as was her appreciation of the intricacies of wine production – and sampling.

She cast a glance towards the vineyard and smiled as she saw a cloud of dust ballooning behind Gianni's tractor as he ploughed his way between the vines, stopping occasionally to inspect the leaves for the scourge of disease. She really hoped that, come the *vendemmia* in September, the quality of the grapes would reflect the hard work he had devoted to their care. What an amazing feeling it must be to taste the wine that you have created yourself, from the vine to the glass. She wondered whether she would be at Villa Limoncello to join in with the celebrations. She wanted to be, that was for sure, but that meant she would have to redouble her efforts to ferret out who was responsible for putting the villa's future in jeopardy.

A surprise honk of a car horn from behind caused Izzie to wobble on the Vespa as she drew to a halt at the villa's front steps that led to the entrance, flanked by a pair of lemon trees proudly displaying the citrus globes the house was famous for. She twisted in her seat to see Luca jump out of the driver's seat of his Alfa Romeo, and stride over to greet her.

'Hey! Just the person I wanted to see!'

Izzie couldn't stop herself from beaming as he dropped kisses on her cheeks, enjoying the frisson of pleasure that cascaded through her veins when his signature cologne hit her nostrils. However, the creases in his forehead warned her that this wasn't a social visit.

'What's going on?'

'I've just had a call from the food hygiene inspectors. They want to come over to the villa next week to carry out an inspection.'

'Oh, no! I thought Carmen was still thinking about things. I thought she would…'

Luca rubbed his palm across his jawline, the over-long stubble testament to the fact he had a great deal on his mind, even though he preferred to give the impression of being confident and in complete control.

'They didn't say who called them.'

'Well, it has to be Carmen, or possibly Hannah, doesn't it?'

'I suppose they are the most likely people.'

'But what happened was a one-off. Everyone's been fine since then, no problems at all, and there's no evidence that it was—'

'I know, Izzie, I know, but we'll just have to deal with it and see what happens.'

'But the group are leaving on Friday. They won't even be here to talk to the inspectors.'

Izzie's heart hammered out a concerto of panic as she contemplated the ordeal that lay ahead. She had no idea how to handle a visit from the Italian food authorities, nor did she have the language skills to explain exactly what had happened. She knew for a fact that there was nothing more she, or Meghan or Carlotta, could have done to prevent the incident from happening; nevertheless, she felt guilty, as though she had let Luca down in some way.

'It's okay, Izzie, I'll deal with them. I'm sure it'll be routine,' said Luca, clearly forcing his features into a mask of nonchalance that did not convince Izzie in the slightest.

'But what if...'

'Let's not stray into the realms of the unforeseeable, eh? Let's just get on with delivering the best Painting & Pasta course we can and then, when it's over, we can take stock of what we are trying to do here. Maybe Villa Limoncello isn't destined to be a venue for cookery classes. Maybe Gianni's plan to produce the best Chianti in the whole of Tuscany will be successful and we can hold wine-tasting evenings, or perhaps we can start producing Maria Rosetti's limoncello again? Or maybe we should continue with the courses but stick to painting, creative writing, yoga sessions, even tennis lessons? There are lots of alternatives. Come on, let's go and see what Gianni and Meghan are up to.'

Luca held out his hand and Izzie slid her palm into his, grateful for his positivity about the future of Villa Limoncello. At least his list of potential solutions hadn't included the sale of the villa. Clearly, he was willing to try anything and everything before resorting to that scenario. It was up to her to join him in his positive outlook, and in order to do that she resolved once again to redouble her efforts to unravel what was going on.

First, Gianni's beloved vines had been sabotaged, and now their very first guests had been targeted. What had Luca done to deserve that?

She strolled through the villa's gardens, her hand tucked into Luca's elbow, enjoying the tranquillity that seemed to descend whenever she was there, listening to the constant symphony of birdsong, inhaling the myriad fragrances of the herbs and the flowers, completely surrounded by nature – such a contrast to the hustle and bustle and toxic stench of car fumes that went hand in hand with life in London.

When they arrived at the gazebo, Luca stopped and pulled her gently towards him, holding her gaze for what felt like an eternity. Her fingertips tingled with anticipation as he leaned closer, his breath caressing her cheek until his lips were on hers. A sudden wave of emotion crashed through her body and she gave herself up to the joy of being kissed by this wonderful man, someone who had guided her tenderly but firmly out from the grey raincloud of grief she had lingered beneath and into the Tuscan sunshine where she could begin to heal.

'Luca, I—'

'Shh, did you hear that?'

Izzie stood still, her ears cocked in the direction Luca had indicated. Did he mean the concerto of croaking frogs, the buzz of a passing bumblebee or the trickle of water from the fountain next to the pond?

'I can't hear anything... Oh...'

Luca put his finger to his lips, reached out to grip her hand, and together they tiptoed forward like a pair of children playing a game of hide-and-seek, or perhaps amateur detectives in search of their next clue. Izzie experienced an almost overwhelming urge to giggle at the absurdity of it all. But within moments she could hear the murmur of conversation from behind the sprawling pink magnolia bush. They came to a standstill next to the marble cherub who watched over the garden fountain and Izzie realised who was speaking.

'That's Tom. Who's he talking to?'

'Not sure,' whispered Luca, stretching to his full height in an attempt to see over the arboreal screen. After a few seconds it became obvious that Tom was on the phone, as they were listening to a one-sided conversation.

'*Laura, listen to me...*'

There was a pause and Izzie held her breath for fear Tom would be able to sense they were there, eavesdropping on his conversation for a second time in as many days. She nudged Luca, intending to suggest they beat a hasty retreat as noiselessly as possible, but the mini Sherlock Holmes on her shoulder argued that if they were to have any chance of getting to the bottom of the mystery of Carmen's illness then this was what they had to do.

'*I* have *told her that, several times...*'

Izzie couldn't fail to detect the strain in Tom's voice and her heart gave a sharp nip of sympathy. As she peered through the foliage, she could see his silhouette pacing backwards and forwards, his mobile phone clutched to his ear, his free hand scratching at the back of his head. She could almost feel the waves of tension emanating from his body.

'*I will, I will, but…*'

Tom's voice had ratcheted up an octave and Izzie knew his grip on his emotions was beginning to wane.

'*Laura, please, I'm doing everything I can.*'

Izzie turned to Luca, discomfort at their invasion of privacy gnawing at her chest. It was clear what they were listening to was deeply personal, something that was causing Tom a great deal of pain.

'Luca, I think we should leave…'

But Luca shook his head, slotted his arm around her shoulders and pulled her close as he continued to listen to Tom. However, the conversation seemed to be over because when Izzie turned back, she saw Tom shove his phone into the back pocket of his khaki shorts, slump down onto the bench next to the pond, and drop his head in his hands.

Luca met Izzie's eyes, raising his eyebrows in question. 'What do you think that was all about?'

'I don't know, but whatever it was about, it was private, so I think we should give him some space to gather his—'

But Luca was already striding out from their leafy camouflage, leaving Izzie with no alternative but to scamper in his wake.

'Tom!' called Luca as though he had just happened upon him whilst out for an afternoon stroll in the garden. 'Hey? Is everything okay?'

Izzie watched Tom raise his head, and when she saw that his eyes were red and swollen, contrition surged through her. Who was Laura? Was she his girlfriend? Had she just terminated their relationship? God, she could kill Luca for being so insensitive – this had nothing to do with them. However, once again her desire to help, to console, to support those who were clearly in need, raced through her veins so she took a seat next to Tom and offered him a tissue.

'Thanks,' he muttered, his cheeks flushing, embarrassed at being found in the uncomfortable position of sobbing into his palms. He quickly blew his nose, inhaled a steadying breath and attempted a weak smile. 'I'm fine, it's all good.'

'Is there anything we can do to help?' asked Izzie, noticing for the first time that his fingernails had been bitten down to the quick and his hands were trembling in his lap. It was clear to even the least observant onlooker that all was not fine.

'No, nothing. Believe me, I wish there was.'

Tom tried to laugh but to Izzie's surprise the attempt morphed into a deep guffaw of distress and again he dropped his head into his hands. She exchanged a glance with Luca, who took a seat on the other side of Tom, placing his hand on the distraught man's shoulder as they waited for him to recover his grasp on his emotions.

'Tom, you have to tell us what's wrong. We might be able to help you. Were you talking to someone on the phone?' asked Izzie, not caring what Tom might think of her for eavesdropping if it meant he would open up. 'Was it your girlfriend?'

That caused Tom to calm down immediately.

'Girlfriend? No, no, I haven't got a girlfriend. I was talking to my sister.'

'Your sister?'

'Yes, Laura.'

'And you argued?'

'No, well, yes, I mean, no. Oh God, it's all such a nightmare. I should never have come to Italy.'

Tom inhaled another long, slow breath, straightened his shoulders and tried to arrange his features into a composed expression before glancing at Luca, then Izzie, and sighing again.

'I wasn't arguing with Laura. I was talking to her about Mum.'

An avalanche of questions tumbled into Izzie's brain and she wanted to fire them off one by one. However, she sensed the best thing to do was to allow Tom to tell his own story at his own pace, so she simply reached out, took his hand in hers and squeezed. The raw agony in his eyes was almost too much for her to bear and her chest tightened as she fought to hold back the reins on her own sadness demons.

'Mum's in a care home. She's been diagnosed with dementia. She has no idea who Laura and I are or why we're visiting her. It's heart-breaking – she was such a vivacious person, with lots of hobbies and interests, until six months ago when the police brought her home after the local supermarket found her pushing a trolley around the aisles in her nightie at midnight. It was a huge shock.'

'Oh, Tom, I'm so sorry,' murmured Izzie, exchanging a glance with Luca.

Tom paused, lost in the labyrinths of his own thoughts for a while.

'It was Laura who insisted I come here to Tuscany. I didn't want to leave Mum, but Laura said I needed a break.'

'And has… has something happened?' asked Izzie, screwing up her courage to hear bad news.

'No, it's not that. Mum's fine, well, as fine as she can be.'

Izzie exhaled a slow, silent breath. She didn't think she could cope with what she had feared may have happened – not so soon after dealing with her own grief. So why was Tom so distressed?

Tom shook his head, clearly struggling with whether to confide his troubles in two relative strangers. As Izzie watched on, all the fight seemed to leave him, his shoulders sagged into his chest, his jaw relaxed and his whole body slumped like a deflated balloon.

'The care home Mum's in is perfect. It's nearby so I can visit her every day on my way home from work and Laura travels over from Bath to be with her every weekend. The staff are kind and caring, and there's lots going on for the residents to get involved in during the day, even painting classes, would you believe?'

Izzie smiled and nodded, but refrained from commenting, keen for Tom to continue.

'Laura and I want her to stay at Castledene; any change in her routine, even the smallest thing, sends her backwards so it's important for her to remain in familiar surroundings with carers she trusts, but it's very expensive. All Mum's savings have gone, and we've cashed in her last insurance policy. Then, at the end of last month, another invoice arrived and the fees had gone up by another five per cent and I, well, I couldn't pay it. I told Laura I'd paid it, but when she visited Mum the manager queried the late payment and she found out. Neither of us have the money to keep Mum there and so… and so… we were asked to move her somewhere else.'

'Oh, Tom…'

'So… I did something I can't even believe I would ever have done in a million years. I hate myself for it and even now looking back I still can't understand…'

Tom paused, unable to continue, his gaze fixed on an indeterminate place in the distance as he relived the trauma of the last few months. Silence expanded through the clearing in Villa Limoncello's garden and Izzie remained motionless, not wanting to break the spell of calm that had descended whilst Tom confided his heart-breaking story. The beauty of the view in front of them receded into the background as her focus remained solely on the drama being played out on that garden bench.

'I paid Castledene's invoice out of Carmen's business account,' Tom blurted, gulping in a lungful of air in order to continue before his courage failed. 'It was a stupid, stupid, stupid thing to do! I don't know what possessed me! A complete aberration, a momentary loss of sanity! For God's sake, I knew it would be flagged up almost immediately by the bank. I knew it was wrong, I just thought… well, I didn't think. Of course, the bank did query the payment with Carmen and what I did quickly came to light.'

Tom shook his head, hot tears now flowing down his cheeks unchecked. The anguish scrawled across his face caused Izzie's stomach to somersault with sympathy for the situation he found himself in.

'I stole from my employer and I'm so ashamed. You should have seen the disappointment on Carmen's face when she asked me about it. I confessed what I'd done straight away. I offered to pay her back, but of course, I don't have the money to do that, *and* there's next month's invoice to pay too, so that's not a solution. Carmen is quite within her rights to report me to the police and to the ICEAW – it's theft after all. But worse than that, I've breached her trust in me and that can never be repaired.

'She kept asking me why I did it. I didn't want to tell her about Mum, didn't want her to know, but I broke down and it all came gushing out. I didn't want her sympathy, but at least she has an explanation. I've promised to repay every penny with interest when Mum's house is sold. It's on the market and there's already a couple of buyers interested, but we can't sell it until… until… until Mum passes away, unless we get a court order. I don't think I could cope with all that, and getting a lawyer is so expensive, and anyway, I don't think it'll be long, if you know what I mean.'

'And what did Carmen say when you told her why you did it?'

'She said she'd have to think about what she was going to do. There was no one more surprised than I was when she insisted that I join them all on their trip to Italy. I really didn't want to come, but, well, I could hardly refuse, could I? She said she'd let me know at the end of the week when she's had time to mull things over. I've tried to block it all out, tried to focus on the classes, but it's like torture being here – trying to pretend to Hannah, Beth and Zara that everything is normal. As Carmen's PA, Hannah knows there's something going on. She asked me about it on the plane on the way over, but I haven't told her. I can't! How can I confess to her that I'm a thief? What will she think of me? She'll have nothing to do with me when she finds out…'

And for the first time Izzie understood that Tom thought of Hannah as more than a mere colleague. He was in love with her, probably had been for some time, but now, not only had he lost his self-respect and probably his job, he'd also lost the chance of seeing the person he loved every day.

'Laura's been ringing me every day to ask if I've spoken to Carmen or whether she's reached any decisions yet. I keep telling her that Carmen has made it clear that she wants to enjoy the week here at the villa and I don't want to press her. But it's eating away at me! I've never been involved with the police before, I'll never work in finance again, and I'll never see…'

This time Tom let his emotions flow freely and Izzie slid her arm around his shoulders, murmuring soothing words, her heart breaking for him and the predicament he found himself in. She knew that when grief descended, a person could do the most reckless and ill-advised things as the brain struggled to cope with performing even the most mundane of tasks. Tom's mother might still be alive, but the grip of dementia had obviously changed her into a completely different person which, in Izzie's view, was a great deal harder to accept.

Izzie had no idea how long the three of them had been sitting there when a voice interrupted the crescendo of cicadas.

'Tom? Tom? Are you there?'

Chapter Eighteen

The gazebo, Villa Limoncello
Colour: Blanched white

Izzie looked up and saw Hannah approaching from the direction of the terrace, the tassels on her short floral sundress flapping in the breeze. Her cheeks were flushed, her hair was still damp from the swim in Riccardo's pool and she looked several years younger than thirty-one. When she reached them, she glanced around the gathering, taking in the strained atmosphere, and wrinkling her nose in confusion when she saw Tom's puffy eyes.

'What's going on?'

Izzie flashed a quick look at Luca, who simply shook his head, clearly preferring to leave any explanations to Tom.

'Tom? Why didn't you come for a swim with us? What are you doing here?'

'Nothing,' Tom said quickly, pushing himself up from his seat and joining Hannah, keen to escape a further inquisition. 'Come on, why don't we grab a coffee?'

Unfortunately for Tom, Hannah couldn't be brushed off that easily; she'd noticed the distress scrawled across his freckled features and how pale his complexion was.

'Don't fob me off with that. I might have my hands full running after Carmen, but that doesn't mean I don't still notice what's happening around me. I know there's something going on, Tom. What is it? What's happened? And why are you sitting here with Luca and Izzie looking like you've lost your pet spaniel? If you need to talk about anything, I'm here for you, you know that, don't you?'

'It's nothing, really.' Tom smiled, making a visible effort to pull himself together and divert the attention away from him. Izzie just wished he'd have chosen a different subject. 'Luca, Izzie and I were just chatting about Carmen's stomach bug, that's all, trying to get to the bottom of the mystery of what might have caused it. You know, I was thinking, as no one else suffered an adverse reaction to eating lunch, maybe it could have been something to do with that vitamin drink she has – what do you think, Han?'

Hannah stared at Tom for a beat longer than necessary. 'But Carmen has the same shake every day and she's never been ill before.'

'Maybe Monday's was different,' said Izzie.

'What do you mean different?' demanded Hannah, flicking her eyes from Izzie to Luca, reading their expressions. 'You think one of us spiked her drink, don't you? You can't just accept that your food was below par, so you have to accuse innocent people instead. Oh my God! You think it's Tom! Have you been interrogating him? Is that why he's so distressed?'

'Hannah, they haven't been—'

'No, Tom, hang on a minute. Is that true, Izzie? Do you think Tom put something in Carmen's drink or not?'

Hannah stood with her hands on her hips, staring at Izzie with a challenge in her eyes.

'Actually, we—'

'I knew it! How can you think Tom would do such a thing? He's the most generous, kind-hearted person I know! He would never do anything to hurt anyone, especially not Carmen. Why would he do that to her? She's our boss! You've seen what she's like, she'd fire him in a minute! She'd—'

'Hannah…' began Tom, reaching out to touch Hannah's arm.

'No, Tom, I won't have you accused of something you didn't do!'

'No one's accusing me of anything…'

But Hannah wasn't listening. 'Come on, Tom, we're leaving!'

Tom heaved a sigh of defeat. He clearly had no emotional energy left to argue with her whilst she was in such a mood – either that, or from the way Hannah's face was burning like a Belisha beacon he was worried she was going to explode right there in the middle of the gazebo – so he simply shrugged an apology at Izzie and Luca, pushed himself up from the bench and made his way to where Hannah was waiting for him.

Izzie was about to let them go when a surge of indignation overtook her. It was time to take control of events and turn the tables on Hannah. There was something that had been burning a hole in her brain and this was the perfect opportunity to ask Hannah about it – after all, she couldn't make her any more angry than she already was!

'Before you go, can I ask you a question, Hannah?' she said, earning herself a quizzical look from Luca.

'What kind of question?'

'What's your relationship with Dalton?'

The shock on Hannah's face told Izzie everything she needed to know, because if her face had been flushed before, it was now positively crimson.

'What do you mean, "relationship"? We don't have a *relationship* – Dalton's my boss's fiancé!'

'But they met through you?'

Hannah hesitated, then tossed a quick glance at Tom.

'Look, Izzie, if it's okay with you, I think we'd both like to go back to our rooms to get ready for dinner at the organic farm this evening. Perhaps your cross-examination of Hannah could be saved for another day?' said Tom, his chin raised, his gaze steady, his eyes brooking no argument.

It was the first time Izzie had seen Tom take command of a situation and she was even more surprised when he laid a firm hand on Hannah's shoulder and guided her down the steps of the gazebo. She waited until the couple were out of earshot before meeting Luca's gaze.

'Well, it looks like Beth was spot on when she said Hannah used to have a thing for Dalton – it was written all over her face.'

'*Dio mio*, I really thought this quest for answers would be much more straightforward than it's proving to be. I thought we'd establish the facts, unveil the culprit – who would apologise profusely and beg Carmen for forgiveness – and we'd all be back to normal before sunset. The more we dig into the backgrounds of these people, the more intricate the web becomes. I wish we'd never embarked on this sleuthing business!'

'I agree!'

Izzie dropped down onto the top step of the gazebo and let out a sigh. From the moment she'd set foot on

Italian soil her emotions had undulated like a runaway roller coaster. First, there had been the mortification when it had turned out the film shoot she was organising was actually a real-life celebrity wedding. Then she had laboured under the mistaken belief that Luca had been reconciled with his ex-fiancée, a bridesmaid at the wedding, causing her to bolt from the scene rueing the day she had come to San Vivaldo. And, finally, it had transpired that the villa's absent owner was in fact Luca, who had purchased it as a home for him and Sabrina before she'd run off with his best friend.

And yet her visit to Villa Limoncello had been instrumental in her emergence from the cloud of gloom that had followed her around with the obstinacy of a rabid Rottweiler. Her renaissance was still a work in progress; nevertheless, she now woke up every morning in a Tuscan paradise with a spring in her step and her heart filled with gratitude. Her relationship with Luca was blossoming, despite both of their initial reticence to revisit heartache, and each day that passed she was getting stronger, just like the ripples of attraction she felt whenever Luca was by her side. She desperately wanted to stay!

Could they have avoided what had happened if she'd been more organised?

She wanted the answer to be no, that her preparation had been meticulous, every recipe carefully collated, every painting technique researched and recorded, and their itineraries planned down to the very last detail and covering every eventuality. It's what she always did, it was her superpower – but as she knew to her cost, life had no truck with best-laid plans.

'I'm even more confused than I was before we spoke to Hannah and Tom.'

'Don't worry, I have the perfect antidote to confusion.' Izzie smiled, a whoosh of confidence elevating her mood because she knew exactly what they needed to do.

'What?'

She sprang up from the whitewashed step, smoothed down her wayward curls and grabbed her trusty folder from the table in the middle of the gazebo, flicking through the pages until she found what she was looking for.

'Let's do this properly!'

'And by that you mean going back to the list you started earlier?'

'Exactly!'

'Izzie,' groaned Luca, the creases in his forehead deepening. 'Why don't we shelve all the Agatha Christie stuff for one night, especially as our guests are having dinner at the farm. We could take a trip ourselves? I know this great trattoria on the road to Siena where a friend of mine from university, and a fellow escapee from the world of high finance, makes the best gnocchi this side of Florence.'

'I'd love that.' Izzie smiled, her taste buds already tingling in anticipation.

'Come on, let me introduce you to Paolo, and maybe a few glasses of Chianti will take your mind off everything that's going on here. Where's Meghan tonight? Oh, don't tell me – Gianni?'

'She's having dinner with his brother and family.'

'Must be serious!' Luca smirked, his dark eyes twinkling.

Izzie relaxed. Luca was right. She needed to take a break from the escalating anxiety, and all the organising and worrying about the guests. And in order to do that she had to follow Meghan's example by spending every minute she could with the handsome man in front of her. After all, if this was what running courses at the villa was about, then it was unlikely she would be staying there much longer and that thought caused her heart to squeeze painfully.

'Let's take the Vespa!'

Izzie dashed to the driveway, crammed the helmet over her curls and climbed onto the back of the scooter, waiting for Luca to take the controls. She leaned forward, snaking her hands around his waist, the warmth from his body sending waves of pleasure tumbling through her abdomen. They headed out to the main road, in the opposite direction to San Vivaldo, and after struggling to reach the brow of a particularly steep incline, Izzie raised herself from her seat and held her arms aloft.

'What are you doing?'

'Ever seen *Titanic*?'

With a whoop of pure delight, she closed her eyes and savoured the sense of complete freedom as Luca coasted down the hill into the neighbouring village, laughing at her antics, joining in with her playful exuberance by singing the theme song at the top of his voice before they both dissolved into a fit of giggles.

'*Izz… a… bel… la Jenkins, sei una donna straordinaria!*'

'And you, Luca Castelotti, are an amazing guy!'

The food at Paulo's trattoria was delicious and they feasted on potato gnocchi, flavoured with saffron, nutmeg and crushed amaretti biscuits and topped with shavings of Gran Padano, and a dessert of home-made limoncello tiramisu, followed by a few passionate kisses under the moonlight on the way home.

Chapter Nineteen

The limonaia, *Villa Limoncello*
Colour: Misty dawn

The following morning, Izzie woke early and spent a few moments luxuriating between the cool cotton sheets as she relived the events of the night before. With Luca as her guide, she was enjoying her gastronomic journey of discovery and their visit to Paolo's had ignited her taste buds as well as her dreams of romance. It had been well past midnight when they'd lingered on the villa's terrace, staring up at the stars, safe in the knowledge that everyone was asleep and she could give herself up to his embrace. The memory still caused her extremities to fizzle with desire.

When she had at last climbed the stairs to her sunflower-bedecked room, she'd smiled at the text she'd received from Meghan, assuring her that all was well after their guests' trip to the organic farm, that she adored Gianni's family and Carlotta should receive a national award for her role in bringing them together, and ended by telling her she was staying the night at Gianni's and not to expect her until mid-morning.

Izzie leapt from her bed, flung back the shutters and inhaled that special fragrance of an early Tuscan morning.

For her, it was the best part of the day, when she could spend a few quiet moments running through her lists of what needed to be achieved before her head next hit the pillow.

She showered and dressed quickly, then fixed herself a coffee and took it outside to enjoy her daily saunter through the grounds before even the cicadas had woken from their slumber. Dawn had brought a low mist that lingered languidly over the hillside, covering the vines and the olive groves in a veil of translucent candyfloss. The sun was just starting to peek over the eastern horizon, its ripples of golden light washing the whole scene in a strange sepia hue, bestowing the valley with an almost Tolkien-esque appearance. She could easily imagine hobbits and elves bustling about amongst the nooks and crannies of the rolling countryside.

Izzie sighed, contentment spreading into every corner of her heart. Villa Limoncello was a truly magical place and the perfect location to learn how to stitch the sadness of the last two years into the tapestry of her life and start to pursue her dreams again.

She plucked a sprig of lavender from an ancient terra-cotta pot and lifted it to her nostril, inhaling the woody scent as she made her way back towards the villa to re-familiarize herself with that morning's itinerary; a trip to Siena, a place that had won a spot in her top ten most picturesque cities when Luca had taken her there as part of their planning for the painting course. It was only a thirty-minute drive away, but they weren't taking the hire car – she'd arranged with Roberto from the village to provide everyone with a Vespa for that authentic Italian experience.

She returned to the kitchen for a refill and to fetch her trusty folder, then headed for the patio outside the *limonaia*. She was about to flop into one of the rattan chairs and indulge in a list-making session when she paused, her ears pricking up at the sound of raised voices coming from inside.

'You made a promise, Zara!'

'I know and I'm sorry, okay? It won't happen again.'

'You said that last time. I'm not sure I can believe you again.'

'Please, Carmen, you have to…'

'Actually, I think you'll find that I don't have to do anything.'

Izzie had just crouched down to peer through one of the windowpanes when she heard the door being wrenched open and saw a flicker of powder-pink fabric dart over the threshold and disappear towards the villa. She was about to follow Carmen into the kitchen when she heard a muffled sob float through the air. She hesitated, unsure whether to respect Zara's privacy or to reveal the fact that she had been eavesdropping, albeit involuntarily, on their argument so that she could comfort her in her distress.

Compassion won, as she knew it always would. She had been the recipient of a great deal of kindness after Anna's death and she would never shy away from offering a listening ear to anyone who needed it.

'Zara? Are you okay?'

She took a step into the *limonaia*, her foot crunching on the gravelled floor, squinting through the foliage until she saw Zara slumped in one of the cane chairs. She couldn't work out whether the elegant Chinese silk pyjamas in a luscious lime-green colour was her outfit for the day or if she was still in her nightclothes, but she moved forward and placed her hand on the woman's shoulder, shocked at the jutting bones and the slenderness of her body.

'Yes, I'm… I'm…' Zara began before crumpling, burying her head in her hands and letting loose with a cascade of emotion.

Izzie fumbled in the pocket of her capri pants, unearthed a clean serviette and offered it to Zara, who accepted gratefully, dabbing the corners of her eyes as she sought to gather her thoughts.

'Sorry, I didn't mean to…'

'It's not a problem. Is there anything I can do?'

'No, sadly there's not.'

'You know, if there's one thing I've learnt over the last few years it's that talking usually helps; whether it's to family, a good friend, but also to a neutral bystander. A different perspective can be all it takes to find a solution to even the most difficult of problems.'

'Sounds like you've learnt that from personal experience?'

'That's true, but let's concentrate on the here and now, eh?'

Izzie met Zara's eyes, gave her a smile of encouragement, and then waited for what seemed like an eternity.

'I…'

Zara paused again, fiddling with the paper tissue as she wrestled with her emotions.

'I don't know where to start. It's all such a mess.'

'Well, something else my mum told me was that the best place to start is at the beginning. Can you tell me why you and Carmen were arguing?'

'It's all my fault. Carmen has every right to be angry with me. She's been a supportive friend and I've let her down.'

'How long have you and Carmen been friends?' asked Izzie, perching on the edge of the seat next to Zara.

'For nearly fifteen years, would you believe! Since we were naïve twenty-year-olds, intent on taking the modelling industry by storm. We had the world at our feet! Over the years, we've travelled to hundreds of photo-shoots and catwalk shows on every continent. We were living the dream. It was an amazing experience and to find such an amazing friend to share it with was the icing on the cake. When our assignments started to dwindle, Carmen decided to chase another dream and she launched her fashion business – and there was no one more surprised by its success than she was. She was thrilled, but then we all knew she could achieve anything she put her mind to. I was so happy for her when she won her award last month.'

Zara paused again, swallowing down on her tears. Izzie remained silent, allowing her the space she needed to corral her memories and her emotions. She knew that once someone started to tell a difficult story it was best to let them finish it, to lance the boil, so to speak, and then allow them the time and space to heal in their own way.

'I know I should have followed Carmen's example. I should have moved on to something else, too, when the bookings started to slide, but I just kept saying to myself, one more show, one more trip abroad, one more photoshoot. Two years later I was getting just one or two engagements a month, and there was always someone else younger than me, prettier than me, thinner than me, waiting to step into my Jimmy Choos. I… I…'

When Izzie met Zara's eyes and saw the raw agony scorched deep in her soul, she was shocked, so much so that she reached out to take Zara's hand into hers and gave it an encouraging squeeze.

'Everything's going to be okay, Zara.'

'No, it's not. I've done something that… something that I never should have done. I…'

Zara's tears resumed. She hugged her elbows into her waist and began to rock back and forth, keening softly like a wounded animal, a sound that cut right through Izzie and caused tears to prickle at her own lids.

'Zara, what's going on? Maybe if you…'

'It's Carmen I need to talk to… to persuade her not to say anything, but I don't deserve…'

'Say anything about what?'

Eventually, Zara's tears subsided. She inhaled a long, ragged breath, averted her eyes so she wouldn't have to look at Izzie before blurting out, 'I've been using laxatives to maintain my figure.'

'Oh…' Izzie didn't know what she had been expecting, but it wasn't that.

'Carmen found out a couple of months ago and challenged me about it. I promised her I would stop, and I did for a while, but then I put on a couple of pounds after a trip to Hong Kong and, well, I thought, if I was careful, no one would ever know, so I started again.'

For a few long minutes, silence coiled around the *limonaia*, interrupted only by the sporadic tinkle of laughter that floated on the air from the terrace where Izzie assumed Hannah, Beth and Tom were indulging in the fresh fruit and breakfast croissants she had left on the kitchen bench. A lone bee went about her daily business collecting nectar and a band of frogs croaked their way through a quirky ballad. It was the perfect place for confessions; she just didn't know what advice to give to help Zara slay her demons.

'So how did Carmen find out?'

'When we were unpacking on Sunday night, she came into my room. I had my headphones in so I didn't hear her knock, and she saw the packets on my bed and blasted me. She told me how disappointed she was, and she… she said she was going to drop me in it with my agent, because that was the only way she could think of to bring me to my senses. I know she's just concerned about my health, but if she does report me, then my career will be over and I'm not ready to move on, I'm not ready…' sobbed Zara, dropping her head to her knees.

Izzie placed her hand on Zara's back, horrified that she could see every vertebra in her spine through the sheer fabric of her outfit. Whilst she, too, had lost a great deal of weight after the sudden death of her sister when the only things she could stomach were coffee and toast, she was relieved to have rediscovered the joy of food, in no small thanks to Luca, and she felt better for the extra pounds.

'Look, Zara, Carmen is your friend. As you said, she only has your best interests at heart. I'm sure she'll come round. She's just upset, that's all.'

'I hope so.'

'But I also think she will need you to be honest about this and maybe seek some kind of professional help, or have some sort of plan for your future beyond the modelling?'

'I know, and I intend to, I really do. But... there's... there's something else.'

'What do you mean?'

'I didn't say anything to Carmen, but the reason the packets were scattered on my bed was because I was counting them, and there was a packet missing.'

'Missing?'

'I brought three packets with me to Italy and there were only two in my handbag.'

'And so you're saying...'

'Someone took one without telling me.'

'Why would they want to do that?'

'I have no idea. I can't get my head around it, but it means they know about my... my... problem.'

'Has anyone else confronted you about it?'

'No, but... oh, I don't know whether I should say this.'

'Say what?'

'I think... I think...'

'Zara?'

'I think someone might have put laxatives in Carmen's vitamin drink. I know exactly what happens when I take too many of the tablets – I recognised the symptoms, I understand the effects.'

'Oh my God!'

Izzie's thoughts swirled through her head like a whirlpool until she felt completely lightheaded – and yet what Zara had said made perfect sense. Luca had been right from the very beginning and whilst it seemed she now had an explanation for the so-called food poisoning incident, the alternative was far more disturbing. Food poisoning was usually an accident, something that could happen to even the most careful of cooks, but she now had evidence of a deliberate attempt to incapacitate Carmen.

'Why would anyone want to do that?'

'You've seen what she's like, how patronising she can be. It's just her way of dealing with things; she really is a good person, but she can come off as arrogant and bullying. But it's only because she wants people to be the best they can. She had a difficult upbringing and the reason she's got to where she is today is through dogged determination and hard work. She always puts in that extra ten per cent, and she's never, ever broken the rules and wouldn't stand for anyone who did. That's why she was so disappointed when she found out about the... about the tablets.'

'Why didn't you say anything when she got sick?'

'Why do you think? I didn't want to say anything because how would that look? Carmen threatens to expose me to my agency, then her vitamin shake is spiked with laxatives? Everyone would think it's me, and it wasn't. It absolutely wasn't. Izzie, you have to believe me, but you also can't tell her either!'

'I don't know...'

'Izzie, you can't, not until I find out who took them!'

Oh God! thought Izzie, a streak of panic shooting through her stomach. Who would do such a thing? And why? Zara was right, the first person anyone would suspect was Zara herself; she had both the means and the motive. Her heartbeat increased as the enormity of what she was facing hit her like a speeding meteor. A rush of heat swept through her body and she experienced an overwhelming urge to escape from the *limonaia*.

'Zara, I have to call Luca...'

'Please, Izzie, please don't call him yet.'

'I have to! This is his livelihood at stake…'

'But wouldn't it be better to tell him when we know who's to blame? There are others here who are much more likely to have spiked Carmen's drink than me!'

'What do you mean? Like who?'

'Like…'

'*Pronto? Signorina Jenkins? È Roberto – con le Vespe!*'

'Excuse me,' murmured Zara, jumping from her chair and dashing out of the door before Izzie could stop her, leaving behind a cloud of Christian Dior's Poison.

Chapter Twenty

A trip to Siena, Tuscany
Colour: Black-and-white stripes

'*Ciao*, Roberto.'

Izzie deposited the regulation two kisses on Roberto's cheeks and followed him to the front steps, where she saw he had already deposited five of the iconic Italian scooters in a variety of colours so they could make their journey to Siena in style. She smiled her thanks, struggling to respond to Roberto's enquiries issued in rapid staccato Italian because every last morsel of brainpower was taken up by the repercussions of Zara's confession.

She fingered her phone, desperate to call Luca, to recount every detail, to ask him what she should do, but within moments everyone had emerged from the villa and, after some wrangling, were seated on their chosen vehicle, listening attentively whilst Roberto gave them a lesson on how to operate the controls and, more importantly, on road safety.

'I love my Vespa!' declared Hannah, who, having mastered the controls quickly, was zooming up and down the gravelled driveway like a professional whilst the rest of the group progressed more tentatively, wobbling with their feet inches from the ground as they built up their confidence for their forthcoming battle with the serpentine roads and the assertiveness of Italian drivers.

'Yay! I've got it!' yelled Tom, beaming with pride as he chased Hannah towards the gate and then back towards the front steps, his handling of the scooter improving with every metre.

To Izzie's surprise, it was Carmen who struggled the most with mastering the technique and Roberto patiently talked her through an extra few minutes of instruction until she was ready to take to the road. Maybe the disagreement with Zara was playing on her mind, causing her to lose her concentration? Although none of the others seemed to have noticed, Izzie could feel the crackle of awkwardness between the two women. Nevertheless, Carmen still looked like she was about to take a turn on the catwalk, and Izzie knew that even if she spent all day, she could never hope to reach her level of glamour.

They waved off Roberto, and Izzie took the lead on her trusty, sugar-pink Vespa which she loved so much that she was planning to trade in her Fiat 500 for a yellow one when she returned to London. It wasn't just the fact that she would be solving all her parking problems in one fell swoop, but the whoosh of unadulterated joy she experienced zipping along the winding roads, the wind whipping her curls into the air like a wild Medusa. On the back of her scooter, she felt so much more a part of the landscape, closer to the fields of bobbing sunflowers, able to inhale their fragrance, listen to the incessant chirp of the crickets, almost taste the wild asparagus that grew beyond the hedgerows, and just for a moment all her problems receded.

'Whee… eeesh!' squealed Hannah, racing ahead of Izzie, her feet in the air as she motored down a short incline.

'Wait for me!' shouted Zara, leaning over the handle-bars to give chase, clearly keen to put as much distance between herself and Carmen as possible.

'Hey! Slow down!' cried Tom, his pale face creased with concern.

'Come on, Tom! Let's throw caution to the wind and become more Italian!' called Beth, as she overtook him and joined the others out in front.

Tom glanced over his shoulder, indecision scrawled across his features until Izzie saw him clench his jaw, tighten his knuckles on the handlebars and fix his eyes on the road ahead.

'Watch out then!'

Izzie exchanged a smile with Carmen as she tootled alongside her. Together, they watched Tom catch up with Hannah and Beth, then, with a spurt of speed, he overtook them, raising his fist in the air with whoop of exhilaration.

'I think he's found his new vocation!' Carmen smiled.

'What do you mean?' asked Izzie.

'Speedway?'

Izzie laughed. 'I'm really pleased to see him relax at last.'

'Yes, me too,' agreed Carmen, a thoughtful expression spreading across her face.

'Did you enjoy your visit to the organic farm last night?'

'Yes, I did! The grounds were amazing, and the view was to die for. We sat outside on this elevated wooden veranda overlooking San Gimignano with another tour group from Montreal and a family who were over from Australia and driving around Tuscany in a campervan! It was like we were one big happy family, all sitting around the table together, sharing our stories, eating whatever the chef put in front of us. And the sunset was stunning, I just stood and watched in complete awe – it would have been so much more romantic, though, if I'd had someone to share it with. Thank you for arranging it, Izzie; we all had a great time, especially Tom.'

'Why especially Tom?'

Carmen clamped her mouth shut in a gesture of comedic horror. 'Oops, didn't mean to say that.'

'Why not?'

'Oh, well, I don't suppose it'll stay a secret for long with Beth around. After we'd had our coffees, we were encouraged to stroll through the owner's vineyard to soak up the ambience, to meditate, to stare up at the stars, or just to chat with each other over a nightcap. We all went our own separate ways, but half an hour later, Tom and Hannah emerged from the bushes with their arms linked, and Tom wore the widest grin I've seen on his face, ever!'

'You think they kissed?'

'Well, in my experience, discussing the relative intricacies of double-entry bookkeeping has never produced anything approaching the same kind of pleasure – although I could be wrong.'

Izzie glanced at the celebrated fashion designer, wondering if she should mention her earlier conversation with Tom, and ask whether she'd come to a decision about his fate. She thought of Tom, emerging from the darkness with Hannah at his side, and her heart blossomed to think that he'd enjoyed a little chink of happiness in what was a difficult landscape for him. She wondered whether he'd taken the opportunity to confide in Hannah about what had happened with the accounts. She hoped so. She knew from her own experience that a problem aired was a problem well on its way to being overcome. As always, her mum was right – when it came to tackling difficult issues, two heads were better than one.

Again, a sharp stab of homesickness needled her chest and she suddenly wished her parents were right there in Tuscany with her, enjoying a few days of relaxation and sunshine therapy. She loved her mum and dad, and witnessing their grief over the loss of Anna had been more than she could bear. Every time she'd gone back to St Ives, for birthdays or for Christmas, her sister's absence had been so immediate, so vivid and raw, that she'd felt as if she couldn't breathe. She was only able to function properly again when she returned to London, to her ordered, timetabled, monochrome life where she could simply focus on achieving the next item on her list rather than dwell on her emotions.

Her strategy had worked to a certain extent, but her stay at Villa Limoncello had taught her that it wasn't a healthy existence, and she was starting to understand how much she needed to embrace her family, not push them away. Who needed the services of a counsellor when there was summer sunshine, tranquillity and an abundance of warm-hearted friends? Perhaps when her time in Italy came to an end, she would find the courage to take the trip to Cornwall.

To Izzie's relief, they survived the journey to Siena unscathed and she led them to a shady courtyard overlooking Il Duomo di Siena, where they parked their scooters so they could explore the city on foot.

'Wow just look at that view!' declared Carmen, yanking off her helmet and shaking out her long golden hair as if auditioning for a role in a shampoo advert. She grabbed her phone, took a few shots of Siena's spectacular Gothic cathedral with its black-and-white striped marble bell tower, before handing it over to Beth. 'Take a couple of photographs of us, will you? Come on, Hannah, Tom, stand next to me! These will look amazing on the company's website!'

Izzie saw Beth roll her eyes as Carmen dragged an astonished Tom into position and ordered them to produce their best smiles for the camera. When they had finished their photoshoot, Izzie gathered everyone together.

'Okay, so we'll be spending this morning learning about pencil drawing. You can choose whatever subject appeals to you; maybe an architectural detail, a pretty courtyard or a shady alleyway, or you could set up your chair in the Piazza del Campo where you'll be spoilt for choice.'

'What are all these flags? Are they coats of arms?' asked Carmen, squinting through her over-sized sunglasses at the emerald and burgundy flags featuring a golden dragon hanging from the eaves of every building in the narrow, cobbled street.

'Sort of. Siena is divided into seventeen separate *contrade*, and each one has its own unique emblem and colours. This one, for example, is Il Drago, the dragon, but there's the snail, the caterpillar, the owl, the eagle, the giraffe, the unicorn...'

'Oh, I'd choose that one!' declared Hannah.

'You don't choose; you're born into a particular *contrada* and you are a proud member of that community for the rest of your life; you'll be baptised in the *contrada*'s font, find your best friends there, get married there, attend food and wine festivals there, but the most important event on the Sienese calendar is the Palio.'

'I've heard of that,' said Tom, walking alongside Izzie as they made their way towards the famous piazza at the centre of Siena. 'It's a horse race, isn't it?'

'It's more than just a horse race – it's a fiercely fought battle for civic pride and the right to display the *drappellone*, the winner's canvas, in your *contrada*'s museum. Only ten of the *contrade* take part in each race, seven who didn't participate in the previous race and three that are drawn from lots, and whilst you get to select your jockey, your horse is allocated by lottery only four days before the actual race!'

'Stops any underhand tactics, I'm sure!'

'And here we are,' announced Izzie as they stepped into the shell-shaped piazza, watched over by the Palazzo Pubblico and the one-hundred-metre-high Torre del Mangia, one of Italy's tallest medieval towers. She was delighted to see the expressions of awe on the faces of her guests. 'Spectacular, isn't it?'

'It's just stunning!'

'See how the centre of Il Campo is paved with red bricks in a fish-tail design, which is then encircled by a walkway which is where the *Palio* is run. Twice a year, on 2 July and 15 August, this whole square is packed with thousands of spectators cheering on their rider.'

'Wow, I mean… just wow!' enthused Hannah.

Izzie laughed, but Hannah was right to be awe-struck at the sight spread out in front of them; the golden façades of the ancient buildings, their balconies draped in matching burgundy canopies, their shutters flung open to embrace the early morning breeze all merged together to create a completely harmonious image. Cafés spilled out onto the piazza, their little cane chairs filled with glamourous locals exchanging cheek-kisses before sitting down to enjoy an espresso and a conversation about renaissance art, the surrounding architecture or the latest fashions from Milan, rather than the storylines of last night's soaps. Knots of tourists loitered in the centre of the piazza, armed with maps and guide books, or listening attentively to their tour guide, not knowing where to point their cameras next.

'Come on, I've found a quiet corner where I can give you a quick tutorial on the essentials of sketching, and then you can all go off to find your own shady niche and let the pencil do the talking. Just make sure you're back here, under the clock tower, by two p.m. because I've organised a visit to a farmhouse where we'll be tasting the local cheeses. Any questions?'

'No,' came a chorus of excited artists.

Forty minutes later Izzie had guided her pupils through the necessary techniques, handed out boxes of coloured pencils and suggested they each find a shady spot for a morning of creative endeavour.

'Well, I'm heading over to that cute little gelateria first,' said Beth, grabbing her sketchbook and pencils and making her way towards the ice cream shop at the edge of the piazza showcasing a rainbow of flavours.

'I'm going back to the cathedral, if that's okay, Izzie. I want to take a few photographs of that fabulous Gothic bell tower,' announced Tom, stuffing his artist's paraphernalia into his rucksack at random, then hesitating before turning to Hannah. 'Do you... do you fancy joining me?'

Tom's cheeks burned as he waited for Hannah's reply, hope reflected in his eyes as he studiously avoided looking in the direction of Carmen, Zara and Izzie.

'I'd love to, Tom.' Hannah smiled, flicking her ponytail over her shoulder, hooking her arm through Tom's and sauntering off across the piazza like an old married couple.

Izzie saw Carmen exchange a look with Zara, her lips twitching with amusement, and was delighted when both women dissolved into laughter and the electricity that had sparked between them since the argument in the *limonaia* dissipated. Zara took a step forward at the same time as Carmen did and they hugged each other tightly whilst Izzie's heart softened at the reconciliation.

'I'm sorry, Carmen.'

'It's okay, darling, really it is.'

'No, it's not okay. You are completely justified in being angry with me. I've let you down, but I have also let myself down. I promise you, hand on heart, that this time I've disposed of every single one of the tablets and I will never touch them again.'

'You don't know how relieved I am to hear you say that.'

'And I promise that when we get back home, I'm going to put what I learned last summer on that jewellery-making course into practice and start my own business.'

'Well, if you do, you already have your first client!'

'What do you mean?' asked Zara, tears sparkling at the corners of her eyes, her face wreathed in hope.

'Me! Is that necklace one of your designs? And the earrings?'

'Yes…'

'They're adorable, and I love that silver ring you gave me for my Christmas present – maybe you could design me a bracelet to match?'

'Oh, Carmen, I'd love to do that! Oh my God, I've got so many ideas – what about a wire-wrapped theme, or maybe a black-and-white geometric design inspired by the cathedral, or what do you think about silk tassels or fringes or plaits? Oh, and I'd really like your advice on a brass ponytail cuff I've been working on for Hannah's birthday next month.'

'They all sound amazing!'

Carmen linked her arm though Zara's, and together they sauntered off towards the Fonte Gaia to plan their joint assault on the jewellery world; two tall, willowy figures, their hair flying in the breeze, dresses floating around their ankles like a pair of woodland nymphs, their disagreement already consigned to ancient history.

With her spirits higher than they had been for years, Izzie made her way to her favourite café and ordered a cappuccino from a waiter whose slicked back hair and pencil moustache made him look like he was auditioning for a part in a mafia film. As she waited for her coffee to arrive, she toyed with her phone, contemplating how to spend the next two hours in one of her favourite cities. She really should call Luca, but she knew he would be in the middle of the lunchtime preparations and she didn't want to disturb him when she only had half a story to tell.

She gazed at the medieval architecture spread out in front of her, wondering what stories were woven into the ancient stones. Church bells chimed, small dogs yapped and the burble of conversation rippled through the air from a melange of visitors keen to soak up the atmosphere.

Once again, her thoughts meandered to her parents, and she knew they would love to spend some time touring the hilltop towns dotted around Tuscany. A spasm of guilt erupted in her chest as she realised that she hadn't called them since arriving at Florence airport the previous month, preferring the distance that emailed updates and postcards offered. They'd been surprised when her first postcard of the Ponte Vecchio in Florence had arrived on their doormat but had been enthusiastic that she was breaking free at last from the mundane, 'snoring boring' life she had made for herself.

She made a decision. She quickly scrolled through her contacts and selected her parents' home number, pressing the call button before she had chance to change her mind.

'Hi, Mum!'

'Darling! How are you? How's Tuscany?'

'It's fabulous. I'm sitting in a pavement café in Siena, just soaking up the culture!'

'Ah, that sounds amazing. It's drizzle, drizzle and more drizzle here, but your dad's still insisting on mowing the lawn! One day he's going to electrocute himself and he'll have no one to blame but himself!'

Izzie laughed at the regularly recurring refrain. Her father had always loved his garden, but since Anna had left them, the time he spent tending his fruit and vegetables had been his salvation and the place could easily take part in the annual Open Gardens competition. She spent another ten minutes filling her mum in on the various guests staying at Villa Limoncello, taking care not to mention the drama.

'So, when do you think you'll get some time to come home to Cornwall?'

She heard the faint wobble in her mum's voice, along with a generous helping of yearning. She wanted to assure her that she would catch a train as soon as she landed back in the UK – after all, she had no job to go back to – but was she really ready to face the tumble of memories such a visit would inevitably dredge up? Every single nook and cranny in St Ives reminded her of her sister; the village school, the sandy beach, the Badger Inn where they'd enjoyed their first cocktail – hers a mojito, Anna's a creamy pina colada.

'I'm not sure yet, Mum,' she hedged, feeling guilty at not giving a straight answer. 'It'll depend on whether Luca decides to run any more courses.'

'Does he have others in mind?'

'Yes, perhaps a yoga retreat, or a wine-tasting course, or a creative writing course.'

'Well, they all sound intriguing. Maybe me and your dad should sign up for one!' her mum laughed. 'Especially if you're planning a horticulture or maybe a flower-arranging one?'

'They are both great ideas, Mum.'

'Perhaps if you did run the creative writing course you could make a start on writing one of those travel memoirs you and Anna used to devour!'

Hearing her sister's name sent a red-hot arrow of agony through Izzie's heart, but she decided to follow the advice Luca had given her when they'd spent an afternoon together in the Boboli Gardens in Florence; that instead of avoiding any casual mention of Anna in conversation, she should make a start on stitching her loss into the fabric of her life. She had to learn to understand that whilst Anna no longer walked by her side, she would carry her with her in her heart every day and always. Tears sparkled at the corners of her eyes, but she smiled.

'Yes, Mum, perhaps I will.'

Chapter Twenty-One

Piazza del Campo, Siena
Colour: Terracotta red

'Hey, Izzie, I hoped I would find you here.'

Izzie flinched with surprise. After her conversation with her mother, she'd been buried so deep in her memories that she hadn't heard Hannah approach.

'I'm sorry to interrupt you. Do you mind if I take a seat?'

'Sure.'

Izzie smiled, and for the first time she noticed Hannah's more relaxed attire; the flimsy floral blouse, hair loose around her shoulders, candy-pink lipstick instead of the more business-like red she usually wore. Maybe it was the tendrils of romance weaving their magic, she thought, until she saw how jittery Hannah was, fidgeting with the café's menu, stammering when she ordered a cappuccino from the handsome waiter. Izzie's heart sank.

'Is there something wrong, Hannah?'

'I… I wasn't entirely honest with you when we spoke yesterday, about Dalton, that is.'

'Oh, I… well, it wasn't really any of my business…'

'It's just that I didn't want to say anything in front of Tom.'

Hannah cast a quick glance over her shoulder to make sure Tom wasn't lurking behind the row of potted palms that separated the café from its neighbour, his camera trained in their direction. Izzie wanted to giggle but managed to control herself.

'I've come to tell you the truth, Izzie, but first of all I want you to know that I no longer have any feelings for Dalton whatsoever and I'm happy that he and Carmen are together.'

'But that wasn't always the case?'

'No. I was in love with him. Or I *thought* I was but looking back it was really just lust.'

'Lust?'

'Yes.' Hannah's cheeks coloured but she pressed on with her explanation. 'When Dalton moved into the apartment next to mine, I was smitten. He was so good-looking, charismatic, talented; it was like a film star had moved in. But he was also really friendly, down-to-earth, and we hit it off straight away. It turned out that we'd both played tennis at county level before moving to London, so one night after a few drinks, we made a pact to join the local club and we played a couple of times a week.

'Dalton was a great mixed-doubles partner, but we had so much more in common. We both loved Formula One, and golf and mountain biking. Would you believe that on the night of my birthday party I was actually hoping he would ask me out on a date? I'd spent the whole day pampering, having my hair and make-up done at an expensive salon, treating myself to an amazing manicure. Carmen loaned me one of her dresses to wear and I felt fabulous.'

'But?'

'As soon as Carmen floated through the door, I knew my dream was over – I knew I'd lost him. Oh, don't get me wrong, I realise he was never mine in the first place, but now I *knew* he never could be. I'm no competition for the glitzy, glamorous, internationally famous, award-winning model Carmen Campbell. I mean, why would anyone look at me, five foot four, mousy hair, a couple of love handles, when there's a golden goddess in our midst?'

Hannah had finished shredding the paper napkin that had come with her coffee and began to scrap the skin at the sides of her thumbnails, studiously avoiding Izzie's eyes as she formulated the next part of her confession.

'Before the evening was over, Carmen and Dalton were an item – everyone commented on the fizzle of chemistry between them. And why not, they made such a beautiful couple; the talented photographer, the celebrated fashion designer, and they've been together ever since, until...'

'Until what?'

At last Hannah levelled her eyes at Izzie, her lips parted, and she hesitated, unsure whether to continue, whether she should disclose the next episode in the unrequited love story.

'Hannah?'

'You wouldn't believe how hard it was to see them together. Whenever he "just popped in" to the office, I had to make an excuse to leave. I think Tom knew how I felt, or at least suspected something wasn't quite right, but he has never said anything. Typical Tom, eh? It was probably obvious now I look back, although Carmen never guessed. Of course, the mere thought that Dalton would even look in my direction was probably hilarious to her. Anyway, after a while things got easier, and I resigned myself to the fact that they were a couple and that it was great they'd found each other, that I'd had a hand in introducing them, and then...'

Hannah paused, her eyes glazing over, her thoughts sliding off on a different tangent for a few seconds before Izzie brought her back to the present.

'What happened?'

'I... one afternoon, Carmen rushed off to a dental appointment – she's always late for everything, it's a nightmare keeping her diary and schedule on track. You've no idea how much flack I get from everyone; no matter how organised I am, I'm constantly fire-fighting. Anyway, she was in such a hurry that she left without her phone. I ran after her, but she'd already jumped into her taxi and was halfway down the street, so I went back to the office to call the orthodontist to warn him she was on her way but would be thirty minutes late, and that's when I saw it.'

'Saw what?'

'A message on her phone.'

An uncomfortable premonition tickled at Izzie's chest. She knew what Hannah was about to say.

'She was having an affair?'

Hannah nodded as she studied her fingernails, unable to speak.

'There was no doubt about it – she'd arranged to meet the guy, someone called Angus, after her appointment at the dentist. I felt sick. You've no idea the range of emotions that flashed through my mind at that moment – from shock, to indignation, to bewilderment, and then anger on behalf of Dalton. Why would she do such a thing when she'd won the ultimate prize? Someone as amazing as Dalton, who loved her? I'd just started to come to terms with the fact that I had to move on, too.'

'What did you do?'

'I burst into tears. Tom found me, but I made up some story about one of my golf matches getting cancelled. I don't think he believed me, to be honest, but he didn't push it. My first reaction was to tell Dalton. We still played tennis, but only very occasionally, and all he talked about was the amazing restaurants, clubs and parties he and Carmen had been to that week. It was just too painful, so I'd started making excuses and I hadn't actually seen him for a couple of months.'

'When did you find out?'

'A couple of weeks ago.'

'And *did* you tell Dalton?'

'No.'

'Why not?'

'What good would that do? It's none of my business, and don't forget, Carmen is my boss! I don't want to risk losing my job, I have rent to pay. I'm just so… so confused. One the one hand, Dalton has a right to know, but on the other, I don't want Carmen to shoot the messenger! Oh my God, it's all such a mess!'

Izzie smiled at the harassed PA sitting in front of her, clearly struggling with a dilemma that didn't have an easy answer. Despite the relaxing holiday vibe that surrounded them, Hannah exuded nervous energy, like a person teetering on the edge, with dark smudges beneath her eyes and less-than-perfectly applied make-up. Izzie felt a nip of sympathy and reached out to give her arm a squeeze when, to her utter amazement, Hannah dropped her head into her hands and started to weep, not quiet, discreet tears, but a long, painful torrent of distress that seemed an overreaction to the discovery that her boss was having an affair.

Chapter Twenty-Two

Emiliano's Café, Piazza del Campo, Siena
Colour: Iridescent Teardrop

'I'm sorry, so sorry.'

'Hannah, what's—'

'Hi there, you two! I hope I'm not interrupting anything?' Tom beamed, appearing at their table with his sketch pad slotted under his arm. He glanced from Izzie to Hannah, the smile sliding from his face when he saw that she was wiping her eyes on a serviette, his expression morphing from shock to concern as he dropped down into the seat next to her and took her hand in his. 'Is… is everything okay? Han, what's the matter? Why are you crying?'

'I… I… Oh, Tom, you're going to hate me.'

'No, Hannah, that's one thing I could never do.'

Despite the weirdness of what was going on, Izzie's heart gave a flop of pleasure when she saw Tom meet Hannah's eyes and there was a click of understanding on Hannah's part before she looked away again, battling with the secrets she was keeping. All around them couples and families, tourists and locals, were enjoying a midday stroll in the sun with their maps and guide books, their children and their pet poodles, every one of them moved by the splendour of the impressive architecture of the piazza. However, the grandeur of the buildings and the chatter of gossip all melted into the background as Izzie waited for Hannah to explain her uncharacteristic outburst of emotion.

'Hannah, what's going on? If you tell us, we might be able to help.'

'No one can help.'

'Try us,' said Tom firmly.

Hannah shook her head, but, after a few moments, she emitted a long, low sigh of resignation as tears brimmed along her lower lashes.

'It's no good, I'm exhausted, absolutely exhausted, so exhausted that I can't keep it in any longer. All I do is work and sleep, sleep and work. I have no time for anything else. I love cooking but all I have the energy for is to grab a takeaway on the way home from work. I love yoga but I haven't been to the studio for over six months. I've put on two stone in weight and I hate myself. I'm tired all the time, but I still wake up in the middle of the night with the next day's schedule circulating through my mind and a ream of never-ending to-do lists. I keep a notepad by my bed and there's always at least half a dozen things scribbled on it when the alarm goes off at six a.m. I haven't seen my mum for weeks and the last time I visited my sister and niece was at Christmas – and it's July!'

'Oh, Hannah, why didn't you say something?'

'What was the point? I made a New Year's resolution to cut down on the hours I put in, but that lasted all of a week until Carmen sent me to Madrid to meet a couple of buyers from El Corte Inglés. Oh, it all sounds very glamorous, doesn't it?' Hannah met Izzie's eyes, shaking her head. 'And I know how ungrateful I sound when I complain, so I just don't. I just get on with it. But it's not glamorous at all; it's manic, incessant hard work and I'm absolutely at the end of my tether.'

Hannah started to twist the tassels on her blouse around her fingers and her tears rolled down her cheeks, but she flicked them away like irritating flies.

'When Carmen told us that she was planning a break in Tuscany to celebrate winning that award, I hoped I'd be able to spend at least some of the time recharging my batteries. I thought maybe a little bit of sunshine-and-limoncello therapy would help me to refocus my mind on what's important; maybe I would even get another opportunity to have a chat with Carmen about employing an assistant to take some of the strain.'

'Some chance...' muttered Tom, heat seeping into his cheeks as he caught Izzie's eye.

'You're right, Tom. I should have known better. Guess who had to organise everything for the spontaneous trip to Italy? Guess who booked the flights, arranged the villa and the courses, sorted out the insurance, and the taxis to and from the airport? For God's sake, I even had to do Carmen's packing! I was even more exhausted than I was before, but I clung to the hope that when we got here, Carmen would relax and let us do our own thing. Izzie, I was so happy when we drove down that driveway and the villa came into view, and when Meghan showed me to the lavender suite, I thought...'

Hannah paused to accept Tom's handkerchief, offering him a weak smile of thanks in return, but her expression was still guarded.

'But why should Carmen change her habits just because we were on holiday? After we'd checked in, she continued to give me a list of things to do – she even asked me to unpack for her and make sure her dresses were ironed before they were hung up in the wardrobe! And she asked me to prepare her vitamin drink for her the following morning so she could have a lie-in, said she needed her beauty sleep!

'When I eventually went back to my own room, I looked out of the window at the whole of Tuscany spread out in front of me. It was idyllic, so peaceful and calm and all I wanted to do was take some time to explore the villa's grounds, meander through the vineyard and the olive groves, linger in that cute conservatory with the lemon trees, but it looked like, as usual, I was going to be at my boss's beck and call for the whole week.'

Hannah raised her gaze from where she had been scraping the skin at her fingernails.

'I just flipped. It was like I was having an out-of-body experience, a bit like sleepwalking. I wanted to do something that would confine Carmen to her room just for the morning, just so I could have a few hours of breathing space to get my head together, to enjoy the tranquillity the villa had to offer. I know it was selfish, but I don't think I was thinking straight or else I never would have…'

Hannah stopped, unable to go on, her eyes wide with anguish, her hands trembling as she reached up to brush a few stray strands of hair from her face. Izzie was grateful they'd been given a corner table, set slightly apart from the rest of the café's clientele, and that the waiter had decided to respect their privacy by giving them a wide berth when new patrons arrived.

'Never would have what?' asked Tom gently, reaching out to take Hannah's hand, his forehead creased in confusion.

'Nothing…'

'Hannah?' said Izzie, her heart pounding with trepidation. 'What have you done?'

'Nothing, I haven't done anything! I *wanted* to do something, believe me, so I suppose I *am* sort of guilty, but I couldn't go through with it in the end. I couldn't. I knew it was selfish and that it was just the exhaustion talking.'

'What were you *going* to do?' pressed Izzie, feeling as though her head was about to explode.

'I'm not sure I can say…'

Izzie stared at Hannah. Sympathy twisted through her veins at the intensity of the misery she saw reflected in Hannah's red-rimmed eyes. She hated to see a fellow human being suffer, and would never seek to prolong anyone's agony, but if this had something to do with what happened to Carmen then she had to know.

'It's really important you tell us exactly what you did, Hannah. I'm sure you're aware that the authorities are paying Villa Limoncello a visit next week. Luca and I need to be able to reassure them that the catering conforms to the highest hygiene standards and that Carmen's illness was unconnected with our food preparation. Please, Hannah.'

Hannah raised her eyes, glanced across at Tom, then back at her hands as she continued to scrape away the skin at the sides of her thumbs, causing tiny globules of blood to appear.

'I can't. I don't want to get anyone else into trouble.'

'Like who? Tom?'

'No! Not Tom.'

Izzie stared at the two of them, sitting hand in hand like teenage lovers, and the penny suddenly dropped.

'Do you mean Zara?'

Hannah nodded without looking up.

'It's okay, Zara has told us about her… her… problem.'

'Has she? What else did she say?'

'That one of the packets she brought with her has gone missing.'

'Packet of what?' asked Tom, his bewilderment almost comical. 'I don't understand. What's all this about, Izzie? Hannah?'

Hannah sighed. 'I didn't want to say anything because I didn't want to get Zara into trouble, but I found out a while ago that she's been using laxatives to stay slim. It's not my place to say anything, but I think Carmen has had a few words with her. Anyway, when Zara was in the bathroom on Sunday night, I helped myself to a packet of her laxatives.'

'But what for?'

Hannah stared at Tom, simply waiting for the realisation of what she had done to dawn and when it did he withdrew his hand and looked at her askance.

'You added them to Carmen's vitamin drink?'

'That's what I *intended* to do, yes, but I swear to you on my niece's life that I didn't go through with it. I can actually prove it to you because the packet I took from Zara's handbag is still in my room and it's still completely intact. I was going to put it back – no harm done – but then Carmen got sick and I panicked. I mean, I actually thought I was losing my sanity! I thought that I'd tumbled into some kind of parallel universe inhabited by the perpetually exhausted and I'd somehow gone through with my plan without realising it and then wiped it from my mind afterwards. I can't tell you the relief I felt when I found the unopened packet of laxatives exactly where I'd left them.'

'But…'

'Carmen's symptoms were precisely what I'd *expected* to happen, and I realised that if *I* hadn't done it, then it must have been Zara. I know how hard it's been for her these last few months with the shrinking number of modelling assignments. Carmen has been constantly berating her for not planning ahead. I wouldn't blame her if she *had* added a couple of laxatives to her drink for the same reason that I thought of doing it – just to get a bit of peace from the constant low-key disapproval and criticism.'

'So, is that why you were so adamant that Carmen had food poisoning? To divert attention from Zara?'

'Yes,' replied Hannah, sheepishly. 'Sorry.'

'But why go as far as to report the incident to the authorities?'

'I didn't call the authorities,' Hannah shot back, shaking her head.

'Then who did?'

'It must have been Carmen. I'm sorry, Izzie. I should never have said the things I did about Luca's food. I actually think it's amazing! He's a very talented chef. I was only trying to protect Zara.'

Izzie stared at Hannah as though she was out of her mind. 'But Hannah, I've already spoken to Zara and she's denied having anything to do with any of this.'

'Well, she would, wouldn't she?' said Tom, indignance suffusing his words as he leapt to Hannah's defence.

'Yes, that's true, I suppose.'

Hannah and Tom exchanged glances, unsure where to go next.

'Well, I can absolutely assure you, Izzie, that I did not, under any circumstances, tamper with Carmen's drink. And if you want my opinion as to who's to blame, you should be looking in another direction.'

Izzie raised her eyes sharply. 'What do you mean?'

'All I'm saying is that I'm not the only person whose heart Carmen has trampled on.'

'You mean someone else was in love with Dalton?'

'No!' Hannah rolled her eyes at Izzie and her mouth curled upwards in amusement. 'Well, not as far as I know.'

'Then what do you mean?'

'I think you should talk to Beth.'

'What about?'

'Ask her why she left university before she graduated.'

'You mean she didn't finish her degree?'

'No, she didn't.'

'But—'

'Oh, hi there, everyone!' Carmen smiled, glancing from Izzie, to Hannah and then Tom, crunching up her nose. 'You did say we should meet back here at two, didn't you? I make it two fifteen and I can't believe that for the first time ever I'm the first person to arrive!'

Izzie groaned inwardly. Far from clarifying matters, her chat with Hannah had introduced yet another thread to follow up on. There were so many unanswered questions buzzing around in her brain that she needed to focus on a different topic for a while.

'What do you think?' Carmen demanded, holding up her pencil drawing of the Fonte Gaia for their inspection.

'It's very good, said Izzie, placing a few euros on the table for their coffee and leading them from the pavement café towards the campanile where she could see Beth and Zara loitering, their artist's rucksacks slung over their shoulders and their sketch pads under their arms.

'Thank you, and that's without the benefit of my artist's pencils.'

'What do you mean?'

'Well, I wasn't going to mention it because I know you've got a lot on your plate, Izzie, but the box of coloured pencils you gave me, well, it was empty – all I had to work with was an old graphite pencil I found at the bottom of my handbag.'

'Empty?'

'Yes,' Carmen laughed. 'But you know what, I think the simplicity works, don't you?'

'Yes, yes, it does,' murmured Izzie, confusion whipping through her mind.

How could the box have been empty when she had bought them new from the artist's supplies shop in Florence the week before? She had only removed the cellophane covers that morning. Yet another mystery to add to the growing pile – and again, one that had Carmen at its centre – but there was no time to ponder the ramifications.

'Right, who's ready for lunch?'

'Me!' chorused Beth and Carmen, whilst Zara rolled her eyes.

'Come on then. Let's grab the Vespas and make our way to Nicoletta's – she makes the best cheese in the whole of Tuscany.'

'I can't remember the last time I ate cheese,' muttered Zara, slinging her colt-like leg astride her scooter and revving the engine.

'Then you're in for a treat,' said Carmen, her expression leaving Zara, and Izzie, in no doubt that everyone was expected to join in with the cheese-tasting session irrespective of their views on eating dairy.

As the group travelled in single file along the narrow roads from Siena to Pienza, the town at the heart of pecorino country, Izzie tried to make sense of everything she had heard that morning, from Zara's confession, to Hannah's aborted plan to spike her boss's drink, to the weird absence of the coloured pencils.

God! It was one step forward and two steps back!

One thing she was relieved about, though, was that she hadn't spoken to Luca after her conversation with Zara, otherwise she would have been in the unenviable position of having to call him up to tell him that she had got it all wrong, that Zara's laxatives weren't to blame for Carmen's illness, and that she was even further away from unravelling the mystery than she had been that morning! He had enough to worry about with the restaurant and the impending visit from the food inspectors without her giving him false hope.

A sudden squall of nausea erupted in her stomach that had nothing to do with the winding roads they were forced to navigate on their journey to Nicoletta's farmhouse, where they would taste different varieties of pecorino and meet the sheep who provided the milk that gave it its slightly grassy taste. Whilst she had been excited about joining Luca's new venture at Villa Limoncello, she had completely underestimated the issues that taking a group of people out of their normal lives might throw up.

Chapter Twenty-Three

The kitchen, Villa Limoncello
Colour: Dark espresso

'Okay, everyone, as you've spent your day in Siena, this evening we will be cooking *pici all'etrusca*, which is a vegetarian dish, and for the meat eaters amongst you, there's a recipe in your folders for *pici con la nana* that you can try out when you get back home.'

Izzie handed round the embroidered Villa Limoncello aprons and they got to work on the pasta, following Luca's instructions with care. Meghan had called earlier to say she was taking a rain check on the final pasta-making tutorial in favour of spending what was left of her short time in San Vivaldo with Gianni, before she returned home the following day. She had confided in Izzie that she loved being with Gianni, that he was different from all the other guys she had dated and that despite loving her job as a window dresser in Harrods, she was considering relocating to Tuscany so she could see where their relationship might lead.

This had come as a surprise to Izzie. She was used to Meghan falling in and out of love like Tigger on speed, rarely spending more than a couple of weeks with the same guy, coming up with some sort of excuse for ditching them ranging from his choice of footwear, his pre-disposition to following carpet bowls or his habit of eating Roquefort with pickled onions as a midnight snack.

'So first we'll make the *pici senesi*, which is local to the Siena area and is thought to date back to the Etruscan era. It's made the same way as spaghetti, with flour, water, salt and a little olive oil and egg for richness, but the strands are thicker and much longer. My *nonna* has been known to make strands of *pici* that are over three metres in length!'

After the pasta dough had rested for a while, each student was given a wooden board and Luca demonstrated how to roll it out, cut it into ribbons and then hand-roll the dough into long fat strings with a flat palm.

'Hey, look!' exclaimed Tom, grinning with pride as he reached for his camera. 'Mine must be at least a metre long!'

When everyone had produced a heaped pyramid of fresh pasta, Luca turned to the recipe for the vegetarian sauce. Izzie handed each student a wide bowl containing two hard-boiled eggs, a bunch of fresh mint, basil and flat-leaf parsley and a small mound of grated pecorino, and placed a jug of extra virgin olive oil in the middle of the table for them all to share.

'This is a type of pesto sauce, but it's unusual because it uses eggs, which makes it much creamier, and I hope you'll agree with me that it's absolutely delicious. So, first we peel the eggs and then we slice them lengthways, retaining one of the yolks for later.'

There followed an animated few minutes as the students tried to peel the eggs without shooting them across the table – Beth – or dropping them on the floor

– Tom – and eventually they stood in front of their wooden boards ready for their next set of instructions.

'Okay, now we peel the garlic. Three cloves should do it.'

'Three?' exclaimed Zara, her eyes widening with disgust. 'That's a lot of garlic! Are we expecting Dracula?'

A ripple of giggles erupted amongst the gathering.

'You can adjust to taste, but for the authentic recipe, I recommend three.'

'What's the point in learning local dishes if you're not going to be authentic!' cajoled Carmen, clearly hoping that on the last day her friend would make something she could eat.

'Okay, okay.' Zara smiled, tossing three cloves of garlic into her bowl.

'Right, now we put all the ingredients into the blender, like this.'

Luca threw everything into the blender, added a generous slosh of olive oil and a pinch of salt and some ground black pepper, and pulsed the ingredients into a rough paste.

'Mmm, that looks, and smells, amazing,' said Hannah, peering into the plastic jug.

'Now it's your turn. I'll put the pasta on to boil and when it's ready, we simply add the pesto, sprinkle on the remaining egg, another dash of pecorino and parsley and *ecco!* It's done!'

For the next five minutes Luca strolled around the table, explaining, commenting, encouraging and praising until everyone had made a passable pesto with which to dress their pasta. Then he drained the huge cooking pan, separated the hand-rolled home-made pasta into bowls and handed one to each of the students so they could add their own sauce and toppings.

'Okay, the table is set outside, let's eat whilst it's hot.'

Izzie grabbed a breadboard with one of Luca's home-made focaccia, the olive oil and two bottles of Chianti, while Luca took a baking tray filled with roasted vegetables from the oven; courgettes, asparagus, artichokes and tomatoes, scattered with cloves of garlic. The fragrance sent her taste buds tingling! They settled at the table beneath the pergola, amongst the frilly wisteria and honeysuckle entwined with strings of fairy lights, and everyone dug in, even Zara.

'It's been a fabulous week,' sighed Hannah, sending a swift glance from beneath her eyelashes towards Tom, who looked away, his cheeks reddening. 'Thank you, Izzie, Luca. I really didn't think I would enjoy it so much. I feel relaxed and a lot calmer than when I arrived, but I've also learnt a whole lot of new things. I'm definitely going to continue to paint; in fact, I'm thinking of enrolling on an evening class at the local high school when I get back.'

'And I'm definitely going to try out some of the recipes in that folder you've given us, Izzie,' said Beth, swirling the red wine around her glass, her enunciation a little slurred. 'I never knew how enjoyable cooking could be. I used to view it as a chore, especially for one, but it's actually quite therapeutic, and the fact that there's a tasty, nutritious meal at the end of it makes it even better!'

'Yes, despite the inauspicious start, I admit that Villa Limoncello has wheedled its way into my heart,' said Carmen, nibbling on a slice of fresh mango that Luca had prepared to accompany his *panforte di Siena*, a fruit and nut cake spiced with cinnamon, cloves and cocoa powder.

'I'll go make the coffee,' said Luca, pushing himself from his seat only to be pulled back down by Carmen, who, like Beth, had overindulged in the Chianti before moving on to the Vin Santo, and was now sipping on a glass of grappa.

'No, I want you to stay right here and tell us how you became such an amazing chef. Who taught you how to cook? Have you always wanted to own a restaurant? What made you buy a dilapidated villa in the Tuscan country-side? What else do you have in mind for the renovations? A swimming pool, perhaps? What are your plans for more courses?'

Izzie couldn't help exchanging a look with Hannah at the deliberate attempt by Carmen to make up for calling in the food inspectors. A coil of unease meandered through her abdomen when she thought of the Dalton situation, and her reaction reaffirmed her suspicions that her feelings for Luca had morphed into something much deeper than a holiday romance under the Tuscan sun. She resolved to talk to him about the future, but first they needed coffee. She counted the empty bottles of wine on the table, shocked to see that between the seven of them they had consumed ten bottles, and she knew that she and Luca had only had one glass each.

'I'll get the coffee.'

'Great,' said Carmen, without looking at Izzie as she continued to fire random questions in Luca's direction and offer her own hard-won advice on the expansion of Villa Limoncello's repertoire. 'Why don't *you* help Izzie with the coffee, Beth?'

Beth clearly hadn't been expecting the command – understandably, as it was usually Hannah who got the orders – and glanced up from the phone she had been checking intermittently during the meal.

'Coffee? Oh, right, yes, okay.'

Beth shoved her mobile into her back pocket and followed Izzie into the kitchen, where she arranged the villa's signature mugs that had been hand-painted with bunches of lemons onto a wide wooden tray with handles, whilst Izzie set the kettle to boil for a pot of Earl Grey tea and fiddled with the coffee machine.

'Thanks, Beth. I think I can…'

Izzie paused as she placed the sugar bowl on the tray, reconsidering her intention to send Beth back to the group. It was the perfect opportunity to follow up on what Hannah had said earlier. She would have preferred to have talked to Luca about her conversation with Hannah at the café in Siena; nevertheless, she couldn't let the chance pass if it meant she could get to the bottom of what was going on – although she suspected even Hercules Poirot himself might struggle to solve this mystery!

'I thought your pencil drawing of the Torre del Mangia was amazing. You're a talented artist, Beth, have you ever thought of pursing it further?'

'Would you believe it's been a dream of mine since I was five years old to earn a living from art in some way,' said Beth, leaning against the kitchen dresser, her cheeks flushed, the wine clearly loosening her tongue. 'I come from a very creative family, you know. My father's a graphic designer, my mum's a lecturer in textiles at our local college, and my older brother is a sculptor. When I decided to study for a degree in fashion design, I was over the moon to be offered a place at Northumbria – it's one of the best in the country.'

'And that's where you met Carmen?'

'Yes, we clicked straight away. We both loved experimenting with different textures, with materials that you wouldn't necessarily associate with fashion design like cork, bamboo, even palm leaves. For the first two years we were not only firm friends, but we collaborated on a number of other projects outside of the university such as creating a stage set for a local theatre production, designing a batch of hessian bags for a charity bash, and helping to style our friend's band for a gig in the students' union.'

As Izzie made herself busy arranging a selection of Luca's *cantuccini* biscuits on a white oval platter to accompany their coffee, she couldn't fail to notice the fire in Beth's eyes as she spoke of her love of design, and she wondered more than ever why she had ended up working in a department store. She hesitated, weighing up whether she should just ask her outright why she hadn't graduated, or to spend the next few minutes working the conversation around to the question that was burning a hole in her brain. As always, she favoured the straightforward approach.

'So why didn't you finish the course?'

She instantly regretted her question when she saw the shock reflected in Beth's eyes and wished she could take back her blunder.

'I'm sorry, I…'

'Who told you that?'

'I, well…'

'Was it Carmen?'

Beth narrowed her eyes, her jaw clenched. Izzie saw her fists were rolled into tight balls and she was clearly poised to fly out of the kitchen to confront her friend over the perils of loose gossip. Izzie couldn't stomach another argument so decided to come clean.

'No, it was Hannah.'

'Hannah? How does she know what happened? Oh, don't tell me, I can guess.'

To Izzie's complete surprise the fight drained out of Beth and she slumped down at the kitchen table, her elbows resting on its surface as she cupped her chin in her palm, tears collecting at the corners of her eyes.

'Beth? Are you okay?'

Izzie handed her a cup of thick, dark espresso, hoping the injection of caffeine would chase away the red wine demons that were clearly taking advantage of Beth's frailties.

'Not really, but I suppose I should be used to being asked that question by now. You want to know why I didn't graduate?'

'Only if you want to...'

'I was asked to leave.'

That hadn't been what Izzie had expected. 'Asked to leave? Why?'

Beth took a gulp of her coffee as though expecting to gain strength from its depths. 'With hindsight, it's a bit embarrassing, to be honest, although at the time it was the most painful episode of my life and I think I was a little bit crazy.'

More silence as Izzie ran through a myriad of possibilities.

'I had an affair with one of our lecturers.'

'Oh... right, and they expelled you for that?'

'No, not for that. You know, I was predicted to get a first? Carmen only managed to scrape a 2:2. Turned out

I'd thrown my whole future away, and for what? Well, at the time it was for love, obviously. I loved Marcus, and he loved me, just not enough to stand by my side and face up to the powers that be. He ended our relationship immediately, and I was devastated, reeling from the shock, and so… and so… I started to follow him, to spy on his every move. I only wanted to be close to him, to see him, to hear his voice, to catch a whiff of his cologne, but they called it… they called it stalking.'

Beth couldn't hold onto her tears any longer and she dropped her head down onto her folded arms and sobbed as though her loss had been yesterday, not over a decade ago.

'I was told that if I left the university without making a fuss, they wouldn't contact the police. What choice did I have? I didn't want a criminal record, but it also meant that I wouldn't have a degree, at least not from Northumbria. I agreed to go, went back to my parents' house in Cardiff, and I intended to resume my course the following year at a different uni, but when the time came around I couldn't face going back to studying.

'It took me a couple of years to get over my broken heart and by that time, life had moved on. I'd found a job at the department store that I loved, a room in the attic of a gorgeous Victorian semi, and hung out with a great group of friends. I started designing and hand-stitching handbags and other leather accessories in the evenings when my friends went out to nightclubs. Carmen stayed in touch and invited me along on a couple of her foreign assignments, even paying for my airfare when I was broke.'

'Oh, Beth, I'm so sorry.'

Izzie's heart gave a squeeze of sympathy for the way life dealt some people a rotten hand of cards whilst others got the royal flush. Love hurt, she knew that from personal experience, but the alternative was much worse. It was true what they said – it was better to have loved and lost than never to have experienced that first delicious glow of a new romance, the skip of a heartbeat, the tingle of desire.

'Have you never wanted to return to your fashion designs, maybe add to your portfolio?'

'No, not at all. I'm happy with the way my life is.'

Beth forced a smile, but her bravado was so brittle that Izzie didn't believe that she had reconciled her misfortune of fifteen years ago. She, too, knew how a person's creative passion could be smothered by sadness, how easily the spark of imagination could be extinguished when desolation came to visit. But it never truly went away, simply lurked beneath the surface, dormant, waiting for the right time to show its face again and shine. It was simply a matter of time and the timescales were different for everyone. She fervently hoped that it wouldn't be too long before Beth's passion was reinvigorated and she either returned to her studies or moved into the industry she so obviously loved, to build on what she had started so long ago.

'Beth...'

'Actually, I was hoping to have a quick word with you before I left. This trip to Tuscany has sown a few seeds of inspiration – oh, I'm not saying I'll ever be a budding Banksy, but I've enjoyed every one of your painting sessions and, Izzie, you are an amazing teacher. Are you planning on holding another Painting & Pasta course later on in the year? I know some of my friends from work would love to come over and learn something new, but mainly to indulge in the great food and the home-made limoncello!'

'I'm not sure. We were hoping to run a course in September – it was going to be Books & Biscotti – but all our plans are on hold until after the food inspectors have been next week.'

'I'm so sorry that happened, Izzie. I've spoken to Carmen, well, we all have, but once she's got something in her head…'

A surge of indignation suddenly welled up inside Izzie, a churning desire to defend Villa Limoncello's reputation, to shout about its attributes from the terracotta rooftops of San Vivaldo, to tell the world that it was an amazing place filled with joy and serenity, a place that could heal a broken heart. She wanted Beth's friends to book a course there, she wanted to build on the knowledge she'd gained both from presenting the tutorials and from the improvement of her own emotional wellbeing. She wanted to help Beth rediscover her lost creativity just like she had.

'Actually,' she blurted before she'd connected her brain to its modem, 'I'm confident that when the inspectors visit, we'll be able to inform them that Carmen's stomach upset had nothing to do with Luca's food preparation.'

'You will?' said Beth, her eyes widening with interest, but before she could say anything further, a voice interrupted from the threshold.

'Hey, there you are! We thought you'd gone off to Columbia for the coffee!' laughed Hannah, depositing a pile of used plates onto the draining board. 'Carmen's asking whether you have decaf, Izzie?'

'Yes, no problem. I'll bring it right out.'

A burst of giggling erupted from the terrace as Beth and Hannah made their way back outside whilst Izzie finished putting the tray of tea and coffee together, berating herself for what she'd said to Beth. Despite all the new information she had gathered that day, she was no nearer to uncovering the truth than she had been on Monday afternoon, and if it hadn't been for the grasshopper incident and the disappearing pencils then she would have had to come to the regrettable but reasonable conclusion that Carmen's illness was indeed food poisoning.

Chapter Twenty-Four

The limonaia*, Villa Limoncello*
Colour: Midnight blue

By the time the group had finished off every last crumb of the *cantuccini* and retired to their respective rooms, Izzie could barely think straight. Random snippets of various conversations had ambushed her thoughts all evening and when Luca suggested a nightcap she nodded, grateful that he had read her anguish and was offering his support. She reached for a bottle of Chianti and carried it out to the terrace, then changed her mind and led Luca towards the *limonaia*, where they could relax in the old rattan chairs and gaze upwards at the magic carpet woven with stars. It was the perfect place to confide every detail of her eventful day in Siena.

God! Where should she start?

It was more like a story from one of Riccardo's crime novels! She briefly toyed with the idea of asking him to join them so they could seek his advice on what to do for the best. As an author, maybe he possessed the kind of thought process that could cut straight to the crux of the matter and he'd be able to tell them straight away who the most likely person was to have spiked Carmen's drink and made it look like food poisoning.

However, she knew that wasn't an option. The person she needed to talk to was Luca, but she wasn't looking forward to hearing his reaction when she related what Zara and Hannah had told her that morning.

'Okay, *Izz… a… bella*, spill! You look like you're about to explode!'

Her heart gave a nip of pleasure at how sexy her name sounded when it rolled off Luca's tongue. For a brief moment, her attention skipped back to the previous night, to their journey home on the Vespa, the laughter, the romance, the kissing, and all she wanted to do was fall into Luca's arms and stay there until dawn tumbled over the horizon. However, the future of the villa was at stake and she had to do everything she could to make things right. With tremendous effort, she dragged her thoughts back to the present and quickly recounted the details of Zara's confession, how she had used laxatives to control her weight, that one of the packets had mysteriously disappeared, and that Zara suspected someone had spiked Carmen's vitamin drink.

'Do you believe her?' interrupted Luca, his voice tight with emotion.

'Actually…'

'She could be saying that to divert attention from the fact that if that were true then the spotlight was bound to fall on her straight away, especially as she has a great deal to lose if Carmen does drop her in it with her agency. I don't know a lot about the modelling world, but I suspect that sort of behaviour is frowned upon, even if it is prevalent.'

'That's exactly what Zara thought people would say, but it turned out she was telling the truth.' Izzie went on to explain what Hannah had done and the reasons behind her actions. 'But she says she didn't go ahead with it.'

'She would say that, though, wouldn't she?'

'I agree, and she did have this weird look in her eyes, but that could have been the exhaustion.'

Izzie glanced across at Luca but he had tuned out of their conversation, lost in the labyrinth of his thoughts, a loose nerve twitching underneath his left eye the only indication of his struggle to keep a grasp on his temper. She got up from her chair and meandered over to one of the lemon trees, absently fingering its glossy leaves, weighing the bulbous fruit in her palm and inhaling its delicious scent.

'Luca?'

Silence ballooned and she felt disorientated and a little light-headed as she waited for him to speak, her orderliness demons spiralling with increasing insistence. Suddenly, she knew exactly what she had to do. Okay, so her slavish adherence to lists, itineraries, schedules and a carefully maintained diary hadn't been enough to save her business from folding – for how could an interior designer with a list of wealthy clients continue to create avant-garde décor when her creativity had packed up its bags and flown off to sunnier climes? – but maybe it could come to her rescue now.

'Luca?'

'Mmm?'

'I've got an idea.'

'What sort of an idea?'

'I'm going to go back to the list I made earlier!'

'Izzie, I don't think…'

But she ignored him and dashed back to the kitchen. When her gaze fell on her trusty purple folder, a smile stretched her lips. She grabbed it and returned to the *limonaia*.

'Let's do this and then I promise I'll ditch the deer-stalker and give you my undivided attention. Do you have a better idea?' She raised her eyebrows as she waited for his answer, her need for order circling with increasing insistence as she craved the release of getting her thoughts down on paper.

'Okay, okay,' Luca relented, looking over her shoulder at the sheet of paper Izzie had turned to in her notebook, a smile twitching at the corners of his mouth. 'Go ahead, Doctor Watson.'

'Right, so there's four people on my list. Who do you want to start with?'

'Zara, of course, my money is still on her. The laxatives belong to her and we only have her word for it that all the tablets are accounted for. And Carmen *was* threatening to drop her in it with her agent and maybe even potential clients – her livelihood is at risk.'

'Okay.'

Izzie jotted down Luca's observations, delighted to find that her earlier feelings of light-headedness were already starting to melt away.

'Next is Hannah and she's the top of my list.'

'Why?'

'I feel sorry for her, particularly after she told me about the way Carmen treats her at the office – even a saint would snap if they had to put up with all that. Perhaps she didn't mean for Carmen to get so ill, just confined to her room for a while so she could have a few hours to herself away from the continuous demands. But the thing that's swung it for me is her feelings for Dalton. She *was* in love with him before his head was turned towards the brightest star in their midst, *and* she told me this afternoon that she thinks Carmen might be having an affair, so that's another reason for wanting to hurt her.'

'Mmm, maybe,' said Luca, the doubt evident in his voice.

'What about Tom?' she asked, moving on to the next column.

'Do you think we could be underestimating what he's capable of?'

'What do you mean?'

'Well, you heard what he told us. He's been so caught up in the trauma surrounding his mum's illness that there's no telling what he might do, especially as Carmen seems to be taking her time deciding how to handle his breach of trust – whether to go to the police or to the regulatory authorities.'

'You know, I actually think it's cruel of her to keep him hanging on like that, wondering, worrying, adding even more pressure to an already very stressful situation, not to mention demanding that he join everyone on their jaunt to Tuscany – that's just plain heartless. It's as though Carmen wants him to suffer as much as possible. Yes, he *could* have acquired something to put in Carmen's daily smoothie, and then sat back and waited for the fireworks, but it's not really his style, is it?'

'I agree with you. He's more Basset Hound than Rottweiler.' Izzie jotted a few words under Tom's name then looked up to see Luca watching her, amusement dancing in his eyes as he asked, 'And what about Beth?'

'Yes, it could have been her. Yesterday, when I asked whether her handbag was one of Carmen's designs, she almost bit my head off, informing me in no uncertain terms that it was one of her own creations. I think she's jealous of Carmen's success as a model, and then as an award-winning fashion designer, when they both attended the same university and she still works in a shop.'

'Okay, so let me get this straight, after all your deductions you think it's... erm, *all* of them? Every one of our esteemed guests could be responsible for spiking their friend's drink to either get rid of her for a while or to teach her some kind of lesson in humility?'

'I...'

Izzie sighed when she ran her eyes down her list.

'God! I'm glad I'm an interior designer and not a private investigator. This mystery-solving is so much harder than they make it look on the TV!'

Luca laughed, jumped out of his seat, reached for Izzie's hand and dragged her up from her chair, the cute dimples she loved bracketing his lips.

'Come on, I've got an idea of my own!'

'What?'

'It's a secret!'

Before she could marshal any objections, citing the fact it was after midnight, that she was bone-tired from the physical and emotional strains of one of the longest days she'd encountered since arriving in Tuscany, she was being guided towards the wall that separated Villa Limoncello from Riccardo's B&B.

'What...?'

Luca released her hand and vaulted the stone barrier like an Olympic gymnast, turning to help her navigate the hurdle in a much less elegant style.

'Luca…'

'Didn't you say Riccardo was in Rome? Meeting his editor?'

'Yes, but he's due back tonight. What if he…'

But she got no further. In front of them lay the swimming pool, its surface reflecting the inky black sky above, and Izzie only had a couple of seconds in which to kick off her sandals before Luca grabbed her hand and they took a running leap into the water, fully clothed, screaming with laughter. She gasped as the water hit her body, but Luca was right by her side, curling his arm around her waist and pulling her closer, kissing her with a passion she had no trouble matching. She met his eyes, her heart performing a somersault of attraction, and she knew the ripples cascading down her spine had nothing to do with the undulations of the pool.

Luca was right. She needed to take a break from the escalating anxiety, and all the organising and worrying about the guests, and a romantic interlude was the perfect remedy. Fortunately, Riccardo was nowhere to be seen and, much later, when her head eventually hit her pillow, she tumbled into the arms of Morpheus within seconds.

Chapter Twenty-Five

The pool house at Riccardo's B&B
Colour: Crimson red

Izzie peeled back her eyelids, squinting at the stream of ivory light shining through the wooden shutters, its beam picking out the dust motes dancing a jig on the window sill. She glanced at her alarm clock and groaned when she realised it was not yet six a.m. Despite having fallen asleep quickly, she had awoken with a start at three o'clock with something niggling at the corner of her brain, something she couldn't quite put her finger on, and the harder she tried to chase it down the more elusive it became. She must have fallen back to sleep only to reawaken again, trying to claw back her subconscious thoughts.

It was something someone had said to her the previous day, but what, and who?

She jumped out of bed, hoping that an invigorating shower would kickstart her brain cells, but as she smoothed a smidgeon of coconut oil through her tresses, she still couldn't put her finger on what was bothering her. She resolved to chat through the details of their trip to Siena with Meghan whilst they prepared breakfast – however, as that was an hour away, she decided to make a start on setting up the gazebo for the final painting session, which was going to be her favourite of the whole week.

Whilst studying at the RCA, Izzie had discovered that what she enjoyed most about design was reusing, recycling and repurposing everyday objects. When she launched her own interior design business she had continued with that passion, introducing as much modern innovation into her designs as her clients would allow. She also loved the uninhibited use of colour, texture and irregular shapes, and, as far as possible, she insisted on using natural raw materials from sustainable sources. This was what she wanted to showcase to her students that morning.

To that end she had titled the tutorial 'Innovate!' and instead of the traditional pastels and acrylics, crayons and sketch pads she had put in their artist's packs, she had sourced other, more unusual products – newspaper, embossed wallpaper, cotton, linen and hessian to pin on their easels; feathers, sponges, rollers and washing-up mops to use as painting implements and to create texture. She had even spent an amazing few hours in the hardware store in San Vivaldo buying up cooking utensils, wooden spoons and pastry brushes for even more experimentation, along with sample pots of gloss paint, varnish and exterior stone paint in a kaleidoscope of colours.

She gulped back a mug of instant coffee and made her way to the outbuilding next to the *limonaia* where she stored everything from rusty old bedsteads, cracked flower pots, a bunch of garden tools that looked more like instruments of torture, and the little pink Vespa that had become her best friend whilst in Tuscany. When she'd first arrived at the villa, the place had been crammed to its rafters with a higgledy-piggledy mess but she had soon created order on the scarred wooden shelves. She flicked on the light, gathered everything she needed for that day's tutorial into one of Gianni's ancient wheelbarrows, and set off along the winding pathway to the gazebo, humming a random tune.

It didn't take her long to set up everyone's workstations and she skipped down the steps back to the wheelbarrow to collect the final pots of gloss that she would open at the last minute and arrange on the table for everyone to share, if they chose to work in that medium.

'Hey, Izzie! Need any help?'

'Oh, hi, Gianni. No thanks, I think I'm just about sorted.'

'Wow, you've got a weird selection of stuff here, haven't you?'

Before Izzie could stop him, Gianni had picked up a tin of gloss paint from the wheelbarrow to inspect the label and she watched in horror as it slipped from his grasp. He spent a couple of tantalising seconds juggling the container like a circus clown, only for it to tumble onto the whitewashed step of the gazebo where it lost its lid on impact. Had it been the tin containing the *white* gloss she wouldn't have been so bothered, but it was the one containing a gorgeous crimson colour and it looked like there'd been a murder, with blood-red liquid dripping from the top to the bottom step. And it was gloss!

'*Spiacente!*'

'God!'

Izzie cursed under her breath until she saw the contrition written across Gianni's handsome features. She should have known what would happen – she should have wrestled him to the ground when he reached for the paint, should have cried out to stop, but it was too late. It was like a scene from the Tuscan Chainsaw Massacre! However, there was no use crying over spilt paint so she mentally ran through the contents of the outbuilding for a bottle of industrial-strength cleaner so she could to clean it up before the group arrived and called in the police.

'I'll get something to—'

'Gianni, there's nothing in the shed that can deal with this – it's *gloss* paint. We need something like turps.'

'Turps? What is *turps*?'

'Solvent?'

Gianni still looked blank. 'I'll go over to the village…'

'But the students will be here in just over an hour. How are they going to get into the gazebo? There's paint everywhere!'

She heaved a sigh, almost giving into a giggle when she saw him bury his hands into the pockets of his ever-so-short denim shorts *and* start to flap his elbows as if considering the complexities of the universe, instead of potential solutions to getting rid of the spillage that was spreading even further and wider like a pool of blood. Then the answer to her problem popped into her mind.

Riccardo!

During the 'vineyard sabotage fiasco', she'd discovered a cornucopia of high-grade chemicals and solvents in the storeroom at the back of his pool house. All she had to do was find something that could deal with the removal of gloss paint and all would be well, although she knew she would have to keep her plan a secret from Gianni, as she wouldn't put it past him to physically restrain her from venturing next door.

'Actually, yes, would you mind zipping over to the village? See what you can get? Maybe you could call in and see Luca at the restaurant, see if he has any ideas?'

She saw Gianni give her a confused look and she thought he might have guessed what she had in mind, but he simply shrugged his shoulders and trotted towards where he'd abandoned his quad bike. Zooming away on his mission of mercy in a cloud of dust, he took a corner at such speed that for a few tantalising seconds she thought he would depart company with his trusty vehicle and end up impaled on one of precious vines.

As soon as he was out of sight, Izzie wiped her hands on a cloth and jogged towards the wishing well, then scrambled over the crumbling stone wall that was held together by a few tendrils of ivy, delighted with the ease of her climb – unlike the first time she had scaled its heights, when it had felt like Mount Everest. Clearly her sojourn in the Tuscan countryside had improved not only her emotional well-being but her physical health too.

She glanced over her shoulder at the decrepit tennis court that was next on her list of renovations projects and a burst of optimism spread through her chest. Once the guests had left, she and Luca would deal with the inspectors, using all the skills of persuasion she possessed to convince them that the incident was unrelated to Villa Limoncello, and then get on with the job of preparing for their next course. She hoped that at least Beth would spread a positive word about them when they got the all-clear.

Now all she had to do was clean up Gianni's mess and start the day's tutorial on schedule. She glanced at her watch – time was running out! She dashed to the B&B's front door and rang the bell, her heart hammering out a concerto of trepidation against her ribcage as she formulated an explanation for her visit that didn't include Gianni's clumsiness.

She rang the bell again but there was no answer. Maybe Riccardo had decided to stay on in Rome? Perfect!

She raced round to the back of the B&B, ignoring the splash of pleasure that entered her chest when she saw the turquoise water of the pool glistening in the early morning sunshine and recalled her moonlight swim with Luca. She would have loved nothing better than to take a flying leap into the deep end and power through a few laps to alleviate the anxiety that was currently gripping her bones. Instead, she made her way to the wooden shed at the back of the pool house, which the last time she'd been inside had been a veritable alchemists' paradise! She had dealt with enough spillages in her time as an interior designer and a professional home-stager to know everything there was to know about hiding snags and tears and removing or disguising stains and spillages. What the eyes couldn't see…

Izzie twisted the handle, but the shed was locked, plus there was no conveniently open window – or any window at all – and the door was made from sturdy wooden planks. Disappointment swept through her until, out of the corner of her eye, she noticed a glint of silver and almost laughed out loud in relief – the key was dangling from a hook under the eaves! She reached up, grabbed it and rushed inside, pausing for a few moments to allow her eyes to become accustomed to the gloom, and when they did her smile broadened into a grin.

Wow! The place was crammed with everything an enthusiastic gardener or avid DIYer could possibly dream of and more! From paint-splattered hammers, screwdrivers, pliers and spirit levels, to spades, rakes, fertilizers and bottles of chemicals to keep the pool clean. She ran her finger along the shelves, searching for the product she needed and when she found it hidden behind a tin of creosote, she let out a whoop of joy. She had just stretched up onto her tiptoes to liberate it from its resting place when there was a crash and complete blackness engulfed her.

'What the...'

Her immediate thought was that her eyes had failed her. The darkness was so absolute that she had no idea where the door was. She spun on her heels before realising that she had just confused her sense of direction even more. She took a step forward, stumbling over a garden rake and giving herself a bash on her head for the trouble. She rubbed the pain away, but within seconds she'd tripped over a bag of mulched bark. When she righted herself, her forearms were tingling with goose bumps and her heart was doing a great impersonation of a *Wacky Races* competitor.

'Hey! It's Izzie! I'm in here!' she screamed, hammering on what she hoped was the door but could easily have been the wall. Nevertheless, she was sure that if Riccardo had been returning from an early morning saunter, noticed that the door was open and shut it, he would have heard her cries of alarm.

But no one came.

'Riccardo! Riccardo!'

She gulped down on the nausea tickling at her throat, struggling to calm her breathing so she didn't hyperventilate, and hoping the sensible side of her brain would kick in so she could consider her options.

Phone!

But when she felt in the pocket of her capri pants she groaned, remembering that she'd left it on the table in the gazebo whilst she mopped up the paint spillage. Stupid! But then how was she to know she would be imprisoned in a dust-filled outbuilding by…

By whom?

Who would do such a thing?

Surely not Riccardo? Whilst it wasn't beyond the realms of possibility when she factored in his past behaviour, it seemed unlikely, and her recent dealings with him had been cordial, especially after he'd agreed to allow the villa's guests to use the swimming pool.

Then a much more ominous thought clanked into her brain and she gasped at the force of the realisation – the spiked vitamin drink, the grasshopper incident, the missing pencils…

Oh God! Did the person responsible think she was on to them? Did they want her out of the way so they could do something even more despicable to Carmen?

Chapter Twenty-Six

The wishing well, Villa Limoncello
Colour: Sparkling sunlight

With her thoughts ricocheting from one dreadful possibility to the next, Izzie forced herself to inhale a long, slow breath and engage her brain, despite the fact that her temples felt like they were being squeezed in Riccardo's bench vice. In the disorientating darkness, she was starting to feel claustrophobic, but she refused to panic and instead ran her fingers along the shelf until she reached what she thought was the door and then felt for the handle.

Within moments, the room was filled with bright, white, glorious sunlight and, like a bat out of hell, she shot from the confines of her wooden prison, only stopping when she reached the edge of the swimming pool, her grazed hands on her knees as she breathed in the sweet air of freedom.

A tsunami of relief swept through her body, washing away the terror, but she knew there was no time to waste. Whilst it had felt like hours, she knew she'd only been trapped for a few minutes and she needed to get back to the gazebo, rescue her phone and call Luca, ask him to come over to the villa so they could stop this craziness once and for all. She was now even more determined than ever to root out the culprit and to bawl them out for bringing their malevolence to the wonderful Villa Limoncello. Instead of feeling shaky and disorientated from her ordeal, she felt empowered, resolute, angry! How dare they do this to Luca, to the villa, to her!

Praying that her jailer was unaware of the shortcut between the B&B and the villa and had taken the longer route back, she ran towards the wall, jumped over it as if auditioning as the next big thing in hurdling, and landed with a stumble. She had just managed to right herself when a spasm of shock ricocheted through her veins, causing her to halt like a participant in a game of musical statues. Through the dense foliage surrounding the wishing well, she could just about make out a dark silhouette stooping over its depths. She couldn't see what they were doing, but when she heard a loud splash, followed by a metallic thud, she realised they had tossed something into the water, and it wasn't a coin!

Indecision coiling through her veins, caught between wanting to launch herself at her assailant to discover their identity so she could confront them, and wanting Luca with her when she did so. She chose the latter course and sank silently into the fragrant embrace of a convenient magnolia bush, straining her eyes to identify the person who had locked her in Riccardo's shed. And, as the figure faded away, she knew immediately from their distinctive outline who she was dealing with, and the final piece of the jigsaw that had been floating through her brain since the previous night slipped into place.

She tiptoed to the gazebo, cringing at the sight of the red paint on the steps. With trembling fingers, she called Luca, gave him a swift abridged version of what had happened that morning, assured him that she was fine, if a little shaken, and asked him to ring Gianni and meet her on the terrace as soon as he could.

Then she went in search of Meghan, her friend, her confidante, her staunch ally through good times and bad, and poured the whole story out to her while Meghan plied her with caffeine and *cantuccini* in the sanctuary of the *limonaia* – her favourite place in the whole of Italy.

'Oh my God! Why didn't you tell me about any of all this? Wait until I get my—'

'No, Meghan, we've got to wait until Luca and Gianni get here. However, there is something we can do before then.'

'What?'

'Come on.'

Izzie lead a confused Meghan from the glasshouse down a twisting weed-strewn pathway to the wishing well.

'Would you mind? My hands are… well, a little sore!'

Meghan's face clouded with anger, but she managed to keep a grasp on her emotions as she wound the wishing well's handle and slowly drew up the wide-brimmed cast-iron bucket from its murky depths. When it reached the top, they both leaned forward, keen to discover what was in there.

'What's that?'

Meghan reached into the water, pulled out a tiny brown bottle and squinted at the label. Izzie knew before looking at it what it was, but that didn't mean she wasn't shocked to her core.

'What on earth is magnesium citrate?' asked Meghan, wrinkling her nose in bewilderment.

'It's a powerful laxative.'

'A powerful...' Meghan's jaw dropped and Izzie watched as the full realisation dawned. 'You mean this is what was used to make Carmen sick?'

'Yes.'

Meghan return to her scrutiny of the label. 'It says it's apple flavour! Oh my God, you're right. Someone brought this with them to Italy with the intention of spiking Carmen's drink and then blaming us for causing food poisoning! It's an absolutely wicked thing to do! Not just to Carmen, but to Luca – he could have lost everything, and for what? Do you think this was some kind of prank that got out of hand?'

'No, not a prank...'

'You think someone wanted to hurt Carmen?'

'Not hurt, but temporarily put her out of action.'

'But who? Who would do such a thing? Izzie? Tell me! Who did you see throw this down the well? Izzie!'

'I...'

'Izzie? *Grazie a Dio!*' exclaimed Luca, rushing through the shrubbery like a knight in shining armour, his dark eyes filled with fire as he pulled her into his arms.

'I'm fine, really, I'm fine.'

A stream of unintelligible Italian flowed from his lips as he kissed her cheeks, her forehead, the top of her head, and squeezed her so tightly she couldn't help but laugh as relief swirled around her body. With Luca by her side, she knew she would find the courage to do what needed to be done.

'Meghan?' said Gianni, stepping into the clearing, his face a mask of concern. 'I thought you wanted us to meet you on the terrace?'

'Oh, Gianni, thank God!'

Meghan promptly burst into tears and Gianni moved forward to envelop her into a bear hug, whispering soothing words into her hair until she calmed down. He opened his mouth to say something, but his brain was clearly still trying to process what was going on.

'What's that?' asked Luca, homing in on the bottle of liquid Meghan was still clutching in her fist.

'This is what was added to Carmen's vitamin drink on Monday morning!'

She handed Luca the little bottle of laxative for him to inspect.

'So we were right?' said Luca, his eyes scouring Izzie's.

Izzie nodded, not trusting herself to speak for fear of imitating Meghan and crumbling into a sodden mess. There was a great deal to do before she could allow herself the luxury of that and now that Luca and Gianni were there to support her, the sooner they got on with it the better.

'Are you saying you know who did this?' demanded Gianni, his arm draped over Meghan's shoulder, but his gaze fixed on Izzie.

'Yes, I do. I had my suspicions yesterday but couldn't quite join the dots until I saw them throw this little bottle down the well.'

'You mean getting rid of the evidence?'

'Yes, I suppose...'

'That's exactly what they were doing and if you hadn't seen them... Do they know that you saw them?'

Izzie shook her head. 'No.'

Prendiamo il bastardo!

Gianni spun on his heels and strode away, taking the path towards the terrace, but Meghan caught up with him and held him back.

'Hang on, Gianni, we need to do this properly, and I think it should be Izzie who handles the matter. She's the one who can identify the person responsible, she's the one who was locked in the shed...'

'Locked in the shed? What shed?'

'The one behind the swimming pool at the B&B!'

'*Sapevo che era lui!* I knew! I knew it would be Riccardo who was responsible for all this!' Gianni raised himself up to his full height and clenched his fists. 'Well, I'm not surprised! Yet another of his ill-fated attempts to sabotage what we're trying to do here at Villa dei Limoni. *Questo è tutto!* I'm going to...'

Gianni swiftly changed direction and marched towards the B&B, fury radiating from every pore.

'Gianni! Stop!' shouted Meghan, sprinting after him and placing her palm on his chest to stop him in his tracks. 'Look, we don't have time to explain everything, just believe me, this has nothing to do with Riccardo – for all we know he's still in Rome.'

Now Gianni's fury was replaced by indecision – he'd clearly relished the opportunity for another face-off with his nemesis, but when he saw Luca nod his agreement, Gianni stood down and followed Izzie, Luca and Meghan to the terrace where, to Izzie's relief, Carmen and her friends had gathered to enjoy their final breakfast under the wisteria-entwined pergola.

In any other circumstances, Izzie would have smiled at the heart-warming image of her guests taking breakfast together under the cloudless Tuscan sky. It really was a perfect day for their last tutorial; a light breeze, a soft medley of birdsong, a faint trickle of water from the fountain.

But the task ahead was far from pleasant.

When she approached the group, she made an effort not to meet anyone's eyes, instead choosing to concentrate on gathering her courage to delivery her exposé in as few words and with as little emotive language as possible. Nerves clawed at her abdomen, but as she ran through what had happened, indignation replaced her jitters and she was ready to confront the perpetrator and challenge them to explain in their own words why they had done such terrible things.

'Hey, Izzie, Meghan, where have you been? We've been looking for you!' Carmen smiled, tossing her sheet of blonde hair over her shoulder and starting to push herself from her chair until she saw the look on Luca's face. 'Luca? Izzie? What's going on?'

Tom and Hannah looked up from their cappuccinos in unison and sought Luca's eyes too.

'Is something wrong?' asked Tom, his face wreathed in panic as he reached out to run his fingers down the strap of his camera. 'Has someone rung from home? Has there been…?'

This got Beth and Zara's attention and they put down their magazines to stare at Luca, both with similar expressions of interest on their faces.

'Luca?' urged Carmen, flicking her eyes to Izzie, then back to Luca.

'I'm afraid this morning's tutorial has had to be cancelled.'

'Cancelled?'

'Cancelled?'

'No, why?'

'What?'

Luca raised his hand and waited for the chorus of objection to fade.

'Because there's something more pressing that needs to be discussed.'

Chapter Twenty-Seven

The pergola, Villa Limoncello
Colour: Apple twist

'What do you mean, something more pressing?' asked Carmen, her sharp eyes fixed on Luca's as she tried to discern what he was talking about.

'I think I should let Izzie talk to you about it.'

'Izzie? What's going on?'

Izzie felt Meghan give her arm a squeeze before she took a seat next to a grim-faced Gianni under the canopy of frilly pink flowers, but Luca remained standing at her side and she drew strength from his sturdy presence. As she inhaled a deep breath, ready to launch into her explanation, the drift of his lemony cologne gave her the confidence she needed to do this – after all, the whole purpose of their search for the truth had been to save Villa Limoncello. The place had given her so much, and it was her turn to return the favour.

'Izzie?' Luca nudged gently.

'Yes, okay…'

Izzie heard the croak in her voice, but she cleared her throat and pushed through her nerves.

'So, when Carmen suffered what she thought was a dose of food poisoning on the first day of our Painting

& Pasta course, there was no one more upset about that that I was. Carlotta, Meghan and I had worked so hard to make sure everything was spotless, from the bedding in the rooms to the towels in the bathrooms and the utensils in the kitchen, everything. Luca and I also spent many long hours creating menus that included the finest, most delicious ingredients Tuscany has to offer. I typed up all the recipes, laminated a set for each of you, along with shopping lists and lots of tips I came across whilst doing the research for Villa Limoncello's first ever course. It looked like all our hard work would be in vain when Carmen became ill, supposedly from something she had eaten during the lunch that Luca had prepared.'

'Supposedly? What does that mean?' demanded Carmen, looking around at the gathering, her eyes widening when she met Luca's gaze and saw him place his index finger on his lips. 'What…?' But his expression was so serious that Carmen stopped in her tracks.

'Both Luca and I were adamant that the food we'd sourced for breakfast, and for lunch, was the freshest on offer and that our hygiene practices were impeccable. However, we were also aware that mistakes can happen in any catering establishment and so we resigned ourselves to scrubbing the kitchen again and dealing with a visit from the health inspectors. But something didn't quite sit right, and now I know that we were right to be sceptical about Carmen's illness.'

'Sceptical? Are you suggesting that I faked it?'

'No, no, of course not. I'm saying that it had nothing to do with the food that Luca prepared. I wasn't absolutely sure until I factored in the grasshopper incident, Carmen's missing pencils, and then when someone shut me in the shed next door…'

'Someone shut you in the shed!' gasped Tom, so shocked that he stopped fiddling with the lens on his camera. 'Oh my God, who would do that? Are you saying… are you saying you think it was one of us?'

'Yes, that's exactly what happened.'

'But why would anyone do that?'

'Because the person who did it knew that I suspected foul play and they needed time to get rid of something.'

'Get rid of what?' asked Beth, flicking the sides of her bob behind her ears and leaning forward in her seat so as to listen more carefully.

'Of this.'

Izzie held up the little brown bottle she and Meghan had recovered from the well.

'But what is it?' asked Hannah, squinting to try and read the words on the label.

'It's magnesium citrate – apple–flavoured, to be precise.'

Silence burgeoned as the group took their time to assimilate that piece of information.

'Sorry, you'll have to be more specific. I have no idea what that is,' said Tom, shaking his head in bewilderment.

'It's a laxative, quite a powerful one,' muttered Zara, her fingers clenched so tightly around her espresso cup that her knuckles had turned white as she anticipated the way the conversation was about to turn.

'Zara's right, and this is what caused your illness, Carmen. I think it was introduced via your vitamin shake.'

'My vitamin shake?' The colour drained from Carmen's face and for the first time since she had arrived at Villa Limoncello, Izzie saw real fear in her eyes. 'Are you serious? You're telling me someone spiked my drink? But why? And who?'

Carmen cast a glance around the table, including everyone in her silent accusation, even Meghan and Gianni, but her gaze eventually came to a stop at Zara, who visibly squirmed under her friend's scrutiny.

'Oh, no, please…' began Carmen, her expression morphing from fear to distress as Zara continued to avoid her eyes.

Izzie wished there was another way she could do this, one where she didn't have to disclose Zara's problems to everyone in the group, but there wasn't. Of course, Carmen already knew, and she hoped that if she were a true friend, she would offer Zara the encouragement she needed to deal with her issues and get back on track.

'Do you want to tell everyone yourself, Zara?'

'Tell everyone…'

Zara paused, her eyes darting from Izzie to Luca, then to Carmen, seeking her support, but Carmen's gaze was still fixed on the bottle of magnesium citrate. Heaving a long, ragged sigh, she straightened her shoulders, lifted her chin and pulled her lips into a smile of resignation.

'I'm sorry, I've been taking laxatives to control my weight, and I brought a couple of packets with me to Italy.'

'Oh, Zara…' began Beth.

'I know I've let everyone down, particularly Carmen, but I promise you that I didn't take any of them. They were just there in my bag, in case… well, in case I needed them, which I suppose is almost as bad.'

'And is that yours, too?' Without looking at her friend, Carmen pointed to the brown bottle sitting in the middle of the table like a fetid fiend.

'No! Absolutely not! I've never used anything like that! I wouldn't, I just wouldn't. Carmen, I assure you…'

But Zara couldn't continue. She broke down, her head dropped onto her forearms, her whole body shaking from the pain of her public admission. After a while, she raised her reddened eyes, misery scrawled across her face.

'I admit I have a problem, but I promise you with every fibre in my body that this has got nothing to do with me, and that as soon as we get home, I'm going to sign up for some professional counselling. I know I should have done it before we came over here, but this time I mean it. Please forgive me, I…'

Carmen was out of her seat in an instant and crouched down next to her friend, draping her arm around Zara's shoulders as she sought out her eyes.

'Darling, there's nothing to forgive!'

'Really?'

'Absolutely.'

'And you… you won't report me to my agent?'

'No! I know I said that, but I would never have *done* it. You and Beth are my best friends. I was so worried about you, and the damage you were doing to your body just so you could eke out another few years on the circuit, that I didn't know what else to do to make you see sense, so I threatened you with exposure. I'm sorry, it wasn't the best way of tackling the issue, I know. I should have been much more supportive, I should have been there for you, helped you to get help, supported you to get to the appointments, and taken you to the spa afterwards! You know, it was one of the reasons I wanted you to come to Tuscany with me!'

'It was?'

'Yes, I wanted you to relax, to swim, to sunbathe. I thought if we spent some quality time together learning how to cook a few delicious meals from scratch, from a gorgeous Italian chef, then we could take some of the recipes home with us and make changes to our lifestyle together. Zara, I love you! I want you to move on from modelling and dazzle London with your beautiful jewellery designs, but you can only do that if you're healthy because, believe me, setting up and running a business is hard work, and it takes every single ounce of energy to succeed. Take it from someone who knows!'

Carmen pulled her sobbing friend into her arms, which only made Zara cry harder while the rest of the group looked on in silence, allowing them the time they needed to marshal their emotions and wipe away their tears.

'Thank you,' whispered Zara, lacing her fingers through her friend's. 'Thank you.'

'You don't have to thank me. I intend to be with you every step of the way from now on. We'll do this together. In fact, I wasn't going to tell you until we got back, but I've arranged for you to meet one of my contacts in the accessories business to pitch a few of your designs for his Spring/Summer collection.'

Zara's eyes widened, her lips parted, and Izzie thought she was about to crumple again, but she didn't. She managed a smile and the two friends returned their attention to Izzie and Luca.

'So, if it wasn't Zara who added this magnesium citrate to my drink, then who was it?'

Carmen's eyes bore into Izzie's as she switched into the professional manner that had helped her to become a successful fashion designer. Under the steely gaze, Izzie almost blurted out the name of the culprit there and then, but there was a lot more to what had been going on at Villa Limoncello than the simple addition of a laxative to Carmen's morning shake and she needed to make sure every single snippet of truth was disclosed – because if she didn't, she knew it would niggle at her conscience for ever.

Izzie mentally flicked through her internal Rolodex and stopped at the next person on her list. When she connected with Hannah's gaze, she wasn't surprised to see her visibly shrink from the spotlight of attention.

Chapter Twenty-Eight

The pergola, Villa Limoncello
Colour: Ash grey

Everyone else had seen Hannah's reaction and stared at Izzie with incredulity.

'Hannah? No way!' cried Carmen. 'I'd trust her with my life!'

'You would?' gasped Hannah, temporarily dumb-founded by Carmen's declaration of confidence, her cheeks flushing with something akin to pleasure. 'Really?'

'Of course. I couldn't run my business without you. I thought you knew that? In fact, I would never have won the award last month if I couldn't absolutely rely on you to run a tight ship at the office whilst I give my complete attention to my designs. Your diligence frees me up to concentrate on innovation and not the mundane admin stuff that gets in the way. Your name should be on that trophy, Han, not mine!'

Hannah opened her mouth in astonishment at Carmen's unexpected compliments, then she closed it again, before parting her lips once more giving the impression of a gobsmacked goldfish. 'I... Oh my God! I had no...'

Now it was Hannah's turn to burst into tears and Tom's turn to comfort her.

'Please, please tell me you had nothing to do with any of this!'

'I didn't. I swear…'

Hannah met Izzie's eyes briefly and the colour drained from her cheeks in seconds. However, she pushed herself up in her chair, gathering her courage to admit that she wasn't entirely blameless.

'But, well… I do have a confession to make.'

'What about?' asked Carmen, dread stalking across her expression.

'I'm so sorry, Carmen. I really am, but we've been so busy recently with next year's collection, then the end of the tax year, then the late nights at those photoshoots for the catalogue, and then the awards ceremony. I was so absolutely exhausted when we arrived here that I was almost clawing at my sanity with my fingertips! I literally couldn't see straight and all I wanted to do was sleep for the week, not learn how to paint or how to make hand-made pasta – sorry, Izzie. Sorry, Luca.'

'So what are you saying?' asked Zara, staring at Hannah with something akin to disgust.

'It was me who took your laxatives, Zara. I'm sorry.'

Hannah couldn't meet Zara's eyes, and instead looked down into her lap, her face filled with remorse and shame. Her fingers trembled and a single tear travelled down her cheek. Eventually she looked up and met Carmen's gaze, but before she could say anything Beth interrupted.

'So it was you! You spiked Carmen's drink?'

'No! I admit that the thought did cross my mind and I'm thoroughly ashamed. I just wanted one day, just one afternoon even, of relaxation, of peace and quiet away from the continual phone calls, the constant demands, the being on call all the time. I was desperate and I wasn't thinking straight, but in the end I just couldn't do it. I'm sorry, Carmen, so *so* sorry.'

The group sat motionless under the infinite sky, their breakfast forgotten as they attempted to process what Hannah had just confessed and anticipate Carmen's reaction. Izzie felt the muscles in her stomach tighten as she waited for the outburst; the anger, the threats, the dismissal even, but none of that came. The cicadas struck up another verse of their perpetual overture, a distant tractor rumbled through the fields and a lone dog barked at a passing Vespa, all of them oblivious to the helix of tension that was mounting under the pergola at Villa Limoncello.

Just as Izzie thought she should intervene to break the expanding silence, Carmen got up from her seat and walked over to Hannah. Everyone held their breath, only exhaling when Carmen knelt at Hannah's side, reached for her hand and waited for Hannah to meet her eyes.

'Hannah, it's me who should be apologising. I should have realised the stress you were under, should have known that there was far too much to do in the office for just one person, but every day seems to be caught up in a whirlwind of activity from first thing in the morning to the last thing at night and I never have a moment to stop for breath and appreciate what those around me are doing to keep the ship afloat – and that includes you, Tom.'

Carmen sent a smile in Tom's direction.

'I've always been a workaholic, "driven", some people call it, but that has negatives as well as positives. Obviously, I knew that the harder I worked, the more likely I was to succeed. I learnt that lesson at a very early age by watching my mum take on three jobs to support me and my sister when my dad walked out on us. I must have inherited her genes, because I worked my butt off at uni for my degree, then, as Zara will confirm, when I landed my modelling contract I took every single job going – even if it meant I got no sleep.'

'It's true.' Zara smiled, an element of pride in her voice.

'And when I realised that my career in modelling was coming to a natural conclusion and I decided to return to my first love – fashion design – my workaholic tendencies went into overdrive. I just had to make my business succeed at all costs. Okay, I'd managed to save a little start-up money from my modelling work, but I didn't have a rich family to fall back on. I now realise that I'm guilty of expecting those around me to be just as focused when I had no right to expect that. I'm sorry, Hannah – this is your *job*, not your passion, your dream, your reason for living.'

Izzie was surprised to hear Carmen's voice, so strong and firm until then, break on the last few words.

'What do you mean, your reason for living?' asked Beth, her head suddenly shooting upwards in surprise at what Carmen had said. Carmen ignored Beth's question and instead walked back to take her place at the table and started to fiddle with her coffee cup.

'Carmen? Are you okay?' said Zara, grasping her friend's hand, concern creasing her forehead.

Carmen nodded but when she looked up, Izzie saw the pain deep in her eyes.

'What's going on, Carr? Are you… are you sick?'

This question seemed to galvanise Carmen into action. 'No! No, it's nothing like that.'

'Then what?'

'It's Dalton.'

Izzie saw Beth exchange a quick glance with Hannah, before saying, 'What about Dalton?'

Izzie was confused. If Carmen was having an affair, as Hannah suspected, why was she worried about Dalton? Unless he'd discovered her infidelity... She hadn't intended to bring their relationship troubles up because it was personal and had nothing to do with the incidents that had taken place a Villa Limoncello. However, if Carmen herself was prepared to reveal her disloyalty to the group than she had no intention of stopping her. Indeed, it would be beneficial to get everything out in the open so that the friends – if they were still friends after all this – could made a fresh start.

But what Carmen said next shocked everyone, not just Izzie.

'He's having an affair.'

'What!'

'No!'

'*He's* having an affair?' exclaimed an astonished Hannah, her face turning an ashen grey.

The only person not to react to Carmen's revelation was Tom, who just sat, watching the various exclamations, his expression impassive. Izzie realised that he had been aware of Carmen's news.

'I knew something was amiss when he was late arriving for the awards ceremony last month. Then he missed the opening night of my sister's play, and when he told me he was going to do the perfume shoot in the US, my suspicions were confirmed. He always said he would never do a perfume shoot, that it was an affront to his talent, so I engaged a private investigator. Angus emailed me his report just before we came out to Italy and, sadly, I was right. I didn't want his cheating to spoil anyone's hard-earned break, so I decided to put the discovery aside until we got back.'

'Oh my God, you should have said something, darling!' declared Zara, sympathy written across her pretty features. 'We could have spent our time here plotting the most embarrassing downfall in the history of the world! Sorry, I don't mean to be flippant, but you're better off without him.'

'I know, and spending this week at the villa has really helped me to put what he's done into perspective. Clearly, he never loved me – so heavens knows why he asked me to marry him. It hurts, but I'll survive. I always do.'

The sadness in Carmen's eyes caused Izzie's heart to contract. Contrary to her impression of Carmen, beneath her tough, business-like, highly polished exterior, she was just as vulnerable as everyone else was to the vagaries of love, and compassion flooded her veins. She wondered how Hannah was feeling about jumping to the wrong conclusion, and she chanced a discreet glance in her direction from beneath her eyelashes.

'I'm going to view the whole episode as a narrow escape.'

'And for you, too, Hannah,' blurted Beth, before slapping her hand over her mouth. 'Oops, sorry, take no notice of me.'

'I'm sorry, Hannah, I know he's your friend and you…'

Hannah's cheeks burned, but she met Carmen's eyes head on.

'He's not my friend, Carmen. Okay, I admit I did have a bit of a crush on him at one time. He's handsome, charming and a great tennis partner, but we haven't played much recently. I thought it was his company I was mourning but, actually, it was probably the loss of a tennis partner. I'm sorry he did this to you, Carmen, I really am.'

Carmen was out of her seat in a moment and dragged a very surprised Hannah into a warm embrace. 'Oh, Hannah, darling, I'm so sorry. I never realised you had feelings for him! If I'd known I would have backed off straight away.'

'It's okay, Carmen. It would never have worked between us, I know that now.'

'I know I should say thank you for everything you do for me more often, Hannah, but I hope you know how much I appreciate you, how grateful I am that the office runs like clockwork because of your hard work and commitment. In fact, until I was thrown off track with the results of Angus's report, I'd been putting out feelers for an assistant for you – and I think I have just the person. I was waiting until Marcie finished her A levels before getting her into the office for a couple of weeks of work experience to see if she meets your high standards, before offering her a permanent job. Is that okay with you?'

All Hannah could do was nod as the tears trickled down her face.

Chapter Twenty-Nine

The pergola, Villa Limoncello
Colour: Russet brown

'Excuse me, Izzie, I really need to take this call.'

Tom's face was the colour of overworked putty as he stumbled away from the pergola whilst the group, including Meghan and Gianni, took the opportunity to fire a cascade of questions at Carmen about the process of instructing a private investigator – which, it turned out, Tom had been involved in. Now that her secret was out in the open, Zara had a wide smile on her face, unburdened from the shackles of guilt she had carried over her slip in integrity and joyous at the speed of Carmen's forgiveness as she made outrageous suggestions on how to seek revenge on Dalton. Hannah, too, was more relaxed, her features softer, the dark rings around her eyes less vivid.

'Who's next on your interrogation schedule?' whispered Luca. 'Beth or Tom?'

'Beth.'

Izzie took a moment to gulp down a glass of the lemonade Meghan had made that morning and to run through her list of potential culprits and their motivations. She cleared her throat and, if the situation hadn't been so serious, she would have giggled at the way the conversation stopped so abruptly and everyone turned to face her, every eye fixed on hers as they waited expectantly for her to reveal the identity of the guilty party. She was just about to resume her explanation when there was a sudden rustle of foliage behind her, sending her heart crashing against her ribcage.

'Oh, Tom!'

'Sorry, sorry,' he gabbled, sliding his mobile phone back into his pocket, his face more desolate than she had seen, and that was saying something. Tom usually looked like the world had it in for him, but when she recalled what he was going through with his mother's illness, that was no surprise.

'What's happened, Tom?' cried Hannah, jumping from her seat and grabbing his arm to lead him to his chair.

'It's… it's Mum.'

'What about her?'

A sharp stab of pain shot through Izzie's heart as her thoughts flew back to the phone call that she'd received that had caused her whole world to tilt on its axis. Only now, two long years later and with the help of Luca and Villa Limoncello, was she starting to regain her equilibrium. She hoped with every fibre of her being that Tom hadn't received similar news.

'She went AWOL again last night. The police found her and took her back to the care home, but the manager wants to have a meeting with my sister and I as soon as I get home to talk about a Deprivation of Liberty assessment – whatever that is.'

Tom looked like he'd been struck by a maelstrom of madness. Everyone spoke at once, offering their sympathy, their support, their suggestions, their own experiences with elderly relatives, until Tom interrupted them, thanked them for their kindness, and then met Carmen's eyes.

'I'm so sorry, Carmen.'

'There's nothing for you to be sorry for. The situation with your mother would be upsetting for anyone. It's a lot to deal with.'

'What I meant was, I'm sorry for...'

'I know what you meant, Tom, but it's me who should be apologising. I shouldn't have made you wait for so long before talking to you about what happened, but if you'll let me explain, I hope you'll forgive me?'

Tom's jaw dropped. 'Forgive you? Forgive you for what?'

'When the bank rang me about the discrepancy in the accounts, I admit I was shocked, but I also understood a little of what you were up against. My gran had dementia, too, and it's heart-breaking to stand helplessly on the side-lines and watch someone who was once so strong, so vibrant, so full of life, deteriorate into someone you no longer recognise. I wanted to do something to help you, I just didn't know what.'

'To help me?'

'Well, to help your mother.'

'But I thought... I thought you were deciding whether or not to report me to the police?'

'The police?' said Zara, confusion spreading across her face.

'Why did you think Carmen was going to call the police, Tom?' asked Beth, also shaking her head as she tried to understand what was happening.

'That doesn't matter,' said Carmen swiftly. 'What does matter is that I've been talking to my financial advisor and he's promised to sort out a short-term loan, guaranteed by me and at preferential rates, which will clear the outstanding fees at the care home and cover the monthly payments until the end of the year. I didn't want to say anything until I knew everything was sorted in case it fell through, but I got the paperwork this morning and it's all been agreed. We'll sign everything when we get back to London and the money should be available straight away.'

'I… I don't know what to say.'

'I don't want you to worry about paying me back until your mother's assets are freed up.'

'I… erm, thank you, thank you so much. I never expected…'

'It's the least I can do, Tom. I wish you'd come to me earlier and we could have saved a lot of hassle, and a lot of stress for you and your sister. It was the reason I absolutely insisted on your coming with us to Italy. You work so hard at the office, I know how many extra hours you put in, all those weekends and late nights when we had to submit the accounts to Companies House, not to mention helping me with engaging Angus. I really appreciate everything you do, and I should have told you more often. But that's going to change. I need to treat you and Hannah more like partners than employees. I know you love the business as much as I do, and I am truly grateful.'

Tom stared at Carmen, motionless, not even fidgeting with his beloved camera, as he struggled to assimilate everything she had said, everything she had done, and how much it would help during what would be a difficult and traumatic time as his mother faded towards the end of her life.

'Thank you,' he managed to whisper before reaching out for his coffee so that he had something to do with his hands, his face aflame with a mixture of relief and embarrassment to match his russet hair and freckles.

Hannah beamed and grabbed his other hand. She leaned over to place a kiss on his cheek and beads of perspiration appeared on his temples, but there was a gentle smile of happiness playing at the corners of his lips. Izzie felt tears prickle at her lower lashes.

'So, is that why you spiked Carmen's drink?' demanded Zara, clearly the only one unmoved by the emotional exchange. 'Because you thought she was going to report you to the police?'

Everyone turned from Zara to face Tom, whose eyes widened in horror at the accusation.

'You think I would do something like that?'

'Well…'

'I can assure you that I was prepared to take whatever punishment Carmen considered appropriate. I didn't spike anyone's drink! I have no idea what magnesium citrate is or what it does to the body!'

Tom's denial was the most forceful speech Izzie had heard him deliver since he'd arrived at the villa and she hoped that the experience had taught him more than just a lesson in integrity, but also the benefits of facing problems head-on and working through possible solutions with those who care about you, listening to their advice and accepting their support.

'If it wasn't you, then who was it?' Zara continued to press, still eyeing Tom suspiciously.

As if in slow motion, every head swivelled towards the only person left.

Beth.

Chapter Thirty

The pergola, Villa Limoncello
Colour: Damson plum

'I don't know what you're looking at me for. None of this has anything to do with me! Why on earth would I want to make Carmen sick? She's my best friend.'

'But that's not true, is it?'

Izzie held Beth's eyes until she was forced to look away and Izzie immediately knew she had been right. However, it gave her no pleasure whatsoever to be the one to reveal to Carmen the fact that her friend had been so envious of her success that she would stoop so low as to attempt to poison her, just to gain a smidgeon of satisfaction.

'Beth? What's going on?'

Izzie's heart performed a somersault of sadness when she saw the hurt in Carmen's eyes.

'Izzie? Why did you say that Beth's lying?'

There was no easy way to deal with this part of the conversation, so Izzie decided to opt for the straightforward approach and to just tell them what she had seen.

'On my way back from Riccardo's this morning, I took a shortcut over the wall between the B&B and the villa and I saw someone throwing something down the well.'

'Who?'

'Beth.'

'Beth? Did you throw something down the well?'

Beth said nothing; she simply remained slumped in her chair, her arms folded across her chest, a look of stubborn disinterest pinned to her face.

'Izzie?'

'When Meghan and I hauled up the bucket, we found this bottle.'

She picked up the little brown bottle that had been sitting on the table waiting for its starring role in the mystery.

'Is that true, Beth?' demanded Carmen, hope disappearing from her eyes as Beth continued to refuse to comment on what Izzie was saying. 'Beth, say something, anything!'

Beth pulled a face and shrugged her shoulders like a teenager confronted by her parents over her drinking habits, despite being in her mid-thirties. But her reaction was tantamount to an admission and Izzie was now more keen than ever to get the final hurdle over with so she could wave the party goodbye and retreat to the *limonaia*, where she knew she would find the calm she needed to get back on track.

'When I spoke to Beth about her time at university, she told me about her relationship with her lecturer – about how he'd refused to stand up to the authorities and how the pain of his betrayal caused her to act irrationally, which led to her being expelled.'

Two dots of red appeared on Beth's cheeks as she stared at Izzie from beneath her long dark fringe, her jaw clenched, every muscle in her body tense as she tried to cling onto her emotions by her fingertips. A loose nerve beat just below her left eye as she chewed on the nail of her little finger.

'Beth also told me that she had no regrets about not resuming her studies; that she was happy working at the department store in Cardiff. She even asked about other potential courses at Villa Limoncello, hoping to bring her friends with her next time. I believed what she told me, and Beth was the first person I crossed off the list as someone who would hurt Carmen. I mean, she was her *best* friend. But something she said came back to me. The way she snapped when I asked her about her handbag design, telling me straight that she'd designed it and not Carmen.'

'Carmen could never design anything as avant-garde as that!' spat Beth, her jealousy bursting through her silence.

'Beth!' cried Hannah. 'How can you say such a thing?

'Because it's true!' Beth shot up from her chair and leaned over the table, stabbing her finger in Carmen's direction. 'Tell them! Tell them what you did!'

Carmen was so shocked at Beth's venomous outburst that it took a few moments for her to register what she had said and then a few more to understand what she meant.

'No? Too ashamed? Then I will! Carmen used my designs to launch her first collection. She stole them and passed them off as her own! Go on, deny it!'

Carmen stared at her friend, whose face was the colour of a ripened damson plum. Years of envy, of bitterness, of simmering resentment were wrapped up in that one sentence, probably a sentence that had been coiling around her brain since she had sat in the front row of her friend's first catwalk show. Whilst Izzie had known the identity of the person who had added the industrial-strength laxative to Carmen's drink since she'd seen her loitering next to the wishing well, she had no idea why she had done such a thing. Now that she did, her indignation over what had happened at Villa Limoncello had lessened somewhat – Beth's reasoning did not justify her actions, but it certainly explained them.

'Carmen? Is that true?' asked Zara gently, placing her hand on her friend's arm.

'Partly.'

'Partly, what does that mean?' demanded Beth, her eyes flashing with fury. 'I came up with the sketch for that off-the-shoulder prom dress in periwinkle blue...'

'Yes, and I changed it to a halter-neck, added a silver chain belt, shortened the length to above the knee, and sourced the printed silk that turned a pretty standard prom dress into a great statement piece so the wearer would be the belle of the ball!'

'What about the candy-striped T-shirt dress with fluted sleeves? I came up with that idea when we were in Milan and we had those Neapolitan ice creams!'

'Again, I remember you mentioning using a candy-striped fabric for a bikini and bathing costume line when we were brainstorming on the flight home, but that's totally different to the minidress I designed for last year's summer collection. That was actually inspired by a visit to Southend where I saw a sweet shop filled with rows and rows of sticks of rock!'

'And I suppose you're going to say that the Hawaiian-tropic jumpsuit with puff sleeves was your idea, too?'

'I think it was a collaboration; not *my* idea, not *your* idea, but something we came up with together, but which I turned into a sample, experimented with different printed fabrics and commissioned the hand-made feathered trim from a women's collective in Bangladesh that gave the design to a kinky Soho vibe.'

Carmen held Beth's gaze, steady, confident, assured of her veracity, until the wind fell from Beth's sails and she sank back down into her chair, defeat coiling through her veins.

'You could have acknowledged my contribution. You could have told me that you rated my ideas, that you thought I had a modicum of talent. I would have agreed to you using them, no problem, but when I saw those designs on the runway, I was flabbergasted that you didn't say anything.'

'I'm sorry, Beth. I guess I was so caught up in the launch of my first ever collection that I didn't stop to think that you were a big part of my inspiration. I had no idea you felt like that. If I had, I would have done something about it, offered you a percentage...'

'It's not about the money! It's about my self-esteem! Okay, you paid for all those trips abroad for me to come with you on those modelling assignments, and don't get me wrong, I appreciated every single one of them. But the whole time I was there, I felt inadequate, pitied for not being statuesque or beanpole thin! You know what your friend Freya called me? Dumpy! I was treated like a hanger-on, the little friend who was riding on her famous friend's coat tails for the freebies, or worse, taking advantage of our friendship instead of paying my own way – which of course I couldn't afford to do. I saw the way the other models looked at me, Zara included, and it hurt.'

Izzie saw that Zara had the grace to study her French manicure.

'I only wanted you to acknowledge that, even though I didn't finish my degree, I still had creative flair, still had something to offer in the fashion business, and, more importantly, that you valued my opinion. And because you didn't, the despondency over not completing my degree, and not getting to work in the industry I've worshipped since I was six years old and designing my Barbie's outfits, festered and grew.

'You know, I hate the way your success makes me feel! I've tried and tried to get over it, to put every last ounce of effort into starting my own fledgling business with the handbags, and I love every minute when I find the time to do that after working at the store six days a week. But then you won that award and I just couldn't suppress my feelings any longer. When you offered to take everyone to Italy to celebrate, all expenses paid, I should have been delighted – like a real friend would be – but instead I was resentful. So, I ordered a bottle of laxative from the Internet and had some kind of vague plan of spoiling the whole trip.'

'Beth, how could you!' cried Hannah, her face flushed with distress.

'I wasn't sure I would actually go through with it until I saw how you went on with everyone at the first painting tutorial, when we were learning the techniques of water-colours. I think something just clicked in my brain and my subconscious took over. I only put a few drops in your drink when Hannah left it unattended on the kitchen bench, just enough to make you feel a little of the nausea I experience every time I see a quote in the newspaper, or a magazine, or an online fashion blog, about Carmen Campbell's brilliance. But, you know what? It didn't make me feel better – it made me feel worse, much worse – but of course I couldn't take it back. When you laid the blame at Luca's door, I thought I'd got away with it and I resolved to get a grip and grow up.'

'Even when Carmen called in the health inspectors?' said Meghan, speaking for the first time since they'd sat down on the terrace. 'You know what you did could have ruined his business, not only here but at Antonio's, too? He might have been forced to sell the villa! How could you do such a thing?'

'I'm sorry. I'll call the authorities myself and explain what I did. I'll—'

'No need to do that,' interrupted Carmen, pulling out her mobile phone. 'I'll call them myself and tell them I made a mistake.'

Carmen jumped up from her seat and stalked off towards the gazebo to make her call in private, the lilt of her voice floating on the breeze as the gathering sat in silence, trying to look anywhere but at Beth. Unlike with Zara and Hannah, no one came to her aid, which caused a nip of sympathy in Izzie's chest. Envy was a terrible thing, but it was also a part of being human and once it had wriggled under your skin it was very difficult to evict without tremendous willpower.

'Okay, it's sorted. Please accept my apology, Luca. Your culinary skills are amazing and the recipes you've show-cased this week at Villa Limoncello have been nothing short of fabulous! And, Izzie, you have been a fantastic host, and a skilled teacher. I'll be returning home with lots of new ideas for my next collection. Now, if you'll excuse me, I think Beth and I have a great deal to talk about before the taxi arrives to take us to the airport. Beth?'

And to Izzie's amazement, Carmen held out her elbow for Beth to take. For a brief moment, she wasn't entirely sure if Beth was going to accept the proffered olive branch, but she did and the two women strolled from the terrace towards the vineyard, their heads leaning towards each other, ebony next to blonde, until they disappeared from sight.

'Want to take a last look at the *limonaia* before we go?' asked Tom, raising his eyebrows at Hannah, who smiled and nodded her agreement immediately.

'Love to!'

Arm in arm they left the terrace, chatting in low voices as they tried to make sense of everything that had just happened.

'Want to help me and Gianni gift-wrap the *cantuccini* and *ricciarelli* for you to take home?' asked Meghan when she saw Zara hesitate over what she should do next.

'Sure, if you promise to give me the recipes?'

'It's a deal.'

Izzie and Luca watched the two women, and a very surprised Gianni, disappear into the kitchen, Meghan's sequined sleeves flapping in her wake like a bejewelled bat, Zara's wide-legged trousers rippling around her ankles.

'I don't know about you but I'm exhausted!' declared Luca, leaning back in his chair and stretching his arms above his head. 'I was crazy to think that the life of a chef was much less pressurised than that of an investment banker – how wrong I was! You know what, Isabella Jenkins? From the moment I ran you off the road on that little pink Vespa, my life has become one long rollercoaster of drama! I thought you thrived on order and routine!'

'I do! Or I did!'

'Well, you could have fooled me!' Luca laughed, his dark eyes creasing at the corners. 'I don't think I'm up to arranging another course at Villa dei Limoni for a while! Give me the manic, high-pressure environment of a commercial kitchen any day! Antonio's is positively serene compared to a day in the life of Villa dei Limoni!'

Izzie smiled, enjoying the way Luca's proximity caused her stomach to churn with pleasure, and all the tension of the last week seeped from her body to be replaced by a feeling of complete calm, a feeling she had grown to appreciate since arriving at the villa. 'It has been an unusual week, hasn't it?'

'Unusual? Crazy, bizarre, stressful, hectic, exasperating...'

'Yes, those too.'

Izzie leaned forward and laced her fingers through Luca's, gifting him with a broad smile.

'Izzie, I...'

But whatever Luca had been about to say would have to wait because the vigorous honk of a car horn announced the arrival of the airport taxi. Zara and Meghan appeared on the front steps carrying everyone's goodie bags wrapped in cellophane and tied with yellow ribbon, along with a bottle of home-made limoncello each. Luca and Gianni disappeared to fetch the suitcases and Meghan went in search of Carmen and Beth, whilst Zara sought Tom and Hannah.

Izzie rushed into the kitchen to collect the individual files she'd prepared for each guest to take home with them, containing everything they had covered over the week and a great deal more. She had also included a questionnaire for everyone to complete later, and a twist of trepidation gnawed at her abdomen as she regretted that decision. Nevertheless, whatever the results, she resolved to take each and every suggestion on board and use the feedback to improve next time.

Next time? Was there really going to be a next time, then?

Chapter Thirty-One

The limonaia, *Villa Limoncello*
Colour: Sherbet lemon

'So, now that everyone has gone, will you be packing your bags and racing off to the airport too? I wouldn't blame you, you know! I certainly feel like ringing the local *agente immobiliare* in San Vivaldo and begging her to hop on her Vespa without delay!'

Izzie smiled at Luca, loving the cute way his hair flopped into his dark eyes, currently filled with uncertainty and not a little regret. Her heart gave a tweak of guilt that everything hadn't gone according to her best-laid plans – there was a lesson to be learned there somewhere but she would leave that for later pondering. She linked her arm through his and guided him towards the *limonaia*, a place where she knew they'd find tranquillity and calm.

As they pushed open the glass door, dusk began to tickle at the treetops and the sinking sun spread rays of golden light across the valley whilst the cicadas performed their final song of the day. She loved Villa Limoncello, not just for the panoramic views of rolling hillside dotted with vineyards and olive trees and crowned by pretty terracotta villages, but the all-encompassing serenity, the aroma of baked earth mingled with wild herbs, the intense feeling of homecoming she experienced whenever she entered its walls, like a warm, welcoming hug.

But the one thing that had made her stay in San Vivaldo, the best thing to have happened to her in two long years, was her blossoming love for its handsome and kind-hearted owner. Okay, running the Painting & Pasta course had been a lot more difficult than she could ever have imagined, so surely that meant that next time things had to run more smoothly!

'Of *course* it hasn't put me off!'

'So what do you say to hosting the Italian Pastries & Pilates course in September?'

'Pastries & Pilates?' she laughed.

'Or Tennis & Tiramisu?'

'What about Wine & Words?'

'Yes, that could work.'

'Gianni could handle the wine-tasting part – but I think we should also include sessions on growing the grapes, harvesting them, and the process of the wine-making too, as well as a few trips to other Tuscan vineyards.'

'Gianni's going to be thrilled! Who do you have in mind for the writing part?'

Izzie met Luca's eyes and he burst out laughing, shaking his head.

'Not Riccardo? No way! It'll be pistols at dawn with them two!'

'Riccardo is the ideal candidate to run a creative writing retreat. He *has* had two bestselling crime novels published!'

'That was five years ago, and he's Gianni's sworn enemy!'

'But there's no need for them to even come into contact with each other. The guests could write in the mornings, learn everything there is to know about viticulture in the afternoons, and taste the wines of Tuscany in the evenings with their meal. Sorted!'

'Or perhaps the other way around if the wheels of inspiration need a little oiling?'

'And then we could do something for Christmas, like Crafts & Cannoli, showcasing the local seasonal handicrafts as well as Italian patisserie?'

'So, does this mean you're planning on staying?' asked Luca, the corners of his mouth turning upwards as he held her eyes.

A ripple of attraction shot through Izzie's veins and before she could answer his question, Luca had leaned forward and kissed her, gently at first, until she stepped closer and melted into his arms. She relished the way the contours of their bodies fit perfectly together, loved how the scent of his citrussy cologne mingled with the fragrance of the lemons in the *limonaia*, and how his embrace caused her knees to turn to jelly.

She had arrived in San Vivaldo with a heart shattered into myriad pieces, and a cloud of despondency hanging over her head like a character from a comic book illustration. Luca had not only introduced her to the wonderful art and architecture that Tuscany was famous for, he had also taught her how to weave her grief into the fabric of life and embroider a new picture. She had a great deal to thank him for, and if she stayed on at Villa Limoncello she could find out what destiny had in store for their relationship.

However, now that the recovery process had started, she found herself thinking more and more about how much she missed her parents. After Anna's memorial service, every visit home had been a distressing experience as memories launched a vicious assault on her fragile emotions, but a trip to Cornwall was beckoning.

'I'd love to stay on here, Luca, I've got loads more ideas for improving the villa, but I need to go back to the UK for a couple of weeks. I'm thinking of spending some time with my parents in St Ives. They've been really understanding, allowing me the time and space to grieve for Anna in my own way, but I know they miss me. And it's time to banish my demons once and for all, to face all those people who loved Anna just as much as we did, to spend some time talking about her, reminiscing about all her fabulous achievements, sharing our stories. I know Anna's no longer with us, but she's still my sister and I want to keep her memory alive, not bury it under a mountain of mourning.'

'I'm so pleased to hear you say that, Izzie.'

Luca smiled down at her, then he kissed her again, and again, and again, until the back pocket of his jeans began to vibrate. He broke away from Izzie, pulled out his phone and glanced at the screen before swiftly replacing it, his expression unreadable.

'What's wrong?'

'Nothing, just a text from Gianni. Come on, let's get a drink. Limoncello?'

'Absolutely!'

Luca hooked his arm around her shoulders and together they sauntered out of the *limonaia*, across the terrace to the front of the house where they paused on the steps to enjoy the view down the driveway towards the road that lead to San Vivaldo. Izzie had never felt so at peace with what fate had thrown at her, and she exhaled a long sigh of contentment.

'I know I keep saying that the *limonaia* is my favourite place at the villa, but the view down this driveway has to come a very close second. When I arrived, it was exactly how I expected the entrance to Villa Limoncello to look; the wrought-iron gates, the avenue of elegant cypress trees welcoming visitors like a guard of honour at a wedding, the… Oh my God, what on earth is that?'

The sound of screeching tyres, followed by a cacophony of indignant horn-bowing, pierced the tranquillity of the early evening. Izzie shaded her eyes and squinted into the dusky light where she could just about make out the shape of a tiny red Fiat 500 bouncing down the uneven surface of the drive, sending up a balloon of dust as it skidded to a halt in front of them.

'What the…'

Izzie turned to Luca, confusion spinning through her brain. Surely they weren't expecting any more guests – she didn't think she could cope with that so soon after waving goodbye to Carmen and her friends! She didn't want to admit it to Luca but all she really wanted to do was lie down in a darkened room and process what had happened during the last week, then fold it all up into a neat bundle and lock it away in a box for ever. But Luca was clearly expecting the new arrivals because, smiling broadly, he stepped forward to open the passenger door with a flourish of welcome.

'*Buona sera! Benvenuta a Villa dei Limoni!*'

For a moment, Izzie couldn't believe what her eyes were telling her. A crescendo of emotion whipped through her body and tears sprang into her eyes as she gasped and pressed her hand to her mouth.

'Oh my God! Mum!'

She flew down the steps and into her mother's arms, hugging her tightly until her father appeared from the driver's side, his familiar face creased into a smile as he patted down his bouffant silver hair.

'I feel like I've spent the last thirty minutes taking part in the Italian Grand Prix! Hello, darling!'

'Dad…'

But her voice cracked with emotion and she couldn't continue, so she simply reached out to draw him into the family embrace.

'Sorry just to land on you, Izzie. I hope you don't mind.'

Izzie wiped away her tears and beamed at her parents, standing there on the steps of Villa Limoncello, surrounded by all the beauty Tuscany has to offer, and her heart overflowed with gratitude and happiness. She knew that the director of fate was smiling down on her and had decided it was her turn to be blessed with good fortune at last.

'Of course not! But how did you know… how did you…?'

Izzie saw her father flick a glance in Luca's direction.

'Luca? You knew about this?'

He nodded.

'Why didn't you tell me?'

'Don't blame Luca, darling. We wanted it to be a surprise for you. We arrived earlier this afternoon, but we wanted to wait until your guests had left before coming over to the villa. We've just had the most amazing meal at Antonio's in the village, *and* we've met a couple of your friends, too.'

'You have?'

'Yes, first Oriana arrived at the restaurant with this huge box of home-made Italian pastries. They look absolutely amazing! I can't wait to try them with a nice cup of tea! But wait until you see what else we've got. Jack?'

Izzie turned to her father, who, with Luca's help, had just finished unloading the luggage from the boot of the car, a quizzical look on her face.

'Ah, yes!'

Jack Jenkins exchanged an indecipherable look with his wife before leaning into the back seat of the Cinquecento and emerging brandishing a huge spray of vibrant orange roses intertwined with dark green foliage and tied with matching ribbons that floated high in the soft breeze.

'Ta-da!'

Izzie gasped as her emotions broke free of their tethers. She recognised Francesca's floral genius immediately, but what caused the tears to flow was the fact that the roses she had used to create the bouquet were those that bore the same name as her beloved sister – Annabel.

'Oh, Izzie, darling, what's wrong?'

It was a few minutes before Izzie found the right words to explain the significance of her friend's generous gesture and then her mother joined her in a few tears.

'Why don't you take your mum for a stroll around the garden whilst I sort out the coffee?' suggested Luca gently.

'Great idea,' said Izzie, linking her arm through her mother's and guiding her towards the gazebo.

287

'So, tell me how your first Villa Limoncello course went! I want all the details!'

'Oh my God, Mum, how long have you got?'

Luca's Recipes

Spaghetti sugo finto

Ingredients

For the pasta:
- 200g durum wheat flour
- 200g plain flour
- 4 eggs

For the sauce:
- 2 onions
- 2 carrots
- 2 sticks of celery
- 1 small red pepper
- 4 tomatoes, their skins removed and finely chopped
- 2 cloves of garlic
- Tomato paste
- 100ml red wine
- Extra virgin olive oil
- Pinch of salt and pepper
- Fresh basil to decorate

Method

Sift the flour onto the table and make a well in the centre. Add the eggs, gently incorporating them into the flour with the fingers until everything is combined, then knead well for at least ten minutes. Wrap the dough in clingfilm and set aside to rest whilst you make the sauce.

Finely chop the onions, carrots and celery and heat in a little olive oil until cooked. Pour in the red wine and reduce for a few minutes, then add the tomatoes, the tomato paste, and the garlic and simmer, stirring occasionally until the *sugo* is thick and rich.

Take a piece of dough the size of a tennis ball, squash it flat and feed it through the pasta machine until the dough is smooth, then pass it through the blades on the spaghetti setting. Cook in a large pan of boiling water for two minutes and serve with the sauce and a generous sprinkle of grated pecorino.

Tortelli con ricotta e ortica

Ingredients

- Home-made pasta dough (as above)

For the sauce:
- 100g nettles, washed
- 200g spinach, washed
- 300g ricotta
- 2 eggs
- 1 tbsp grated pecorino
- Pinch of nutmeg and salt

Method

Blanch the spinach and the nettles, squeeze out excess water, and then add to the ricotta and stir. Add the parmesan, the beaten eggs and the nutmeg with a pinch of salt and bind together.

Next, roll out the home-made pasta until 1mm thick and cut it into two uniform strips eight centimetres wide. Then place teaspoon-sized portions of the ricotta mixture onto one of the pasta strips, cover with the second strip and press down with fingers to remove any excess air. Cut the *tortelli* into squares using a toothed pasta wheel and place them gently on a plate dusted with semolina. Cook in a pan of boiling salted water and serve with a drizzle of extra virgin olive oil and a sprinkle of pecorino.

Pici all'etrusca

Ingredients

- Home-made pasta dough (as above)

For the sauce:
- 2 hard-boiled eggs
- 3 cloves of garlic
- A bunch of fresh mint, basil and flat-leaf parsley
- 50g of grated pecorino
- Extra virgin olive oil
- Salt & pepper

Method

Roll the pasta into a flat sheet and cut into strips. Starting at the centre and using the flat of the palm, roll the strips into long thick strings. Don't worry if it's not uniform – that is part of the home-made charm. Cook in a large pan of boiling salted water for three minutes.

Remove the shell from the hard-boiled eggs, slice in half lengthways and remove one egg yolk. Peel the garlic, then put all the ingredients in a blender and pulse, adding a generous splash of extra virgin olive oil. Add salt and pepper to taste, then stir through the warm pasta, finishing with the egg yolk crumbled on the top and a sprinkle of parsley and pecorino. Serve with a green salad.

Schiacciata alla Fiorentina

Ingredients

- 250g flour
- 200g caster sugar
- 2 eggs, beaten
- 7 tbsp warm milk
- 4 tbsp olive oil
- 1 tbsp baking powder
- One large orange
- Icing sugar, cocoa & orange zest to decorate

Method

In a large mixing bowl, beat together the caster sugar, olive oil, milk, eggs, and the zest and juice of the orange. Stir in the sifted flour and baking powder and combine. Pour the batter into a 13 x 9 greased baking tin and cook for 30 mins, at 350 degrees F until golden. Turn out onto a wire rack and leave to cool.

Whilst waiting, print off a picture of a fleur-de-lis (the symbol and coat of arms of the city of Florence), and cut out a stencil. Decorate the top of the cake with a generous dusting of icing sugar, then, using your stencil, create a lily with cocoa powder and finish with the grated zest of an orange.

Izzie's Limoncello Tiramisu

Ingredients

- 100g caster sugar
- 100ml limoncello
- Zest & juice of 3 lemons
- 50ml water
- 500g mascarpone
- 500ml double cream
- 10g icing sugar
- 100g lemon curd
- 200g sponge fingers

Method

Place the caster sugar, water and the zest and juice of two lemons into a small pan and heat until the sugar is dissolved. Add half the limoncello and simmer until syrupy. Set aside to cool.

In a large mixing bowl, beat the mascarpone until smooth, then add the double cream, the remaining limoncello, the zest and juice of the remaining lemon and the lemon curd and stir together.

Carefully soak the sponge fingers with the syrup and place in the base of a ceramic dish, or individual glass dessert dishes, then spoon over a generous helping of the cream mixture and repeat, finishing off with a sprinkle of finely grated lemon zest and a dusting of finely grated milk chocolate. Refrigerate for at least 3-4 hours. Serve with home-made limoncello cocktails.

Buon Appetito!

Acknowledgements

A book is never the product of just one person, so I'd like to extend my grateful thanks to everyone at Canelo who have supported me in my dream to write a story set in gorgeous Tuscany, especially my fabulous editor, Laura McCallen, and the wonderful Ellie Pilcher.

I also want to thank my amazing friends Carol, Hilary and Jane for the breakfast brainstorming sessions fuelled by copious mugs of coffee and rounds of buttered toast. This would have been a very different story without your contributions.

And finally, as always, a huge hug to my family who have encouraged me to follow my dreams wherever they may take me.

Tuscan Dreams

Wedding Bells at Villa Limoncello
Summer Dreams at Villa Limoncello
Christmas Secrets at Villa Limoncello